ABOUT THE AUTHOR

« The seed of this book was planted on September 18, 2007, the day I learned of an explosion at the Baghdad morgue: looking for an explanation became an obsession! »

Edward Subut is an alias ; the writer, a traveller who handled his first AK47 at age fifteen in the Djibouti desert and who has a past in military intelligence, is very happy to remain anonymous… He can be reached at edwardsubut@gmail.com or @edwardsubut on Twitter.

PRELUDE

Forward, forward, forward, forward,
Without ever retreating, never surrender,
Forward, forward, forward, forward,
Undefeated Warrior, sword in hand kill them!

Kill the devil's soldiers without hesitation,
Make them bleed even on their doors,
Don't be afraid of anything, go straight for vindication,
The field of battle is the field of honors.

In this war you have everything to gain,
One fine day your sweat and your blood will bear witness,
Fight until you meet the Almighty
Running towards your prey, you are there, Roaring Lion!

Forward, forward, forward, forward,
Without ever retreating, never surrender,
Forward, forward, forward, forward,
Undefeated Warrior, sword in hand, kill them!

INTRODUCTION

Babel Muaddam,
   Baghdad, Iraq,

September 18th, 2012

The heat was excruciating, the post-summer September noon sun leaving little shadow to hide for the few pedestrians daring enough to walk the street, along the cemetery, from the parking lot to the Ministry of Health.

The southern side of the square was occupied by an ugly and functional building, whose color had taken the dirty beige that seemed to be the ominous trademark of the city, blasted all year long by dust storms, and whose cleaning services had long been stopped by the war. It hosted Baghdad's largest morgue and the Institute of Forensic science, where remnants of teams of dedicated people tried to find cause of death for some of the many bodies that would be sent to them, relentlessly, every day.

A crowd of people would always linger close to the building: relatives of those, who had passed away or - more than often - had been killed in the past hours, would come and wait by the large doors at the entrance for information; some would come looking for missing ones, dreading the news, yet willing to find an answer; ambulance drivers would wait for the next explosion to take them away into another bloody furnace; the usual street vendors would also try and sell poor food and tepid drinks to the captured crowd.

Today was a slow day: no bombings had occurred in the vicinity and the night had been blessed by few exchanges of gunfire between American forces and insurgents, whom ever they might be; the endless chorus of helicopter engines patrolling the sky over Baghdad was the only sound in the somewhat silenced environment; close to thirty people were huddled in the few batches of shadow next to the entrance of the Institute.

The silence was broken by the approaching noise of heavy duty engines, the ground slightly shaking as they got nearer; a Cobra gunship flew over the street, grazing the rooftops, a sure sign of an approaching US convoy. A silhouette appeared at the corner of the block, two hundred and fifty yards to the West, moving carefully and kneeing by the remnants of a lamp post.

*　　　　*　　　*

« *All clear Sarge* » said Turner, « *the street is good all the way to the Ministry.* »

« *Right, Martinez, Johnson, move across the street to that tree by the playground and give me a line of fire into the street* » ordered the Sergeant, then turning back: « *Porty, keep covering the North-West, across that yard!* »

* * *

« *Yes, Sarge* » and the burly man behind the machine gun on top of the huge Hummer moved his sights to the walls of the building three hundred yards away.

« *Bravo five, this is Blue Jay, do you read? Over* »

« *This is Bravo five* » said the Sergeant, pressing the handle from his radio, « *Loud and clear* »

« *What's holding you up? We are getting late on the schedule* »

« *This is Bravo Five: just making sure that the next turn is safe; we're kinda exposed here Sir* »

« *Well, we're kinda exposed in the whole funkin' city! The Cobra said that there was no one on the roofs and intel says this part of the city hasn't had an attack in months. So move your ass and let's finish this patrol! Out!* »

« *This is Bravo Five: roger, out* » rumbled the Sergeant as he wiped the sweat off his eye brows.

« *You guy heard the LT; move. Turner, Brody: to the next building on the right hand side of the street.* »

The men started moving forward on both side of the street, checking the windows and roofs; the three recon hummers followed them and turned right into the street.

« *Fuckin' moron* » murmured the Sergeant in a breath, « *All this to be on time for his ball game with the Colonel…* »

A hundred yards further down the road, Turner, the point man, stopped, bent a knee and raised his right fist.

* * *

« *All stop* » said the Sergeant who walked up to his man and put a hand on his left shoulder; « *Wassup Turner?* »

« *Can't tell you Sarge, but something don't feel right; I know there're no cars down the street, but with all those people waiting out there... don't like it!* »

The Sergeant took his binoculars and went through a pattern: first the facade of the buildings from roof to bottom, the pavement, then the road, and finally the small crowd by the parking lot where a few rusted cars and ambulances were parked.

« *Bravo Five, Blue Jay here, what the fuck again?* »

« *Argh, common man* » said Turner

« *This Bravo F...* »

First the flash,
    Then the blast,
    Then the dust, the bodies, the blood,
    And the cries...

Lying on his back, the Sergeant looks at the sky, tries to stand up and falls grabbing his thigh, his right foot missing.

The pain soars, then blackness comes mercifully…

*   *   *

« *That was too soon; why didn't you wait: we could have gotten the Hummers* » said the man in Arabic looking out from a half-opened window in a dark room two hundred yards to the West.

« *I know, I KNOW!* » said his partner, already destroying the telephone that he had just used to blow up the IED hidden in the ambulance, parked next to the Institute.

Then came a whisper through his closed teeth: « *Et merde*[1]… »

---

[1] French: shit

CHAPTER 1

Indian Avenue,
   Middletown, Rhode Island,
   USA

January 2014

There were a handful of people in front of him in the queue at his local sandwich shop; an overweight black lady was undecided between turkey or ham and a couple of rowdy teenagers were comparing their scores on their latest video game fight, using names and words that had only meanings to them; John was third in line and the only one not looking at some kind of device,

« Move, move! He's behind you! » said an unidentified male voice next to him.

« What? What did you say? » said John.

« Watch out for the bomb! »

« Wait a minute: what bomb? Who's behind me? Who are you? » yelled John, frozen by fear.

* * *

« He's gonna blow it! Move! »

John turned around and saw a guy dressed up in traditional middle-Eastern clothes: he was small; its beard was long and unkempt, yet could not hide an ugly smile and some missing teeth; he spat and yelled:

« I'm gonna blow it all if you don't give it to me. »

« What? Give you what? » cried John looking right and left, as he tried to move away from the terrorist and find the exit door.

Yet, the more he walked, the closer the mad smile was; he started to run but couldn't seem to loose that damned yell; no, not a yell anymore now, more like the loudest whisper he had ever heard.

« Give it to me or I'm gonna blow it all! »

« Give you what? » an exhausted John replied as his voice broke.

« Your leg! » and the maniac chuckled, *« Your leg! »*

John sat up suddenly, his heart beating, his breath short; his shirt was drenched with sweat. Looking down, he saw the ugly stump – his "residual limb" in the fucking VA doctors' jargon – lying in front of him in place of his right leg.

On the floor by the bed, the alarm clock displayed the time in a red halo: 3:21am.

* * *

« *A nightmare,* » he thought, « *just another nightmare.* » Not the worst, not the nicest but, for once, pretty clear and easy to understand.

« *Write them down!* » had said the shrink, « *It will help you understand your inner thoughts and work through your negative emotions…* »

« *Negative emotions my ass; just as if I did not know what my problem was* » had he yelled: « *my leg is gone and there is nothing that you or any one can do about it! And don't start talking to me about some anger management issue: YES I'M ANGRY, I'M MAD and there not a fuckin' person on the planet that can do nothing about it!* »

The sympathetic VA[2] shrink had actually taken it quite well; there seemed to be nothing that John could do or say that hadn't been done or said to him by the many young men and women coming back from Iraq missing a limb or, more often than not, simply their sanity.

His return from Iraq was, still today, some kind of a dreadful dream: he had woken up in a hospital in the middle of the green zone where a blood-covered doctor - he was his third case in the past hour and a half - had broken the bad news to him: his right leg had been amputated four inches below the knee, which, according to the weary man, was as much good news as possible because « *modern pneumatic prostheses do wonders these days* », his damaged back was OK, his knee would recover flexibility quickly and he'd be able to walk and maybe even run in the future... The doc probably meant it or maybe was simply relieved that John had not died like his

---

[2] Veteran Affairs

first two patients.

It took him a couple minutes to ask the obvious question:

« What of my men? »

« They were my first two patients… » He sighed: *« Sorry Sergeant »*

It hit him hard, maybe harder than losing his leg: Turner and Brody, though they had been a hundred yards from the truck when it blew up, had taken the full blast; John had only been hit by a piece of shrapnel that had neatly severed his leg; "luckily" the rest of the patrol had suffered only minor scratches and concussion: they would be back to the streets within a week.

He actually lost it when Lieutenant Brown came later in the afternoon with his sorry feelings and *« how it was going to be difficult for him and the Colonel to break the news to the families of his fallen men! »* The nurses actually had to quickly sedate him as he was trying to assault the man responsible for the death of his men.

He grabbed his crutches and limped to the kitchen; he poured himself a glass of water, drank some and sighed; it had been a pretty good week so far with three nights in a row without nightmares: three nights in a row that had been a sad relief to his pains and ugly memories…

The big house was so quiet it felt abandoned: it was in a way since his wife, exhausted and fed up with yet another fit of self-inflicted rage and ranting, had taken their little boy back to her parents' house up in Providence. She had not bothered nor dared taking the time to bring along any of their belongings. Her father had shown up the next morning, filled a few suitcases and told John to stay away from his daughter and grandson until he was « *a normal decent human being* » again.

The worst for John was that he quite agreed with his father-in-law and couldn't fault his wife for giving up on him: between his remorse for his men and his rage against the people responsible for his plight, he did not even know who he was anymore! This had been four months ago and John had not yet found the courage to call his wife.

Surprisingly and in some kind of hopeful life-line, his father-in-law had actually sent him an email every two weeks with a picture of little Josh; he had opened the first one, broken up in sobs and filed away the next ones unopened, finding the sight of his happy little man too much to bear.

He opened the freezer, checked for a beer and cursed when he saw none: beer was his night drink to chase away the whiskey vapors of the evening.

He popped open a tube of the ubiquitous Vicodin, took one and engulfed it with some water. He then hopped to the big sofa in the living room and let himself fall into it, panting. At six feet, he was now weighting two hundred and five pounds, a lifetime away from his Marine days: a daily regimen of fast food, soda and alcohol had seen to his transformation that had wrecked quite a few mirrors in the house.

He awoke with the sun coming up through the windows after a thoughtless sleep and took a shower, trying to clear his mind; coming back home after his discharge, his wife had made sure that the shower was equipped with a hand rail and a seat, a design that would « *make life easier for customers with impaired walking ability* » had said the salesman; he had ripped both off one morning, hating this permanent reminder of his weakness.

He limped to his car and exited the driveway; the neighborhood was, as usual, quiet: a nice rural road surrounded by secluded houses did not make much for excitement. At least, money was not an issue: his parents, real-estates moguls apparently, had died when he was nine, leaving him with a seven-digit fortune; he was taken in custody by an vaguely known uncle in Washington DC, his only family left, and had moved back to his house in Middletown as soon as he had turned eighteen.

*   *   *

Though rich, John Quirston was anything but a spoiled brat: raised and pushed forward by his uncle who had little time for a kid, he had quickly built on a competitive inner streak and had become the captain of his boarding high school rugby team; always the over-achiever, he had started his valedictorian speech by asking his fellow students « *not to wait upon life's decisions for you, but to pursue actively and rough life into what you will want it to be!* »

Being accepted in Yale came like a breeze and was simply logic as, as well as close to home, both his parents had been students there; he had spent the next five years getting his double major in Global Affairs and International Finance, including one year in Paris playing the educated citizen of the world and studying at '*Sciences Po*', the top French political science school in Paris. A Yale alumni, fluent in Spanish thanks to a caring house maid in DC and in French, he was on a direct course to a brilliant Political Officer career in the Department of State.

In 2003, he was invited by his activist girl friend of the time to a meeting with the then not-yet defeated presidential candidate, John Kerry; a moderate conservative himself, he could not but be impressed by the man and his willingness to serve his country; he also realized cynically that some years in the armed forces could also do wonders to his resume, both at the Department of State but also in a future glorious all-American life...

Fresh from Yale, having aced the various tests and physical requirements, he had resisted joining Officer School and enlisted as a grunt at the local Marine recruiting office on West Main Road in Middletown; the recruiter was quite skeptical upon seeing his resume, needed him for his numbers, but had probably felt that he was going to last just a few days in Pendleton.

Life in the Marines was as tough and demanding as he had expected: the first weeks were the toughest he had ever gone through and he surprised himself in savoring the camaraderie of the rough bunch surrounding him; at twenty two, he was older than most and had quite the intellectual upper hand; yet, feet deep in the mud, exhausted after going through an extra obstacle course – he did have a bit of a loud mouth after all – he had reveled in the power of a hand extended to him by a fellow muddied aspiring Marine.

The first years came and went, alternating between Camp Lejeune and Pendleton; his first tour in Iraq, followed by a second one in Afghanistan; he asked for and was sent to

MARSOC[3] selection and training. He settled in a high paced combatant life, somewhat disconnected from the others: only his officers knew about his academic past, no one about his wealth.

During one short leave, he went back on a whim to a high school reunion and met Kate, a friend's cousin; the romance was hot, unexpected and, in a whirlwind, he found himself engaged, then married.

Little Josh was borne in 2012, during his third Iraq tour. He had gotten inexplicably mad at the news of Kate's pregnancy, received upon returning from a tough patrol in Fallujah. Abortion was not an issue in Kate's world and holding his newborn son for the first time three months later had been an awkward event.

He was a changed man: the six years spent fighting in the Marines, mostly away from his family, had hardened him more than what he had thought. Life home was a mix of happy moments, disappointments, painful routines: the boring visits to church, the in-laws, shoppings and plans for the following vacations.

The more he excelled at his job, the worse it became home.

*   *   *

When he arrived in the convenience store, there were a few customers milling about in the aisle of the shop; he picked up some frozen food, soda and several packs of beer. As he moved to the counter, he saw that two people were already

---

[3] Marine Corps Special Operations Command

waiting: a cute looking young woman and a fifty-something man wearing a turban; the woman looked at him and quickly looked away, her posture stiffening, a definite assessment of his drunkard looks; the guy with the turban raised his eyes from his bag and moved to give John some leeway.

That and, more probably the girl's judging frown, pushed John over the edge:

« What the fuck, rag head, don't want to be close to a real American hero? »

Clearly startled, the guy did not say anything.

« What's wrong with you? Can't talk? What the fuck are you doing here anyway? What don't you go back home fucking camels and goats? »

The girl at the till said: *« Sir, what's wrong with you? Leave him alone! »*

« Shut up bitch! This is my country and no'ne's gonna tell me what to do, especially some goat fucking alien! Why are you still here? Get the hell out of my country! »

« I'm calling the police! » she said, picking up the phone. The cute woman was nowhere to be seen; the turban guy was looking sadly at him. The other customers were carefully keeping away from the counter.

« Yeah, you do that, » he said, *« I'll tell them what I lost so that you guys can enjoy all those foreigners messing up the US of A! »*

He then threw several twenties at her and left the store.

* * *

As he was driving out of the parking lot, his path was blocked by a police car, lights blazing. The driver exited the car, gun in the hand:

« *Ah common man!* » moaned John as he recognized Mike Tyndall, a Marine classmate, not the brightest of the bunch...

« *Hand on the wheel! Show me your hands, NOW!* »

« *Mike, it's me John, John Quirston* »

« *Right, hands on the wheel John, now!* »

« *What going on? What's wrong?* »

« *Get out of the car John!* » said the police officer as he opened the driver door, his pistol was back into his holster.

« *I need my crutches!* »

« *Ok, you get them* »

John grabbed his crutches and clumsily got out of the car.

« *Have you been drinking?* » said the police officer

« *Not this morning,* » chuckled John: « *ran out of booze...* »

« *Well, we are going to check that!* »

« *Hey, what's wrong with you Mike? You know me!* »

« *Yeah, that's why we're gonna check that!* »

* * *

« You still angry with me cause of that girl… What was her name? Celia? Sylvia? Yeah, Sylvia? Not my fault that she liked my good looks… » he chuckled. *« Errr, gonna have a hard time walking straight with my crutches. »*

« You are one sorry dude, John; I know that you got it tough in Iraq but still… Blow this! » he said, presenting a breathalyzer.

The device cleared him, which actually came as a surprise to John: running out of beer the previous night was getting him out of a shitload of trouble.

« Now, come with me in the store! » said Mike

The cashier and the turban guy were still there looking at them through the window.

John and the Police officer walked up to them:

« Good morning folks. » said Mike, *« Is this the guy you called about? »*

« Yes Officer, » said the cashier *« He was all exited and mean; I was so scared; he called the man here all kinds of nasty names! »*

« Sir, did he physically harm you? » asked the police officer to the turban guy.

« No Officer, he just called me a rag head and asked me to leave this country. »

« Do you want to press charges? »

* * *

« No, the guy's obviously had a bad streak; is he really a vet? »

« Yes Sir, a Marine, Bronze Star, Purple Heart and all. » Said the Police officer, surprising John.

« Then surely no; mind if I go Officer; gonna be late for work. »

« Not at all, thank you Sir; have a good day! »

The turban guy picked up his bags and looked at John as he left with dignity: *« Very sorry for what you went through Sir. »*

« Jezzzus » muttered John through his closed teeth.

« You don't come back here no more! » said the cashier

« He won't! » said Mike *« Right John? »*

« Nah… »

Mike walked him to his car, closed the door and leaned through the window:

« Get your act together John; next time, I'll get you in for disorderly conduct or maybe assault… And that might not be the best way to get your wife and kiddo back… »

« You know that? »

« The whole city knows about you John: the poor rich boy, the fallen hero… » He said with a smirk.

« Move! » and he slapped the roof of the car.

* * *

The rest of the day was eventless and John spent it pretty much like any other in a stupor, half-looking at a ball game on TV, half-sleeping on the couch.

The night came, the good part of a bottle of vodka went...

*   *   *

Some heavy pounding on the door walked him up:

« John? John? Are you here? Open the door! »

« Uncle William? » said John through his Russian-induced mist

« Yes, open the door! »

As John opened the door, he took the full brunt of the sun in the face.

« Jesus, you look terrible! » said his uncle *« Let me in; I'll make some coffee! »*

« Su, sure. » said John tentatively, following him; *« Err, what are you doing here? »*

Six feet tall, thin, as ever dressed in his black suit, dark burgundy tie and pocket square on a starched white shirt, his uncle cut quite a figure. He walked to the kitchen and started foraging the cupboards to find coffee: *« Ah, there they are. »* as he found the coffee pods and brew two cups. *« Double extra strong for you! »*

« Uncle William, what are you doing here? » John almost

chocked on the first gulp of the strong, burning coffee.

« Heard that you got into trouble yesterday; couldn't let you screw up your life like that... » He said between two sips. *« And I thought losing Katie and the boy would have you grow up a backbone again! »*

« What? How? » stuttered John; *« What the fu... »*

« Don't swear at me young man; there is no one else here who is messing up his life but you! »

John shook his head: *« You don't know, you can't understand: my life got fucked the day that damn ambulance ... »*

« You know the funny thing John? You think that you know everything there is to know and yet, you are as aware of the world around you as a toddler »

His uncle said that with such a tone that John felt stupid and compelled to ask: *« What do you mean Uncle William? »*

« Do you think that you are the only one in the world with problems? Do you think that no one else ever went to war? »

John realized that he actually did not know much about his uncle's past; he knew vaguely that he was working in a rather high position within the Washington administration. The wound of his parents' death and the boarding school in DC had not left him much time for mutual introspection.

« Look up Signal Hill, Vietnam, when you're sober enough; I was there, I fought there, and when I came back missing a kidney and several friends, my fiancée had dumped me in favor of a hippy that

played the guitar and opposed the war... Think that was easy? Do you think that I gave up? No, I grinded my cursed mood on, day after day, until I was back on my feet! And you are going to just do that! »

« *What's the point Uncle William? My mind's banged up, I can't walk half a mile and Kate won't see me... »*

His uncle took a deep breath: « *That's where you get it all wrong son: all this is a consequence of your cowardice; you have given up the fight... »*

« *Well, look at me: how can I fight? Can't even walk? »*

« *There are different ways John, not only the gun... »*

And he left it at that for a moment.

« *Listen to me: I'll be back in exactly three months; you'll either be ready to fight again or not. If you are ready, I'll take you right in the middle of it: you'll get your payback! »*

« *What if I'm not ready? »*

« *That's the last you'll see of me! »*

With those brutal words, his uncle walked out of the kitchen; John heard his car leave the driveway towards the road.

He struggled to the fridge, opened the door and picked up a beer.

What he could get his payback? What if he could make those fucking Arabs pay for his leg? He realized suddenly that his hatred had been burning within him, unused, wasted... He emptied the beer in the sink.

*   *   *

As he was driving to Providence Airport and catch a return flight to DC, William Brandson dialed a number:

« Good morning, could I talk to the Chief of Police please? »

« ... »

« Tell him Director Brandson would like to speak to him! »

« ... »

« Good Morning Chief, How are you? »

« ... »

« I wanted to thank you again for calling me; I had a talk with him: let's see what happens next. »

« ... »

« Yes, we'll see; anyway Chief, I owe you one; have a good day. Goodbye. »

And he hung up.

*   *   *

Three months later, 09 am

* * *

William Brandson turned right into the driveway at 228 Indian Avenue; he drove along the recently cut lawn and parked his rented sedan in front of the house, next to his nephew's car. He walked to the door and rang the bell.

No one answered.

He heard some music coming from the back of the house and walked around the den; coming from behind a bush, the music got louder, very loud actually.

There was a bench on the terrace and a man was doing some lifting.

« *What is that?* » yelled William.

« *Metallica* » answered a sweaty and grinning John; then his face took a serious, nasty look: « *I am getting ready for some payback, Uncle William, I'm almost there!* »

His uncle couldn't suppress a smile...

CHAPTER 2

Pierrefite-sur-Seine, France,

February 23rd, 2014
  04:15am

A gun was pointed at me and I shrugged.

I killed my first man on my twentieth birthday; it wasn't a very difficult decision: he was aiming a rifle at me. I also had a gun... To make it short, I was faster and aimed better than he did. He took three bullets in the torso and never stood up again. I did not have the time to reflect on that and, still today, I wonder what his name was.

Strangely, I did not have nightmares as the more experienced killers had told me that I would; the horrendous dreams would come later. I did think of him though, once in a while at odd moments. Such was one right now...

I was standing in a rarely used parking lot behind some dilapidated buildings; several cars were parked along a dirty black wall, but I doubted that any of them would ever see a road again. One BMW sedan was facing me, its back to the disused landing dock, its lights off. The parking was hidden away from the main *Nationale* 1 road and served on Fridays as an extension to the mosque by the corner of the block. There were few lampposts still working and most of the lot was bathed in a dark orange light.

I wasn't too happy to be so close to those worship grounds as they were a place of obvious interest to the members of the DGSI – *Direction Générale de la Sécurité Intérieure,* the French equivalent of the FBI counter-terrorism Division – as several of his regular tenants had left France to go fight the Jihad in Iraq and Syria; on top of that, the *Police Nationale* maintained a regular presence by the nearby city hall, as it had been already attacked twice at night in the past year by some *jeunes*[4] wanting to have fun or pretending to fight the social distress they struggled in... with Molotov cocktails! No Police tonight though, as we had carefully checked driving south from Sarcelles. As a matter of principle, I had kept a lookout on the *Nationale* 1 road, ready to beep me in case of a problem.

Yet, work is work and I needed to be there to finalize the transaction: I had to deliver a kilogram of fifty percent pure, high quality cocaine to some local hotshot... who had decided to jump me and my load as soon as I had gotten out of the car...

Mohamed and Chuppa were still seated in the car, a black Renault Laguna, the ubiquitous Uber sedan: Chuppa in front, the plastic bag worth its weight in gold still carefully hidden between his feet... along with an old but deadly nine millimeter mini-Uzi; I, for myself, had a nicely concealed

---

[4] French: teenager

Glock nineteen in a holster inside my waistband and a smaller Glock twenty six – what can you say, I am a Glock fan! A boy's gotta have his fads - in an ankle holster inside my right ankle and an emergency ceramic blade in the small of my back along my belt. Big Mo was in the rear seat with a twelve-gauge shotgun.

« *Don't move man!* » The young beur[5] said. « *Give me your gun!* »

« *Where is Ahmed?* » I said calmly.

« *Gimme your gun now! I won't repeat it!* » and he closed the gap, holding his gun in a cool-looking, idiot sideways hold. The barrel stopped a couple inches from my chest.

Always the cooperative guy, I slowly put my hands in the air in front of me. I was wearing latex gloves.

I always go for a suit when I am doing business: no hoodies, shiny stuff or anything camo-style; it really reduces the risk of a random arrest by the police: what police officer is gonna frown upon a Caucasian thirty-something guy in a suit? I am also a pain with the people working with me and Chuppa and Mohamed were decently clothed, at least as properly as they could be.

I have a great tailor, who thinks I am some kind of plain-clothes Police officer: my pants have been altered to host my side holster and my suit is made of a nice Italian stretching material to offer full flexibility of movement, which I sometimes put to good use...

____

[5] French slang: Arab

* * *

« What the fuck? » I say, looking left towards the building.

He cannot help it and his eyes leave me just an instant; my left hand shoots forward, catches the barrel, push it sideways to my right, as my other hand moves inside his wrist. His gun is ripped off his hands and lies in mine.

I drop it behind me and draw my gun – I never trust one that I don't know – grab him by the collar and put the muzzle on his head. Can't believe he fell for that...

« Ahmed, » I call; *« stop fucking around! »*

« Ok man, I am coming out; cool down. » Said a guy from within the car.

He came out of the car and walked up to me.

« Do you realize what you were doing? » I said; *« stealing from the brothers… »*

« Putain mec[6], business is business, » he replied but I could see that he was unsure of what would come next.

« You got the cash? » I said

« Yes, in the car. »

« Go get it, » the kid next to me shivered; *« don't fucking move! »* I said.

* * *

---

[6] French: Fuck man

Chuppa was now out of the car, Uzi in hand, keeping an eye on the surrounding buildings. Mohamed was by the trunk looking at the road.

Ahmed came back to me, carrying a bag; he opened it and showed the money... An amateur really; nothing prevented me from putting a bullet in his head and leaving with the money: luckily for him, I rated efficiency way over money and leaving two corpses by a mosque was not going to help the cause. Efficiency meant discretion, stealth. None of those guys knew my name; Ahmed knew my voice and could probably rat me out, but doing so would mean death to his family and he knew it. The kid was so scared he would be useless to the cops.

Chuppa came over to me and quickly counted the cash: a hundred and fifty thousands euros!

He nodded and went to pick up the Carrefour plastic bag holding the coke; he handed it to Ahmed, who tried to test the product.

« *Move!* » I growled and he backed up.

I released the kid, kicked his gun away and moved backwards to the car; I climbed in, started the engine; Chuppa and Mohamed jumped in and we drove away...

I dropped the guys in Gonnesse, not far from the Concorde jet crash, and headed back towards Pantin where I was expected to deliver the money to my boss; I parked the car rue Mehul and walked across the gardens to the entrance of one of the towers. The buildings around me were pretty well maintained and the people living there would be blue collars, chased out of Paris by the ever-rising cost of rental; the neighborhood was a decent one and not a main focus of Police activity.

An elevator to the fifth floor, a door on the right.

« *Hello brother,* » said the man who opened the door; he closed it behind me, embraced me and walked to the living room.

« *How did it go?* »

« *As expected,* » I said: « *he tried to get the coke and keep the money… »*

« *You did not… »* I interrupted him.

« *No, that would have been too noisy.* »

« *Good; it's a little early for the Fajr prayer[7] but we won't have time later; come and pray with me!* »

He kneeled on a prayer mat; in it was incorporated a little compass. I always found it funny that such a dangerous man had such a kitschy device, kids all went for a compass app on their phones now. There was one mat for me and I joined him.

I had been introduced to him by a friend at the local mosque: he had heard of my stay in Afghanistan and wanted to talk to me; I had suggested that we meet in a local *café* in the nineteenth district one Saturday. We had discussed the latest news, then, over a second coffee, he had gently prodded me

---

[7] First prayer of the day for Muslims

about Afghanistan; I had remained evasive and averted to go into too many details: there was always a chance that he would be working for French Intelligence.

At five feet and limping, he was a small man but there was a ruthlessness about him that he tried to carefully conceal under a long grayish beard and a round belly, hidden under his kameez[8]. His name was Kamaal Hassani: from the whispering at my mosque, I knew that he was a recruiter who, under the guise of Koran teaching, attracted a bunch of followers: one of his students had actually just left discreetly for Iraq...

Our little dance lasted a few weeks every Saturday morning, until one day, he asked me what I felt about the fights against the *mécréants* – the miscreants – that were taking place all over the world. I replied that I had done my share of fighting and that I expected my brothers in France to do their share as well.

« *What was the fight in Afghanistan like?* » he said.

« *Tough,* » I replied; « *We had so little equipment compared to the Americans that it was very frustrating. And we spent half of our time deciding what we would do next and half of our time with whom... or against whom.* »

« *How did you get into Iraq?* » I was surprised at his level of information; I did not think that anyone in Paris knew about that and I had certainly not told anyone.

---

[8] In the Indian subcontinent, both men and women wear these long tunics over loose trousers in matching suits. *Shalwar* refers to the pants, and *kameez* refers to the tunic portion of the outfit.

* * *

« Long story that nearly killed me. » I carefully replied.

« Yet, you went there and managed to come back to Paris. »

« I had a good passport... and no trace on it of my travels to countries that would attract attention from an immigration officer. » I had even avoided entering Turkey officially.

« Amir said that you were a decent man for a kafir[9]. »

I nodded; there was the connection I was missing: Amir had been my go-to guy at the end of my stay in Baghdad and regularly joked that I was a decent kafir and that he did not even know those two words could go together.

« How is he doing? »

« Not very well I am afraid, » said Kamaal, *« He was killed in a fight with Iraqi Army forces several months ago. »*

« Poor Samira, » I said.

« You mean Fatima surely? » He smiled. I grinned: *« A little check never kills the man. »*

« You are a cautious one. » he said.

« I am very much alive: a dead man does not fight effectively! »

He nodded and leaned towards me: *« I might need some help from you. »*

---

[9] Arab: miscreant

* * *

I thought: there we go; « *Tell me!* »

« *You know I have a little school; some people from the community support us and help the cause financially, in many different ways.* »

« *Hmmmm...* »

« *My health is not so good anymore and I need some friends to visit our brothers once in a while and collect the money; would you?* »

« *Why don't you use the association from the Mosque?* »

He grimaced: « *I am quite sure that the association is infiltrated by the French police... and the Imam, holy may he be, wants to know nothing of that.* »

That is how it started: one errand at a time, then more, many more. It actually became a full time job after a few months. Kamaal asked me to slowly stop visiting the mosque and fade away from the brothers I used to frequent since my return from Iraq.

One evening, after collecting the money of my four visits of the day, he asked me to shave my beard and to stop wearing a thobe[10]:

« *You are a Gaulois[11]; look like a Gaulois, act like a Gaulois: you are too visible in Paris!* »

* * *

---

[10] Ankle-length robe, usually with long sleeves
[11] Gaul, original people in France; usually refers to a white man (by contrast with a black man or a beur)

« *You want more from me.* » I said, looking him in the eyes.

« *Yes,* » he said and he explained to me the basics of taqîya[12].

As instructed, I changed my habits, got into normal street clothes, started missing out on some prayers at the mosque; I even stopped visiting him at his apartment. The idea was to do that slowly, in an organized withdrawal from the community: a brutal change of habit is visible and likely to have people, from the community and from the French Intelligence services, notice and ask questions... Which Kamaal wanted to avoid at all cost.

As I slowly became a Gaulois again, he introduced me to a few other collectors and asked me to manage them; I quickly realized that their effectiveness and discretion was wanting: they were young, enthusiastic and awfully, dreadfully proud.

Chuppa was the first one I met; his nickname came from the Chuppa Chups, some lollipops he was always sucking noisily. He was full of bravado and walked the street like he owned it; when he visited "customers", he was aggressive, unthankful and very, very loud.

He took my arrival and my request for a new style of management quite well... That is, after I had beaten the shit out of him and his buddy: it is never a good idea to challenge a guy to a fight when you don't know the guy's street credentials and, to be fair, at one meter eighty and seventy five kilos, I did not look very threatening; he realized his mistake quickly when, having taken his buddy out of the

---

[12] Concealment of practice of Islam to avoid persecution, or more recently to fight more effectively against enemies of Islam

fight, I blocked his savvy looking move with ease and understood that very well when he was out cold five seconds into the fight!

« *Where did you learn to fight?* » He later said when he was conscious again.

« *Not where, what,* » I said. « *I have been practicing Krav Maga for a few years.* »

« *Wow mec[13], that's cool stuff; can you teach me?* »

« *I'll teach you if you'll listen.* »

« *You're the boss,* » he said. « *where do I start?* »

« *First, you're gonna get rid of all that gangsta rapper bullshit: the gold chains, the rings the rolling gait; what are you? A fucking American or a soldier for Islam?* » He winced.

« *Second, no swearing on, no threatening our brothers: that works until they have enough and then, they'll either disappear or rat us out!* »

Chuppa was a quick learner and, from street fight, we moved to a little CQB, close combat battle, the art of gun fight in the street and in buildings: I needed a guy who would not shoot me in the back by mistake and who would be able to support me in the more complicated assignments that I knew would come to me...

Our usual customers were either believers who were putting

----

[13] French: Man

some money on the side for us or outright thugs who wanted some moral standing and some protection within the community: we would visit a family and retrieve two hundred euros, an Uber driver working cars and bicycles – in a booming Paris food delivery business - with several undocumented immigrants, and in a few cases the local drug dealers; more rarely, we would ended up paid in kind, product that needed to be sold; that's where my newly trained muscle proved handy...

Six months after my initial discussion with Kamaal, I had a team of eight collectors and, on good weeks, we would bring back to Kamaal close to fifty thousand euros; I had an "allowance" of ten percent of the collected cash to pay the team and a vast number of informants...

« *I've got a problem,* » I told Kamaal one day: « *I think that Jamaal is cheating on us... *»

« *Let's make some tea and you'll tell me.* » He said quietly. Sugar with tea was his addiction, he used to grin. We moved to the small kitchen and waited patiently for the water to boil. We came back to the living room; he chased his veiled wife away and sat.

« *I have noticed that the sums collected by Jamaal are declining; so I had him followed by Chuppa – they don't know each other... *» He nodded. « *He is doing drugs and apparently also has a new girl friend... Expensive needs... *»

« *What do you want to do?* » he said while caressing his beard; his black eyes were narrow and very, very focused.

« *Get rid of him ... permanently and discreetly! His behavior is not one of a proper believer and I am afraid that, running out cash will get him into trouble and… »*

« He will have only one option: the police! » He said.

« Yes. »

« How much does he know? »

« Not much: he only knows me, never heard of you, thinks I'm a low-level swindler using the Faith as a scam… »

« He is obviously very wrong: what do you need from me? »

« An approval and a way to dispose of the corpse… »

He nodded and we started working on the details.

As fate would have it, he was arrested a few days later before we could launch the plan: a random police control at *Porte d'Ivry*, an exit of the *périphérique*[14]; Still high from the night's partying, an alcohol level three times higher than the accepted norm, no insurance, no driving license and a stolen car! He ran away and tried to hijack a vehicle but failed to see that the car he had gotten into was the supervising police officer's own; the cops are probably still laughing about the face he made when he turned around and faced one perplexed and very armed colleague in the back!

He went through *comparution immédiate*[15] faster than a TGV[16],

---

[14] Main three lane ring around Paris
[15] French legal process: immediate referral to court
[16] TGV, train à grande vitesse: name of the French high-speed train

was sentenced to jail for three years, send behind bars in a Strasbourg[17] prison, where his big mouth immediately got him into trouble, and spent the first three weeks in isolation…

It was a bit tense for a while and I told my team to keep a low profile but Kamaal informed me one day that Jamaal had not spoken about me from inside his cell and that I was safe…

« Are you sure? He breathes to lie… »

« I have it from inside police sources! »

We resumed our operations and life was back to normal until one tense Monday morning…

---

[17] City in Eastern France

CHAPTER 3

Washington DC,

Two months later

As it turned out, Uncle William was a big shot in the American intelligence community. John discovered that on the long drive down to DC; his uncle had decided that a road trip was in order as a proper start to John's new life.

After packing an essential kit for a month in the car and informing the neighbors and a relieved cleaning lady, they drove off; they remained essentially silent for an hour and it is only upon turning onto the I-95 that his uncle started talking.

« *You look better,* » he said.

« *Haven't touch a drop of alcohol for thirty five days,* » John said, looking out at the highway ahead of us. « *I've been exercising as well…* »

« *I noticed: you have crutches but, is that a prosthesis I saw in the trunk?* »

* * *

« Yes, finally moved my ass... The doctor was surprised to see me; I think he had written me off... »

« Yes, a lot of people might have, » he said. *« When will you be able to walk without a cane? »*

« A few more months; I'll need to find a physio in DC. »

« Good, » and he remained silent for a while.

After a couple of hours, they stopped for lunch at a Mobil petrol station in Darien, Connecticut: there was a Subway shop and they both grabbed a six-inch sub and a drink. They sat on a bench outside, in the noise and the fuel vapors of traffic; Uncle William said:

« There is someone I know that I would like you to meet; he operates a small, dedicated team within the CIA that is focusing on something that seems to be gaining some traction. »

« In Iraq? » Said John.

« Yes, but also probably in Syria; the team is working on the identification of their leaders and evaluation of potential evolution. They could use your skills and determination. »

John had an ugly grin: *« Everything as long as I can make the bast... pay! »*

« He will need you focused, not crazed upon avenging yourself! » said his uncle. *« Be clinical and ruthless and you will have results! The money is not great but that is not a problem I reckon? »*

* * *

John nodded and finished his sandwich.

They drove another five hours and finally reached Georgetown, Washington DC, where his uncle lived; the house had not changed much since John had left it to go to Yale; his old unchanged room was still quite spartan, with no sign that a teenager had visited it every other weekends for many years.

He woke up the next morning around 7am and found a note from his uncle on the breakfast table: he had an appointment for lunch with a Mike Willow at a steakhouse on M Street North-West, noon sharp.

After having a cup of tea and some eggs, bacon and toasts, he hobbled carefully down into the basement: the old gym was still there: an old and worn-out punching bag, an exercise bike, some weights and a tatami. He sat on the seat of the bike and tried to slip the tip of his right sole into the strap of the pedal but could not make it stable enough at first to start pedaling: the tip was too loose in the large strap; nothing that a little tinkering could not remediate... After fumbling with his uncle tools, he was able to have a nice fit. He climbed up to his room, changed into gym clothes and went back down pedaling for twenty minutes: it was tough: he could not put much weight on his right leg; his right knee was still reluctant to fully bend after having been ignored for some months and a full extension was painful; he had set the resistance screw at an eerily low level for a start and just getting the right movement of his right leg had taken its toll.

He took a quick shower: after several falls and close calls on the wet slippery surface, he had developed quite a technique in his now handle-less shower in Middletown – he actually had now dedicated shower crutches... He then sat at the dining table with his laptop: no hit on Google for a Mike Willow living or working in DC, that sounded about right for a spook! He familiarized himself with the organization chart of the CIA, hoping to gain some kind of credibility.

As the morning went, he thought of calling a Uber to get to his lunch and cursed through his tight lips: « *Dammit, can't you walk one mile, you faggot!* »

The walk that should have taken him slightly more than ten minutes dragged along for more than twenty five and it was a sweaty and clearly angry young man that entered the white brick building; the restaurant was quiet as the noon crowd had not arrived yet; he told the waitress at the entrance that he had a meeting with Mike Willow; the cute red hair girl nodded and asked him to follow him: she was, as a lot of people interacting with John now, overly cautious and glanced repeatedly at his right leg.

They arrived at a table in a quiet corner, where a pretty fit sixty-something years old, bald Afro-American was seated.

« *Mike,* » she said: « *your guest has arrived!* »

« *Thanks Judy.* » She beamed a lovely smile to him and left them: « *I'll be right back to get your order.* »

« *Have a seat John; I am very happy to finally meet you.* »

« *Thank you Sir,* » replied John nervously as he sat down; « *Jesus, how can you have the shakes like a teenager on your first date,* » he moaned internally...

* * *

« Let's order now before it gets crowded, then we'll get back to business; the salmon's pretty good but I always come here for their "Steack Frites"... Sounds pretty French but don't expect any typical French stuff in here: you've been to France for a while right? »

« Salmon's good for me, thanks and yes, I have spent a year in Paris. »

« Any starter for you? »

« No thanks... »

« Your uncle told that you were pretty intense on getting back into shape! » The red hair waitress came back to their table: « err, my usual, Judy please, and a salmon for the young man here! And I'll have a glass of your Merlot, what's the name again? Can't ever remember it! Old age it is... »

« The Drumheller, Mike? And funnily you can still remember my name... » she smiled and turned towards John, « anything for you Sir? We have an amazing list of beers along with some good wines! »

« No, I'm fine: I'll have water. »

« Righto then, order's on the way, » and she left them.

« You know, your uncle has told me quite a lot about you! He is very proud of you, of your service to our country; deep down, he is still in shock that you joined the Marines: that's tough for an Army die-hard like him but he's getting slowly over it! »

« Where did you meet him? » Asked John.

* * *

« We worked on a project together some twenty years ago; we saved each other's asses several times in a row and we've kept in touch since then. »

« You did not tell me where, » John said abruptly.

« Nope, I did not, » replied Mike smoothly and the small talk went on for a while until he smiled: *« haaaa, there's our order, brilliant! »*

Mike went through his meat like a connoisseur, savoring each bite and commenting the wine; John was not so hungry and, deep down, actually felt that food was just a basic synonym for body fuel; Mike's bonhomie kept him on tip toes and it started to get on his nerves.

« My uncle William told me that you might need me for a job; what is it exactly? »

« Hmmm, yeah, your uncle asked me whether I could do him a favor… »

« What? » Said a startled John. *« I do not need a favor, I… »*

« Stop the nonsense, young man. »

Suddenly, Mike' smoothness had gone and been replaced by a scary hardness; his eyes were like steel: John was shocked by seeing Mike go all out Terminator on him.

« You're an overweight drunk, a potentially violent, self-harming brat, who hasn't been able to get his shit together since he came back from Iraq; Your wife has rightfully dumped you and you'd be a frickin' poor example of a man to your son… »

* * *

John simply fell back in his chair, stunned by the flood of truth handed at him by the low and brutally determined voice.

« Will you listen to me? » Said Mike. John paused, then nodded.

« Good, I'm gonna give you some stuff to do, some papers to read and, in a month from now, we'll have lunch again here and I'll let you know whether I need you or not! Are we good? »

John nodded again. Mike's transformation was immediate and there was again the flirty, smooth, perfectly educated corporate executive who had welcomed him earlier in the restaurant.

Judy came over and cleared the table: *« Would you like a dessert? »*

« I'll have the "crême brulée" and an espresso, » said Mike. *« Nothing for me, »* said John, still recovering from the brutal barrage…

« You're staying at your uncle's place, I suppose; will you be looking for a place of your own? »

John thought about it: *« Yes, probably so, there is nothing for me back in Rhode Island. »*

« As I understand, you have quite the money; I would recommend Palisades as a place to live at: you can find a nice quiet house close to the river and yet close to the center. »

* * *

He went on for a few minutes like a professional real-estate broker, picked up the bill that Judy had just placed on the table and left a card with a phone number.

« I've got to go; I will have stuff delivered to you tonight at our uncle's; let me know what you think about it! »

And left.

John remained seated thinking of their discussion and how he had made a mess of it. Judy came to him and asked: *« Would you like something else? Like a coffee or what? »*

« No thanks; do you know Mike well? »

« He's cool, ain't he? I like him: he's my oldest customer... I mean, he was already coming here before I started working here two years ago when I came to study at GU[18]. » She paused: *« you know he was a soldier for a while, a friend of his came with a picture of the two of them together, with lots of medals... And now he's some kind of professor, I mean he must be, like he's always reading reports and books when he comes on his own... He is, right? »*

John muttered some agreement, stood up and hobbled out of the restaurant. He walked up to Potomac Street, then up 33rd, a bit of Wisconsin and there he was.

At six thirty pm, a man wearing a dark suit rang at the door, asked for an id and delivered a heavy binder full of documents: news clips, accounting sheets... John went to the dining room and spread the documents on the dining table.

---

[18] Georgetown University

CHAPTER 4

Pantin, France,

April 25, 2014
  8:00 am

I was driving on the Périphérique Est[19], coming from the South; Chuppa was seated next to me in the black Renault Laguna, sucking yet another lollipop. Traffic was the usual nightmare as thousands of commuters were coming in from the A4, the main Eastern highway going some four hundred kilometers all the way to Germany. This morning, no German cars were to be seen, but simply bored drivers not willing to add their sorry persons to the already over-crowded RERs and métros[20].

We were coming from an errand in the south of Paris where we had visited a few supporters of the cause: we had recovered some cash and, quite unusually, some very virgin

---

[19] East ring around Paris
[20] French. RER: regional train lines, métro: subway

and apparently totally legit cartes d'identité[21], that would, with no doubt, be useful to help undocumented workers find a job or evade police scrutiny.

Thirty minutes later, we went off the Périphérique at *"Porte des Lilas"* and drove through the morning-busy streets: a mix crowd of Caucasians, North-Africans and Asian milling about, kids hurrying off to school, lorry drivers stopping and blocking the streets every now and then, to furious honking from angry drivers, more and more people on moped and bicycles; those areas that used to be rather run down were being slowly gentrified by the white collar families being chased away from Paris by the crazy real-estate prices.

We turned into rue Méhul and drove east; as we neared the sports ground on our left, I noticed some kind of a commotion ahead of us.

« *What's going on?* » Said Chuppa, suddenly alert and looking ahead.

Cars were stopping in front of us, some of them doing a U-turn in the narrow street; blue lights were blinking ahead. A couple of cars were already behind us.

« *Putain, les keufs[22], we are fucked.* »

« *Don't sweat it.* » I said. « *Stay cool.* »

We moved forward as the cars ahead of us got diverted; two

---

[21] French: National identification card (document given by the French State establishing identity)
[22] French slang: fuck, the cops

police officers were standing in the middle of the street, next to their cars; they were wearing black overalls with POLICE inscription in the back, bullet-proof vests and side guns; one of them was carrying a 9 mm HK UMP sub-machine gun, a rather unusual sight and a sure sign of trouble. Further down the street, a sea of blinking blue lights, baklava wearing officers in various civilian or uniform attires, trouble indeed.

They walked up to our car.

The officer carrying the UMP remained a few feet away from us; his colleague made the universally practiced roll with his hand: lower your window…

« *Bonjour Monsieur, Police Nationale.* » he said, saluting. « *You cannot go any further: the street is blocked. You have to turn around here.* » And he looked at Chuppa. I think that Chuppa couldn't breathe anymore: a lovely, red face shouting: « *I'm guilty as hell…* »

I flashed the Police badge that I had pulled out from the side of dashboard.

« *Bonjour Collègue*[23], *I am going a little further down the street; is there a way around?* »

« *Oh, bonjour Lieutenant, non, the whole block is off-limit.* »

« *Ok, what's going on?* »

« *An anti-terro op by the BRI*[24]; *we are here to support them; don't*

____

[23] French: colleague
[24] French. Brigade de Recherche et d'Intervention: Paris SWAT team

know much more. »

« Great, that's gonna last for a while... Ok, hang on in there! » I sympathized.

« You said it... Have a good day... Hey you! » and he turned his attention to a guy on a scooter who thought that going ahead in spite of the blockade was a good idea...

A three-point turn and back we went.

« What was that? » asked a recovering Chuppa, lollipop forgotten.

« What? The op? »

« Yes, but no: your police badge! You a cop, man? »

« Chuppa, stop being stupid: do you think that I would be driving around all day with a gun without a good excuse if I got pulled over? »

He paused: *« Is it legit? »*

I smiled: *« As legit as it comes buddy; it's a real one that an ass dropped in a bar a couple months ago; I got it for two thousand Euros and had someone change the picture; and there I am: le Lieutenant de Police Michel! »* I grinned. *« First time I use it though... »*

We stopped at a bistro rue Jules Auffret and ordered two espressos. We needed to find out what was going on and agree on a course of action; reaching out to Kamaal was out of question, even on Telegram[25]: if the cops had come for him, all his calls would be monitored... and had probably already been for a while...

I told Chuppa to head home, lie low and wait for my instructions. After finishing a bitter and truly bad coffee, I drove back home.

I rented a sixty square meter apartment rue Albert, in the thirteen's arrondissement[26] in the east of Paris; it was a quiet place with a heavy police presence due to the Police training center that stood at the beginning of the street: sometimes, it is better to hide in plain sight,   though I didn't think that Chuppa would cope well with that! There were more than thirty apartments in the building which offered some sense of discretion, without attracting too much attention like the « barres, » the huge run-down blocks inhabited by the tunnel and bridge crowds, that had been built in the sixties and seventies all around outside Paris.

I parked the car in the underground parking and, seeing no one as usual, went up to my flat on the third floor; I walked in, dropped my jacket on a chair and left my Glock 19 in the drawer of the console table next to the living room entrance. My apartment was neat and tidy - I'm a sucker for order - and had some decoration and a lone ficus, though a girl that I had, for once, brought back home, had told me that it lacked any kind of imagination, personality and warmth; she never came back! I turned on the television and switched to BFM

---

[25] Instant messaging and voice over IP service whose communications are encrypted and 'impossible' to access for a third party
[26] District: Paris is made up of twenty administrative districts

TV, a 24/7 news channel and there was the confirmation I expected: *'Breaking: anti-terrorist operation in the Paris suburbs, several people arrested; guns and cash seized!'*

The ankle holster went into another drawer in a night stand by my bed; I changed from my usual working suit into more casual clothes: chinos, polo shirt, worn-out Sebago boat shoes and a fashionable hoodie that everyone seem to wear these days; I was the normal thirty year-old pretending to a cool attitude. I also picked a small 13 inches laptop that I never powered home – I had another one for fun and official work – and left to roam about the streets with a satchel on my shoulder.

I strolled at random for some twenty minutes and sat on a bench in the sun; I had chosen a location some ten yards away from an Haussmanian[27] seven stories building, the traditional nineteenth century edifices that populated most of Paris' center. I powered my laptop and launched a WiFi sniffer; it was only a minute or two to access a poorly protected internet box via a VPN[28] and an emergency online email account that I had opened six months ago and never used yet; I opened a new mail and typed: « *K gone, waiting for next step!* » I saved the email but did not send it. I logged off and went to have a proper coffee in a little café I knew.

I walked home, stopping only to buy some food and some wine at the local Carrefour convenient store. I cooked a bacon and cheese omelet, poured myself a glass of *Moulin à Vent*[29] and ate quietly in front of the television. As Chuppa and I

---

[27] 19th century architectural style, named after Baron Haussmann
[28] Virtual private network, protecting identity and location of user
[29] Beaujolais red wine (Rhone valley, France)

had started our errand at four that morning, it was time for a well-deserved siesta.

I woke up at three, showered quickly and left home again: I took the line 14 subway and arrived at Saint-Lazare rail station; A Starbucks latte later, I was seated in the waiting departure lounge, logged to the public WIFI network and opened my email account; there was my template with a few words added: *'Unexpected, don't think that you are on Police radars – waiting for some confirmation from inside source. Will contact you soon with instructions'*. I erased the email and went to see yet another Marvel movie in a theater across the Seine River from my place.

I came home, had a light diner and did some yoga for fifteen minutes; yoga has been in my life for a while, since just before my time in Baghdad actually, as I found that it helped relieve me of my stress; I had founded my very own dynamic mix of Balasana, Viparita Karani and other poses: you should have seen the perplexed faces of my fellow fighters at the time...

I then went to bed and reviewed the latest evolution in machine tool amortization rules as decided recently by the French tax office: a proper way to fall dead asleep...

I am officially an accounting software consultant: I work from home and visit my clients when needed; I invoice them monthly, which drives home some three thousand euros per months. It's a legit business that pays for the rent and most bills; it is also a fine way to make sure that curious people do not follow too much on this line of questioning: who gets a kick from analytical accounting, let alone machine tool amortization? The fact that my two major customers are companies owned by brothers and never see, nor need, me allows for a full time work on my collection operation.

From what Kamaal allows me to take every week, most is used to pay for the team and their expenses: I have offered a few times to provide Kamaal with some reporting but he won't: « *Too much of a security risk.* » He said. « *And besides, I know you don't skim: your heart is pure!* » I learned later that he had me checked out thoroughly and still today regularly, including with a discreet visit to my apartment; the purity of my heart be wonderful, hard concrete evidence is truthful...

Good for me that none of the emergency cash that I have put on the side was well hidden in my flat!

I woke up the next morning at five, put some running clothes on and went for my routine run at the nearby George Carpentier sports center; It was opened 24/7 for runners who used the kilometer-long track round the football and rugby pitches extensively.

Not in the rain, not in the cold, certainly not at five fifteen am...

I ran alone ten kilometers that morning; it took me close to forty minutes and I welcomed the hot shower back home. Two Colombian espressos, some whole grain toasts with butter and I was off at six thirty.

I had decided to keep the collection process on, hoping that the operational security measures that Kamaal and I had put in place were enough to keep me out of trouble; besides, if the Police knew about me, there was nothing that I could do about it to prevent them from picking me up from the street and, in the meantime, I might as well cash in from our different sources...

I drove out and went to the south of Paris to pay a visit to Pierre in Vitry-sur-Seine: it had been some time since I had last heard from him and he had been expected to deliver seven thousand euros a few days ago. Stupid Jamaal had been removed from the street before we could make an example out of him and Pierre was my direct next likely target, an sorry inheritance from Kamaal... A late convert at thirty, he alternated between religious overdose and spits of « depravation » when he would party for a few days, only to repent remorsefully of his debauchery. He had a schizophrenic streak to his personality that threatened to tear him apart and I had the feeling that the climax was near...

I arrived at seven am at the Total petrol station in Vitry-sur-Seine, our meeting point; I was in early, as per my usual basic security routine, and drove along both ways and around the block before parking next to the station. Nothing stood out. I went in and bought a poor coffee from a vending machine.

Half an hour later and very unusually, he still had not arrived and I decided to pay him a nice home visit. I drove for an extra ten minutes before arriving to his place. It was a group of old five-stories white buildings that needed a good renovation. Almost eight am, the school rush was in full force: teenagers were pouring out of the buildings and walking to the nearby high school. The parking lot was emptying as those lucky enough to have a job were driving away to confront the dreadful traffic towards Paris.

I parked fifty yards further down the street where I still had a good view of the surroundings and waited for half an hour. I walked out of my black Laguna and entered the parking lot on the side of building A; I followed the path across the grass leading to building B. There was still some activity, enough for me to blend in. For that job and with some foresight, I had opted out of the suit and had donned casual all-purpose street wear, a PSG[30] cap and picked up a cardboard box that allowed me to walk along with purpose and a delivery to handle.

I entered the building: the elevator door was broken and, looking at what was inside and experiencing the ungodly smell, the cabin had been used by someone as a makeshift bedroom for some days. I leaped up the stairs to the third floor, turned right and stopped at his door. I rang the bell a couple time, just a normal delivery guy... At my fourth ring, I heard some noise.

« *Ok, OK, I'm coming.* » The door opened.

« *Bonjour Pierre,* » I said, as I was inserting my foot in the doorway.

« *Merde*[31]*, what you doin here?* » He started pushing the door distressingly. « *How do ya know where…* »

I shoved the door in and he fell backwards. I entered and closed the door behind me.

« *You forgot our meeting!* » I murmured.

« *What, today? Whasstheday.* » he slurred

* * *

---

[30] PSG for Paris Saint Germain: Paris main pro soccer team
[31] French: shit

« Today is the day when we meet and you were not there... »

« Er man, I guess I forgot... »

« That's cool. » I said. *« I'm here now, so let's do our meeting here! »*

« Su... sure, » he said and moved towards the living room.

« Are you alone? » I asked. *« Don't want anyone listening on us... »*

« Hu? Oh yeah, yeah, my girlfriend's gone now. » And he sat on his couch.

The living room was a graveyard of bottles of beer; dirty clothes were scattered all over; a lingering smell of cold cigarette was a welcome relief from the reeking of the whole place.

« Yeah, I can see that. » I said looking around.

« Hey man, you know, I'm a bit back behind my cleaning. » His voice was uneasy, his eyes blurring vaguely at me.

« Not only the cleaning... Where is the contribution from the brothers? »

« Ahem, you gonna laugh... » I didn't! *« Hum, I've got it there but not all is there; there's some dough missing 'cause I had to... I had to... You know, cover some expenses and that's okay 'cause I gonna get some more back in a coupla days... »*

« That's ok. What do you have right now? »

* * *

He stood up uncertain, walked to a dresser and opened one of the doors: « *It's there...'* »

And he turned around suddenly with a gun in his left hand!

I was already just behind him, having quietly followed, my ceramic knife in my right hand: I caught his left forearm with my left hand and drove the knife into his right kidney; he opened his mouth to cry but the excruciating pain took all the air out of his lungs; he dropped the gun and fell to the ground. I pushed the pistol away, left the knife in his body and, my heart rate slowly coming down, quietly pulled some latex gloves on. There was a plastic table cloth partially covering on the table. I covered Pierre with it after pulling the knife out and stabbed him randomly more than a dozen time until he stopped breathing.

I toured the apartment, found some cash which I pocketed and some drugs, ecstasy and what looked like cocaine, some of which I scattered around the room, the rest I picked. I found a plastic bag in the kitchen; I then folded carefully the bloody tablecloth into the bag, closed it and hid it into the carton box along with the drug I had taken; the knife went in as well, wrapped in a dirty tee shirt found on the floor. I walked out the apartment, closed the door behind me and, as I came down the first flight of stairs, I removed the gloves and slid them in the box. I walked casually through the courtyard, turned to the left in the street, crossed the road and put the box in the trunk. I drove away...

I went east until I reached the Seine River and turned left on Quai Jules Gesdes ; it was a quiet one-way road following the water: on one side, the water, on the other, mainly storage buildings with no one in sight; I stopped the car on the left side of the road and went to the fence overlooking the river: a casual 360° lookout and down went the knife in the brown water.

A few streets later, I found myself stopped behind a trash truck; I overtook it and parked two hundred yards later behind a white delivery truck: large green trash containers had been pulled out of the many buildings along the street in anticipation of the truck's arrival: I dropped the plastic bag in a container and walked away, just a normal guy heading home. After touring the block for five minutes and getting rid of the carton in another bin, I got in my car and drove home.

As I entered my flat, it suddenly hit me hard: I had murdered my first man in cold blood, a stark difference from being part of a group of soldiers shooting at an enemy; I went to my bedroom, unfolded out my praying mat with shaking hands, knelt and started praying: after a while, my breathing eased and I did twenty more minutes of yoga while singing softly a nasheed[32] that I had learned in Afghanistan.

« Remember the mission, focus on the mission. The mission supersedes all! »

The next day was off for me, with still no news from Kamaal, not that I expected any really and I decided to pay a visit to Louise in the afternoon; she held a massage parlor in the 14th arrondissement; I had become a regular customer and we enjoyed some casual sex together once in a while. It was good to be close to someone's skin, to confide, to feel human.

---

[32] Acappela rap favored by Jihadis

CHAPTER 5

Washington DC,

The same day

After quickly scanning the documents, John decided to sort them by type and date: news reports, bank slips, heavily redacted notes from various three-letter agencies. He quickly realized that he needed a map to understand the geography of the story unfolding before his eyes and powered on his laptop, launched Google maps and started looking for a story to follow.

What appeared immediately was that it was about radical Islam, taking its roots in Jordan and Iraq; it all started with *Jama'at al-Tawhid wal-Jihad or JTJ,* a militant Jihadist organization that John knew quite well: it was at the roots of the violence he had faced in Iraq for two consecutive tours. He actually remembered cheering and opening a so far well-hidden bottle of Lagavulin, to celebrate the death of its regional leaders al-Masri and Omar al-Baghdadi in Tikrit, Iraq.

The evident route was to follow individuals: this was

complicated by the fact that, quite obviously, some targets would hide behind different aliases; that some names or locations were repeatedly redacted off behind black stripes made it an additional challenge...

Name after name, location after location, action after action, a whole story of a country at war was painted before his eyes... and he could make nothing out of it; sure, he could identify individual stories here or there but they all met the same dead ends! Nothing to be learned from that.

He looked up from the pile of papers facing him and sighed in frustration.

« Tough isn't it? »

John jumped at the voice and turned around: Uncle William was standing just outside of the dining room, by the door frame with a smile.

« Oh, it's you, » said John. *« I didn't hear you arrive. »*

« I've actually been here for close to an hour but you were so absorbed by your reading that I chose not to disturb you! »

« Really, I... Err, what time is it? »

« Close to nine, » and John's eyes widened: he had been grinding at it for two hours without knowing.

« Feels good to use your brain, right? »

John nodded and grinned, then he frowned: *« I'm getting nowhere though: I can't make sense of anything that I've been reading so far. There is so much stuff: it's hard to know where to start. »*

« You did think that it would be easy, didn't you? All those years crawling in the mud and criticizing analysts who didn't know better behind their desks? » He did not wait for an answer: *« Diner is ready, clear the table. »*

That brought John back quite a few years back.

*   *   *

The same house, June 23, 1993

It was on a rainy Tuesday morning that John arrived in his uncle's house; the previous weeks had been a whirlwind of visits, sleepless nights and transfers from one adult's care to another: from the State trooper who had collected him at his school with a Rhode Island Department of Children, Youth and Families representative to the various judges and clerks of the Family Court, from the temporary foster home to a man, his uncle, his father's much older brother, that he barely knew.

« I am your Uncle William, » he had said the first time that he had met him at the Family Court. *« I will take care of you and you will come and live with me in my house in Washington, DC; it will be a few weeks to get all the authorizations settled and I will visit you every Saturday until then! »* He took his hand, shook it and left.

John had remained mum, still crushed by the harrowing loss of his parents.

* * *

True to his word, Uncle Williams had come the following Saturdays and spent the whole day of his parents' funeral alongside him; John had, to this day, a blurred memory of the event: it was lost in the fog of his tears and those of his parents' friends who seemed more bereaved than he felt. Yet today, he still could not enter a church as the souvenir of the entrance of the two coffins towards the altar made the loss overwhelming.

Uncle William had been the only relative interested in him, and not his money; none of his parents had siblings and his guardianship quickly became a financial issue rather than an emotional and educational project; two remote aunts that he had never seen offered to take him, only after hearing about the 13 million dollar trust that John would be inheriting!

The custody process was unusually fast and Uncle William was appointed as John's guardian until he would turn eighteen; it was a few years later that John learned that the Senator of Rhode Island had been a personal friend of his uncle...

He had been welcomed in the house by his uncle's maid, Azucuena, a stout divorced woman in her fifties, who took him in and looked ready to take on the entire world to protect him; at twenty-five and twenty-three, her two children were now living their own lives, thanks to Uncle William's careful vigilance. She would sleep in the house when he was away and spent quite a few nights by John's bed, singing him back to sleep after a nightmare.

Breakfast at seven am, lunch at noon, diner at six thirty, table set up by John, cleared by William: Uncle William, when he was home, lived by strict rules and would not tolerate deviations; for his birthday? A book. Christmas? A book. Discussion at the table would revolve around school, lessons learned, book read... Azucuena was the butterfly creating the far-away storm in the perfectly settled environment and would discreetly talk on weekends about sports, girls, games, whatever would pass through the brain of a young lonely boy...

*　　*　　*

Azucuena was gone, having retired and moved to South Carolina to take care of her two grand-children; how happy had she been when he had called her to invite her to his wedding, when he had Josh, her 'third grand-son' had she said. She had come to visit him at once at the Walter Reed military hospital when he was flown back from Iraq, after a brief stay in Germany. His bitterness and angst had scared her away in a quiet stream of tears.

Amalia, Azucuena's niece, was serving diner; eyes still wide after meeting John – no doubt phones would ring in South Carolina tonight...

« *What did you think of Mike?* » asked his uncle.

John winced.

He laughed: « *got yourself fooled by his nice grand-pa act?* » John nodded; « *You are not the first one though: Mike is a hard man and can be quite abrupt some time; behind his good nature, he is dedicated and ruthless; note, his is one of the best minds you'll find on both sides of the Potomac these days. He liked you apparently!* »

* * *

« I'm not so sure about that, Uncle William… »

« Believe me: if he gave you some documents to read, he liked you. Nephew of mine or not, he would have kicked you out of the restaurant before the main course if he had felt that he was losing his time! »

« Hmmm… » Was John's unconvinced answer.

They were silent for a while as they ate the entrée, a chilled avocado soup, one of Azucuena' signature dishes, that brought John back in time, a very ancient déjà-vu...

The rest of the diner and evening was spent quietly, his uncle recommending a physio nearby to pursue his physical therapy or commenting the news and the latest bombing of civilians in Aleppo; John had pretty much lived as a recluse for the past year and was surprised by the complexity of the Syrian conflict, a twisted playground of local, regional and world power plays...

*   *   *

John woke up the next morning at 7am and went down to the basement for some cycling on the exercise bike; twenty minutes later, he switched to some weights for an extra half-hour. A quick shower, breakfast and he was good to go.

First the physio: he did not want to go to Walter Reed as the hospital was too reminiscent of a past that he was trying to forget; he called the number that his uncle had given him and was rewarded with an appointment four weeks later, that was moved to the present day at 2 pm when asked for a referral! He shook his head: Uncle William's wizardry at work again!

He picked up the stack of documents in one hand and used one of his crutches to hobble back to the dining table: time to give it another go... Three hours later, he sighed in frustration: he was getting nowhere and had too many names, locations, numbers juggling in his mind in no specific order of significance: it was obvious that he needed a method!

He realized that he did not even know why he was doing that, what was Mike Willow's goal in handing him such a mess with no explanation... What was the purpose of the batch of documents? What was the goal: identify players? Predict what will happen? Design and recommend a policy? Identify one or many targets?

« *Only one way to know* » he thought, as he picked up his phone and keyed Mike Willow's number.

There was no personalized message, just an electronic voice asking to leave a message.

« *Good morning,* » said John. « *This is John Quirston; I would like to have a quick conversation about the documents that were delivered to me yesterday; could you call me back at a time of your convenience? Thank you.* »

This done, he went to the kitchen to grab something to eat, opened the door of the fridge and saw that a container with his name marked on it; he took it out and opened it: a salsa chicken, his all-time favorite dish... He made a small smile: phones had indeed been working all night... He heated it up in the microwave, no Azucuena around to balk at that, and ate it in the silence of the kitchen.

The physio was too far away to walk to and John ordered an Uber drive to reach the rehab center; he put his prosthesis on and, twenty minutes later, was dropped off a modern white building ; in a lobby that could aim for the cover page of Vogue, a cute brunette at the welcome desk made him sit on a lavender couch and fill in a complex questionnaire, aiming mostly at making sure that he understood the expensive cost of the care and that he would be able to pay for it…

« Mr Quirston? »

John looked up from the paper. A tall, muscular white man in his forties stood before him: dressed in an immaculate white, nameless set of tee-shirt and pants.

« I am Will Jones. Would you please follow me to my office? »

John struggled a while as, grabbing his crutches and his bag, the questionnaire escaped from his hand and the pen rolled to the ground below the couch. The man did not bother to offer any help and waited patiently for John to be ready.

They walked along the pristine corridor, surrounding by obscure modern art. The physio stopped at a door, opened it and let John enter first. The contrast was stark: the floor was pure concrete, the walls covered with some dark grey alabaster resin; there were no pictures; a lone desk and two chairs stood in a corner. The rest of the room was occupied by various medical equipments, a massage bed and parallel bars.

« Have a seat, Mr Quirston, » said the physio as he sat; *« tell me what you need from me! »*

* * *

« *Well it looks pretty obvious, doesn't it?* » said John whose nerves were slowly being challenged...

« *No Sir, it does not: you obviously had a below-knee amputation; the sutures have healed properly otherwise you would not support the prosthesis and it took place a few months ago as your gait with the crutches indicates that you have not yet fully absorbed your new equilibrium; apart from that, what can I do for you?* »

« *I was operated twenty months ago?* »

Will Jones raised an eyebrow: « *Was there any complications?* »

« *No!* »

« *When did you get the prosthesis fitted?* »

« *One month ago.* »

« *Is there a specific reason why it happened so long after the operation?* » John suddenly felt like a jerk...

« *Err, I... I wasn't ready to have it...* »

The physio looked at him: « *You had a rough ride.* » It was a statement that called for no answer.

« *You have a family?* »

That simple question raised another awkward moment...

« *A rough ride indeed,* » said Will. John nodded... « *How exactly did you get hurt? Jenny forgot to ask you.* »

* * *

« IED[33] in Iraq, I mean a bomb, a roadside bomb… »

« Yes, unfortunately, I know very well what an IED is; Army or Marines? »

« Marines. »

« Which unit? »

« Raiders… You've been there? »

« Yes, and some of my patients have too... Walter Reed bringing up too bad memories for you? »

John looked away.

« Right, so Mr Quirston, back to my original question: what do you want from me? »

« I want to get better… »

« Yeah, sounds logical to me; anything more specific? »

Suddenly, John knew: « I want to run again. »

Will Jones sat back in his chair and smiled: « Now we're talking: you see, I happen to choose my patients: I'm no priest, no confidant, no massager; I won't care about your sentiments, your moods; you don't come whining to me! Either you follow my way or you're out! You want to run; I guarantee that you will! Ready to suffer, sweat and conquer? »

---

[33] Improvised explosive device, often a road-side bomb

* * *

John grinned.

After doing a quick series of tests and agreeing on a schedule of visits for the following weeks, John left the rehabilitation center and hailed a cab back home.

As he was arriving at his uncle's house, his phone rang, the caller id undisclosed:

« *John? Mike Willow here, you left me a message.* »

« *Yes, err, I wanted to know: what do you expect from me?* »

« *What do you mean?* »

« *Well, I reviewed the documents but, truly, I'm getting nowhere: do you want me to look for something? Someone? I'm not...* » Mike interrupted him.

« *You're telling me you don't know what you're doing?* »

« *Err... In a sense... yes!* »

« *Good! Tomorrow, same place, same time!* » and he hung up!

The call was terminated so fast that John found himself looking at his phone, wondering if there had been a miscommunication.

« *Man, this is something,* » he muttered and he went to the kitchen to make himself a nice espresso.

Before having a look again at the documents, he powered his

laptop and checked his emails: in the middle of the usual spams, there was a fund raiser call for the family of yet another Marine from his former unit who had gotten killed in action... Instantaneously, he was transported in the zone, the killing zone: the smell of cordite, the sounds of the various guns, myriads of M4s, AKs, an M40 sniper round here or there, the cries of the injured, the orders barked around, the dark red painting the dead, the sweat glistening on the living; his heart went beating like a drummer on acid and he started panting from the tense burst of stress... The nightmares had come less often since he had given up the booze; they had also been less threatening. He had almost forgotten about them: the wakeup call was brutal.

He was in the middle of the living room, stuck and recovering, when Amalia entered: « *Buenas, Señor John, how are you?* »

« *I'm good,* » he breathed. « *I'm good,* » he repeated, more to persuade himself than to answer her question. She looked at him with worried eyes.

« *Thanks for the chicken; it was great!* » She beamed, then frowned.

« *You did not put in the microondas, did you?* » He did not answer.

« *Dios mio, she told me you would... Now, that is not good Señor John, not good!* »

The familiar, if ancient, ranting finally brought him back to the living room: « *I won't do it again!* »

* * *

« *Si, si, si, you say but you no do it... Am gonna destroy this maquina del diablo...* » And she left towards the kitchen grumbling in her teeth.

There was so much of Azucuena in her that John couldn't help himself and smiled.

The rest of the day went quietly: half reading a book on the history of Middle-East conflicts, half looking at a football game on TV. Diner was quick as Uncle William was away. And John entered a dreamless night.

The next morning was eventless: some time on the bike, a few basic stretching-for-dummy exercises that got him feeling stupid but that had been required by the physio, some reading again of the documents.

At 11:40, he left again towards the restaurant where he would have lunch with Mike Willow.

« *Hello Sir, how are you today?* » said Judy with a lovely smile, as he entered the Steakhouse; « *Here to see Mike?* »

He nodded.

« *He hasn't arrived but let me take you to his table!* »

« *There you are; would you like anything to drink?* »

« *No thanks.* » He sat.

He did not wait long for the CIA man to arrive; they quickly ordered some food and Judy left them on their own.

* * *

« So you don't know what to do with the docs that I gave you? Well, you know what? That's good: I don't need people in my team who speak when they don't know; in my team, we don't make up stuff when we don't know; when we don't know, we don't know, period. »

He smiled and asked in Arabic: *« How good's your Arabic? »*

« It's a bit rusty; I mean, I haven't had the opportunity to speak the language for a while... » replied John in Arabic.

« Your file at DoD[34] says that you could interact pretty easily with the locals during your third tour; your CO[35] actually commented that on a patrol with no translator, you were able to gather actionable intel on a local person of interest in Fallujah... And how's your Pashto? »

« Not so good, only went twice... » Said John; he was a bit rattled by the easy access Mike had to his file: this operation in Fallujah had been pretty highly classified; it spoke at length of his reach at the CIA. *« Well, what did you expect from a spook. »* He thought.

« Here's what you gonna do: first, get your Arabic in shape; how? Your problem; second, call Asal Afghan at that number. » He handed a card to him. *« She's from Kandahar and will be expecting your call tomorrow; you have twelve weeks to get your Pashto back into an appropriate level; in twelve weeks, you start in my team, question? No? Good! »*

« Aaaaah, here's my lovely Judy again; did I tell you John that she

---

[34] Department of Defense
[35] Commanding Officer

was secretly in love with me? » He winked to Judy.

« *Hush Mike, you should be ashamed of yourself: I could be your daughter... Besides you only interested in the horribly rare meat I'm bringing you!* » She laughed, served them and left.

« *If only she would believe me,* » sighed Mike, with a mischievous spark in the eye... « *Let's eat!* »

And thus, started John's new life, to the rhythm of the physio excruciating exercises and the Pashto lessons with a quiet Afghan woman...

CHAPTER 6

Paris, France

May 22nd, 2014

I had a problem, a money problem; since Kamaal had been arrested, I had kept the operation on and was slowly accumulating thousands of euros; I had so far hidden the bank notes in a sports bag, at the top of a closet in my flat, talk about an inventive hide...

It had been two weeks since Kamaal had been taken and the DGSI people had not stormed my apartment yet; the counter-surveillance procedures that I always had in place had highlighted no suspicious activity that I could notice. Knowing Kamaal, he wouldn't talk: being arrested officially, there would be no waterboarding for him! A lawyer was already by his side and the very protective French legal system would keep his mouth shut and me out of trouble.

Still, what was I gonna do with all that cash? As a loyal servant of the cause, I was certainly not going to indulge too much... The money was needed to support our fighting brothers!

* * *

Then, one afternoon, I received a message via an unexpected mean.

As I went out for a cool run, I saw a very old man standing on the other side of the street, looking at my house; while leaning quite heavily on a cane, there was a sense of purpose in the way he looked at the building I lived in. I turned left and headed for the park. An hour later, I came back at a comfortable pace: the old man was still there; he had crossed the street and was looking at me. Of North-African origin, with a medium height and a fragile built, he nodded to himself as I came about him: I realized that I had seen him the day before as I was going out for some errands; he had beeped on my inner threat assessment radar but I had dismissed him, as the DGSI[36] was not known to operate with eighty plus year olds…

« *I have something for you,* » he said in slow, heavily accented French and extended his hand: in his trembling pawn lied a cell phone, not your usual smartphone but a sturdy old-fashioned Nokia.

« *Kamaal told me to give it to you if he disappeared for more than two weeks* »

« *Who are you?* » I said, taking the phone.

« *Kamaal's neighbor, he visits me every Wednesday to play dominos and bring chocolates; he is a good man, he helps me pay for my rent. You see, no one ever comes to visit me anymore. And he did not come last week and not this week and I do not know who will come*

---

[36] French FBI

*and see me now... So I came here to find you: I had your address
and knew what you looked like. »*

« How did you know? »

« He gave me a picture of you. »

That was a shock: a picture of me in Kamaal's hands or
apartment was a sure way for me to get in trouble.

« Do you still have the picture? »

« Yes, here it is! » And he clumsily pulled out a folded paper
out of his pocket and unfolded it; it had been taken at this
precise location in the street, probably several months ago
from the way I was dressed up for the cold weather. I
carefully took it, frowning at my failure to notice the person
who had taken it.

*« You see; with the picture of the building and you, it was easy to
find you... Are you going to come and visit me? Do you play
dominos? Kamaal is a very bad player you know, I always beat
him. »* He smiled, then paused. *« No, no, of course not, you're
young; Kamaal will come next Wednesday; he is a good man you
know, helps me pay the rent... So I will go, my legs do not carry me
well anymore and waiting for you has made me very tired. »* He
walked away slowly.

I looked at him as he hobbled down the street and climbed up
the stairs to my apartment. As I was enjoying the luxury of a
warm shower, I started thinking about Kamaal: he obviously
had a back-up plan and I was part of it: what part? I would
have to wait to find out.

* * *

As it happened, the phone was out of battery; my course of action was simple: buy a charger, turn on the phone, hope that there is no PIN number required other than 0000 … and wait!

Buying the phone was easy thanks to the many Chinese IT shops near Bastille and waiting was part of my DNA: so many fighters die early for all their eagerness and impatience… PIN number was - wow! - 0000. I rested the phone on the table in my living room and waited.

My wait lasted a week: on a Sunday evening, around 11:30pm, the phone rang; a sharp ancient ring woke me up.

« *Hello,* » I said very appropriately.

« *Bonjour, we need to talk; can you be in Lausanne next Saturday?* »

« *Yes, where and when?* »

« *2pm, next to the kids roundabout on the harbor.* »

« *How will I recognize you?* »

« *I will; just be there!* » And he hung up.

Now the question was « *should I stay or should I go?* » Kamaal being neutralized, his contacts could have been compromised. Yet, if the French wanted to grab me, they would already have done so and, for others like the Americans, I was small fish and Switzerland was not an open country for extraterritorial renditions. So I decided to go but take my time…

* * *

The following Thursday, I packed for a few days and left home at my usual morning hour. I drove north on the Périphérique[37]; I turned on the A3 highway, then back south on the A86 and finally on the Eastbound A4.

Still cautious about being tailed, I had arranged for a car swap with the help of a small garage owner in Montry, near Disneyland Paris: a brother would lent me a Volvo with a decent mileage, whose owner had asked him to sell; my car would then be driven to one of the main parkings at the Disneyland railway station.

Nearing Montry, I stopped by a railway track, bent through a hole in the wire fence and quickly walked across the tracks; after a few minute walk through some bush, I found the car and the brother. We embraced: he gave me the keys to the Volvo and walked away to my car. The nearest bridge across the railway was six kilometers further, my two phones were off: no one would be following me now.

I had decided to avoid toll highways and remain on the Nationales[38] roads in order to limit the possibilities of interception and detections as each highway toll barrier had video surveillance. That multiplied the driving time to some eleven hours but I had an early start and I felt the security was worth it.

I slept in a cheap hotel in the morose suburbs of Dijon, which I paid in cash, and entered Switzerland at the Creux crossing around noon, one of the many French people entering

---

[37] Ring around Paris
[38] French main toll-free roads

Switzerland, either to drive to work - Swiss salaries are double that of the French ones - or just enjoy a weekend away. I bought the Swiss national highway toll sticker and sticked it on the windshield of the car: I did not expect to use it but not having it would make me stand out in the traffic and more likely to be stopped by the local cops, always eager to fine the careless tourist…

I had booked a room in a small hotel in Crissier, North-West of Lausanne: an hour after entering Switzerland, the car was safely parked in the hotel parking and I was enjoying a nice shower in my room. Diner was light and, after a quieting bout of yoga, I started praying.

Keeping the rhythm of the five prayers a day was complicated as I had to pray in places where no one would ever see me. Kamaal had told me one morning: « *Get off their radars; there are so many of us now to surveil that one who does not seem too zealous, skipping the Friday Prayer once in a while, will be invisible! Be disgruntled by your time in Afghanistan, in Iraq! Move away from the community! Shorten you beard! Drink alcohol, enjoy the French whores… But, once you are alone, repent, pray and meditate the preaches of an Imam who understands and support our fight; I'll give you an internet address where you'll find them … »*

Once, he took me apart:

« *You do know how to surf the net without being caught, no ? I know a brother who can teach you how, hijack wifi, VPN and so on! He works in a big IT company. A lot of brothers, they are young, reckless and stupid! They want to fight but have no discipline, no organization, no method; they think throwing a grenade in a deli like in Sarcelles[39] makes them great warriors like you! I tell you: they had to throw a stone in the window of the shop because the grenade explosion was so inefficient! They were in jail or dead within a month... I don't want that and you neither! We have bigger things to do and our enemies, believe me, they are not stupid; if an infidel like you can find truth in our fight, Al-ḥamdu lil-lāh[40], there are bastards who pretend to believe in the Faith but enjoy this kafir country and work for the police or the secret services... »*

He paused, boiling with rage.

« They look like us but are dead inside!»

And so, disappear I did; It felt strange drinking some whisky in a bar, getting naked and fucking a girl I had known for a few hours only; I started wondering whether the purity of my fight allowed for this, or whether deep down, it was convenient and that, frankly, I enjoyed bathing in sin...

*   *   *

I had a pretty eventless night and woke up at 7am; I worked through my routine of push-ups and squats, showered, shaved and prayed with a clear head. I went down to the restaurant of the hotel and had a continental breakfast with a surprisingly good coffee.

* * *

---

[39] A terrorist attack took place on September 9, 2012 in a Jewish deli in Sarcelles, a city in the Northern suburbs of Paris
https://www.telegraph.co.uk/news/worldnews/europe/france/9591892/French-police-kill-terrorism-suspect-and-arrest-11-in-nationwide-raids.html
[40] « Thank God! »

« *Time for some recce!* » I told myself and I drove into Lausanne to have a feel of the meeting place. I parked near the railway station and made my way down to the harbor, descending the steep streets, surrounded by the Saturday morning crowd of shoppers and tourists. As I neared the roundabout, I purchased a newspaper and stopped by a café and found a table with a good view of the surroundings.

I wanted to understand the dynamics of the place, where cars went, people crossed - Swiss are surprisingly respectful of traffic lights - and counted how long the main red light in front of the subway station lasted; all kinds of details that could prove useful should the situation go south. Crossing at the last second would make a potential tail quite obvious should he or she decide to cross the street, or would buy me some precious distance without disclosing that I had made the tail... Call me paranoid but I wasn't on my turf and I didn't like it!

After enjoying the morning sun, going through the news from the local newspaper and sipping a coffee just like the other people seated next to me, I crossed the street and walked along the pier, looking at the formidable mountains above Evian-les-Bains, the sail boats on the lake: « *I could live here* » I surprised myself thinking...

« *STOP IT!* » I yelled in my head, hitting the railing before the water and cursed myself silently: « *YOU HAVE A MISSION! YOUR DUTY IS TO FIGHT... You shall have no respite until the fight is over; your duty is to fight; you shall have no respite until the fight is over, your duty is to fight...*»

I took me several minutes to recover my calm and my sense of attention: to my right, a little girl with a pink mermaid dress was looking at me, frowning; our eyes met: she ran away!

I walked back up to my car and drove back to the hotel; I changed in running gear and drove south to the Parc Louis Bourget and ran at a good pace for an hour along the lake, careful to stay well away from my meeting point.

Back to the hotel to shower and prepare my meeting.

At 12:30pm, I left the hotel and drove again to the center of Lausanne; I left the car in an underground parking near Rue Centrale and walked down to the lake. At 1:20pm, I was seated at that same café a couple hundred meters away from the roundabout and I ordered lunch: a Steack-frites and a glass of Bordeaux wine, which I sipped slowly, scanning my environment behind my dark-shaded Ray-Bans.

The continuous flow of people and cars felt as normal as it had that morning: nothing was out of place, no delivery truck hanging around, no works being done on the streets, and because of the configuration of the Avenue de la Navigation, no parked cars in sight.

2pm: I paid my lunch in cash and, staying on the same side of the road, walked east along the avenue; I paused to look at the Chateau d'Ouchy, crossed the street and headed towards the harbor. The sun was glorious, dozens of people were strolling about, kids on their scooters, tourists taking pictures, of themselves mostly… I walked along the peer, looked at the ferries traveling back and forth to the other side of the lake in France, and finally arrived next to the roundabout.

It was a nice, one hundred year old machine, filled with

laughters and music and, right next to it, a man, holding two cups of coffee, was looking at me!

« *Ah, there you are mon vieux*[41]*! Just in time for a hot coffee… »* he said in perfect French, as if we had last seen each other just the day before. « *Here, take it! And let's walk along the peer! »*

I took the cup and followed him. He was a thin man, in the mid-forties, about 1.75 meters tall, with a dark complexion. He had a nicely trimmed beard and was dressed in a casually expensive way: a banker on a week-end!

« *My name is Ibrahim. »* he said softly, « *Kamaal has told me a lot about you… »*

I remained silent, drinking my coffee.

« *Now that Kamaal is out for a long time, we need someone to pick up the French operations that he has built over the past years; he told me sometimes ago that you would be the ideal person to replace him… »*

He paused; I waited…

« *Kamaal told me that your team was the most efficient of all our brothers in France; his exact words were: « Alain is my best guy; he knows how to listen, stay low profile; he is always cautious when we meet and keeps a steady stream of money coming towards the cause! » You know: Kamaal wasn't precisely the guy to offer praises like that to anyone. »*

« *He isn't dead yet! »* I said.

---

[41] French: « buddy »

* * *

« No, but he is off limit to our cause for many years, now; we cannot wait for him and need to move on: we are fighting against the most powerful enemies; they have all the money, the equipment they want; it is crucial to us to keep those many springs of money flowing to our cause. Do you understand? »

I nodded: I knew that helping fighters travel to Iraq, buying weapons, paying officials to look the other way, supplying our men with near-perfect passports, supporting the families in our cities, all this exerted a heavy financial toll.

« Yes, you do: you were in Iraq and in Afghanistan; you saw what we are fighting against… And you are a resourceful man… How did you manage to get out of Baghdad? You were hurt in a fight against some American soldiers I understand? »

I was expecting this, but wasn't ready to give him the full truth: « A good friend of mine helped me drive to the Turkish border; I pretended that I was his cousin, that I had been injured in a roadside bombing near a market and that I was going back to our village to see our family since I couldn't work in Baghdad anymore… And I had money to ease through the checkpoints! »

« Your friend is a very loyal man indeed; who is he? »

« We fought together and I saved this life once! » I paused. He looked at me intently. « Yusuf Al-Rahman »

« Are you still in touch with him? »

« No, when I came back to France, I decided to remain low. I did not think that the French police had picked me up and was not willing to take the risk. »

* * *

« He is dead, you know? »

I sighed and said very softly: « *salaa Allah ealayh wasalam*[42]! *How, when?* »

« Not long after you left apparently, an air strike… »

« The bastards kill too many of our brothers… »

The scene was surreal: here were we discussing war, surrounded by families, to the gentle sound of the small waves crashing on the peer, the singing of the sea gulls and the ever-hungry ducks…

Memories came back to me brutally:

Seated in the back of a white dusty Toyota Camry, the ubiquitous cheap and unbreakable car, driving for hours, waiting for ever at checkpoints, bribing our way when we could, hiding at friends of friends' places, sleeping on squalid mattresses, sweating at night, sweating in the day, chasing away the persistent flies, eating poor soups in which one was desperately looking for something recognizable…

The crossing of the Turkish border, the payment to a smuggler, the extra driving to a hotel far from the border to avoid Turkish security… The first bath in three weeks in a stream in the middle of nowhere… The recovery of my stash, a legit French passport and cash, hidden below some rocks near Tatvan, the crossing of the Armenian border near Igdir, the relief of a nice shower and shave in Erevan and an

---

[42] May God bless him!

eventless flight back to Paris…

« I can pick over from Kamaal; how many people does he have working? »

« He has five teams; and probably one which is obviously… »

« Compromised, » I cut him off. *« Do you know which? »*

« Maybe, that's going to be your first job. » He paused: *« Listen, I'm not too happy with this organization, too many people depending on one person, but it is as it is and the benefits have been truly remarkable. Are you familiar with the battle of Algiers? »*

I was but was not ready to let him know about that!

« No, History always bored me at school… »

« It's a movie[43], old but still excellent: watch it; you'll learn a lot about how to do your job and run your teams. »

« Right, » I shrugged. *« I will. »*

« You might have to rough the teams up; not hearing from Kamaal might have given them wrong ideas… »

« Like helping themselves with the cash? » I smiled; he did not.

« Precisely, you need to collect it and transfer it to a broker I will introduce you to. »

* * *

------

[43] https://www.imdb.com/title/tt0058946/

« How will you know that this guy will not skim some of it? »

« That's a good point; I forget that you have an accountant training: after each delivery, you send a WhatsApp message to a number that I will give you; You'll write whatever you want but will incorporate two numbers in your text : the first one for the thousands, the second for the hundreds; $50,800 will be blablabla 50 blablabla 8; Got it? »

« Yes; is there a minimum amount that I need to have before I call the broker? »

« No, but you'll have to balance the amount and the number of visits; every visit is a security risk for him… and for you! »

We went on like that for thirty minutes, covering every aspect of the ring I was going to take over, how we were going to communicate, strolling along the lake, two ordinary guys basking in the sun.

Once done, he gave me an email and a password for an obscure Australian internet provider account: all the details I needed - names, addresses, etc. - were written in a draft message that I would access, use and delete. This would be our preferred communication tool on top of the Telegram application that would be used to communicate the email name and the password.

We shook hands and separated; I took the long road back to Paris, spending several days in a guesthouse north of Lyon.

On my first night in Paris, I had some trouble falling asleep: the scope of my mission had suddenly widened and the stakes, and the risks, had gone way up!

CHAPTER 7

Washington DC,

May 2014

John quickly fell into a comforting, yet, active, routine:

Wake up at seven am.

He would visit Will Jones three times a week at 8 am in the morning and would train with him for an hour; he would shower at the therapy center and then drive ten minutes to Asal Afghan's study, in the heart of Georgetown University. There, from 10 am to 1 pm, he would alternate between conversations, readings, writings and lectures on Afghanistan; a forty-five minute break at the local sandwich shop - not a Subway though, as his lasting nightmares still gave him the creeps at the sight of one - and he would be back on the library for some more Pashto.

Home at five, time for Al Jazeera, Nile or El Sharq TV in the background for two hours; twice a week, he studied the Quran and listened to preaches from various countries. Most were incendiary, some were moderate, a few highly educated and complex. He specifically focused on the differences in thoughts, vocabulary, cultural habits between the various branches, the Sunnis and Shiites of course, but also the more obscure such as the Sufis. He made it a game to be able to identify them as quickly as possible in a speech or a picture.

Diner at seven with Uncle William and some reading - his uncle provided him with an endless string of geopolitics essays and books - before going to bed at ten pm.

The only different days were those without a physio visit: he would walk down to the basement and spend the following hour working out, following Will's training plan.

Saturday mornings were for swimming in the physio center pool: he hated it! It had been first an advice, then a request, and finally an order when Will Jones realized that John had not gone swimming for the first three Saturdays.

« *We need to talk,* » said Will one Tuesday morning after a rather demanding session that had left John panting hard and feeling pretty happy with himself.

« *What's wrong John?* » He had asked.

« *I reviewed the records and you still haven't attended a single swimming class! Swimming is an essential part for your recovery; let's be clear: if you don't attend, we'll be done with you…* »

John' smile left his face… He felt like a tool and yet: he couldn't tell him that he was afraid, that showing what was left of his body, the missing limb, the shrapnel scars on his right side was mission impossible, that he couldn't bear the pity that he saw in other's eyes while hobbling up and down the streets with his crutches, that look that he had first seen in a cute nurse's eyes… The young twenty-years old braggart who would drop his shirt at every opportunity to show off his abs was an alien long gone!

« *I'll be waiting for you on Saturday at ten.* » Will said and he left the room: « *session over!* »

So he went…

The following Saturday, he got up at eight, had a quick shower and a light breakfast. As nine o'clock was ringing on the old marine clock in the entrance, he ordered in a Uber and left home. The driver wasn't very talkative, which suited him well: he had tried on his swimming trunks the night before! Looking at himself, his less but still flabby body, his profound misbalance had confirmed everything he was afraid of; it was, incredibly, the first time he had fully looked at himself in a mirror in months and the result was…

« *Here we are Sir,* » the surprisingly polite Indian Uber driver interrupted his thoughts, « *do you need help with err… ?* »

John shot him a murderous look, opened the door and grabbed his crutches; once out he grabbed his gym bag and slammed the door shut! He turned, looked at the building and sighed. He hadn't been so deeply embarrassed and afraid since freaking out in front of his Marine buddies during his first parachute jump: there had been only one way forward and he had jumped!

« *Fuck, let's get it done then!* » And he walked: there, he saw Will chatting with the brunette at the reception desk. He looked up, saw John and nodded.

* * *

« Good, follow me! »

They followed a corridor on the right and entered the swimming center.

« Changing room's on the right there; I'll meet you on the other side. »

There were three other guys in the locker room when John stepped in. They were discussing the latest Red Skins' game, disagreeing in a friendly way, full of banter, provocations and useless threats. This was such an expected norm, carried out in every sports center in the world that John froze... The contrast with their broken bodies was something he couldn't comprehend.

« Hi, you're here for the training at ten? » A tall bald guy on the left said, as they all looked at him, *« I'm Matt by the way. Nice to meet you. »*

« Better hurry up, » said another, *« the boss's pretty strict on timing! Last time I was late, I had four extra laps to... »*

« Bullshit Ryan, » interrupted the third, *« You only did two! »*

« Hey smartass, I am missing an arm if you haven't noticed... So two laps count double for me... » He smirked. *« Joke aside buddy, she doesn't like it when someone's late! »*

They left the room and headed for the showers, discussing loudly the competitive advantage of missing an arm or a leg...

* * *

That improbable conversation left John in stupor for a short while. He shook his head and started to undress. In the past year and after many, many shameful spectacular fails that had often driven him mad, he had mastered the act of undressing standing on one leg. Swimming trunks on, he picked his crutches and walked to the shower room: there were bright orange 'pool only' crutches available on the left, so he left his in a box, showered and entered the swimming pool, very much aware of his figure.

« *Ah, there is my laggard,* » said a blond woman in a black sport swimming suit, as he came into the sunshine beaming from the glass roof. She was five feet four, athletic and slender, and exulted a no nonsense energy that John had known very well, crawling in the mud and yelled at by some instructor!

« *John, this is Jenna, your instructor; Jenna, this is John; he will be with you every Saturday from now on.* » Will had appeared from the side. « *See you Tuesday John!* » And he left.

« *Welcome John, get in the pool; just follow what the others are doing; we'll just go easy on the intensity and the repetitions with you as you are just starting…* » She turned abruptly towards the pool with a mischievous smile: « *and I won't hear any whining from you guys, unless you want me to add some high intensity amusement to today's session!* » Thus cutting in mid air the smart replies that were about to land!

Forty-five minutes later, he was exhausted, what had seemed rather dull at the beginning had transformed into a brutal crescendo; he surprised himself by climbing out of the pool without much afterthoughts, almost not caring about what the other swimmers would think of him… Jenna was there and handed him his crutches.

« You did well John, » she said with a big smile: *« see you next Saturday! »*

« Thanks Jenna! »

As he entered the changing room, Matt looked up and said: *« Hey, we usually go for a beer after the session, are you in? »*

« Err, yeah, sure. »

« Cool; let's meet outside and we'll walk there together; it's just a couple block… »

Fifteen minutes later, they arrived in front of John's Hyde, a small bar, hidden behind a blackened weather-worn facade and darken windows; it was calm, with some cool jazzy music in the background. The other two guys were already seated in a booth on the left.

« Hey, I'm Ryan and this is Phil, » said a red hair chubby guy, the one missing an arm.

« Hi, I'm John. »

« Have a seat, » said Ryan. *« We usually get a Bud, except for Matt who can't live without his Corona. »*

« Bud's fine. »

They ordered and introduced themselves: Matt was a former police officer turned PI, who had lost his right leg above the knee in a high speed crash on the Beltway; Ryan was a banker, also hurt in a crash, this time on a bike; Phil, missing some toes and fingers from a freak winter trek in the Great Smoky Mountains, was a software specialist.

The beer felt wonderfully fresh and great.

« *What do you do John?* » Asked Matt.

« *Nothing right now, working on a project.* » John was taken aback by the question: are you actually allowed to say that you work for the CIA? Did he actually work for the CIA? Too many questions that he would have to find answers to later.

« *How did you get hurt?* » Asked Matt.

« *Iraq,* » said John

« *IED? You were lucky… »*

He was right: in a sense, he was the lucky one, though he would have probably have a hard time acknowledging it looking at himself in a mirror.

« *Where are you from?* »

« *Rhode Island* »

« *Well, being a vet, you might have a go at government jobs… »*

« *Yeah, that and I have family here.* »

The conversation switched to sports and some obscene sign-on bonus a quarterback had received: Ryan, the banker agreeing with it, law of demand and offer and all that, Matt playing the communist. For the first time in a long time, it felt good to be with people, not to empty a bottle alone…

« *Guys, gotta go,* » said Phil, who had been typing furiously on his smartphone with his remaining two fingers…

They all emptied their bottles and Matt paid: « *my turn,* » he said, « *you'll be up next time!* »

On his Uber ride home, John felt the most relaxed he had in months… No, not relaxed: being just almost a normal guy was something new!

The following weeks went by swiftly; he was getting in better shape and his newly found bunch of friends brought him some balance that he had not realized was missing.

« *You look better!* » Mike had also noticed when they had lunch a couple months later at their usual restaurant. His call had taken John completely by surprise in the comforting routine that had become his life.

« *Let's talk business before I enjoy my Steack-frites! My people tell me that you have been true to our agreement; Asal was quite impressed by your progress in Pashto.* »

*   *   *

« *Haunted and driven,* » she had actually said, « *I don't like him: too many ghosts in him…* »

« *Yes, but his Pashto Asal?* »

* * *

« *Oh, good, quite good for a* [44]بهرنی*; he has made surprising progress... He understands pretty much everything, even when I speak quickly. Like I said, driven...* » She paused. « *Don't send me another dead one like that.* »

« *I won't; thank you Asal.* »

*   *   *

« *Thanks, I have actually enjoyed it; I mean, having something to do... I have also started looking at a place I could live at, not too far from Langley...* »

« *You're not going to Langley.* » Said Mike.

« *What? What do you mean? I am out before I even started?* » The rage that John suddenly felt was sudden and surprising. How could Mike do that? How come that dead-upon-start job abruptly felt so important to him, lifesaving to be honest!

« *It's time I give you some more details about our collaboration,* » said Mike, oblivious of the storm he had initiated. « *You will work for the CIA, but not in Langley, not far from here actually.* »

John had nothing to say to that, his eyes alight with emotions.

« *John, I am a senior Director at the CIA; I run an independent department called the Red House. My role is to provide the CIA's senior leadership with an independent, apolitical, iconoclast opinion on various matters of interest. You see, Langley's full of politics, analysts take in the data and look at it - willingly or not - through the prisms of their bosses, who spent a good part of their time*

---

[44] Foreigner in Pashto

fighting turf wars… One opinion - should I say a trend supported by an agenda - usually wins and all dissident voices are muted, to the detriment of the truth and the very mission of the Agency. »

« My role is to carry that lone, dissident voice and present it to the seventh floor[45]; they then act on it or not, it isn't my problem anymore… For this, I need two things: the best possible intel and the best and most diverse people, hidden away from Langley »

He chuckled: *« consider me as a start-up within the CIA, but with no cash issue! The team uses all the new techs available, with a special focus on data; you'd be surprised by what raw data can tell us… »*

John's head was spinning…

« The office is at Georgetown park; here's the address, » he gave him a card, *« I expect you there Monday at 8am; dress code is startup casual! »*

Judy arrived, her usual smiling self.

« Enjoy your meal Gentlemen! »

« How did your semesters go? » Asked Mike.

« Come on, Mike, I've aced them, you know me! Time for me to go to SFS[46], that is, if they take me in… » She left as another table caught her attention.

* * *

---

[45] The seventh floor at Langley hosts the office of the Director of the CIA
[46] Walsh School of Foreign Service, Georgetown University

« Oh, don't worry, you will, » smiled Mike once she was gone.

« Are you monitoring her? » Asked John.

« Fluent in four languages, 4 GPA for as long as she's had one, one philosophy essay published and paid for by a newspaper, no parents, few relatives, no steady boyfriend and a sharp tong... » Mike closed his eyes, savoring his meat.

« You are actually growing her? »

« I look for talent, » corrected Mike, *« I don't care where they come from or how damaged they are... »*

That shut John for good...

CHAPTER 8

Paris, France

June 1st, 2014

That trip in Switzerland had left me both energized and confused: it was a big leap from overseeing a few guys that I knew very well to meeting people who I didn't know and who, at least for one of them, might have ratted away my mentor…

I had very good knowledge about the five guys I had been working with: I would sometimes follow them, visit their apartments, check out their girlfriends, and for one of them, scare the hell out of him on a healthy monthly basis… Needless to say that none of them knew the others and that no one knew my real identity, nor where I lived.

I would visit them once a week, in random places and at random times, once in a while showing up unannounced; money would be collected in uneven amounts: at the end of each meeting, I would tell them to get in touch with me when they had collected a specific amount of cash, an amount that changed every time, thus confusing any one looking at patterns.

I had also started taking in alternative means of payments: one of my guys was bringing in some bitcoins; another shared with me logging credentials for various PayPal and Western Union accounts: he would put the money on those and I would empty the accounts from a distance…

But what Ibrahim had given me was something else: a list of eleven associates, some of whom had had no contacts with Kamaal for months.

*   *   *

Right, let's get organized:

Step one: get rid of the money that I already have,
    Step two: identify the mole,
    Step three: visit the associates and persuade them to collaborate,
    Step four: survive that mess!

*   *   *

    First, the money.

Ibrahim had given me a contact: Fazil, a French guy of Turkish origins who lived north of Paris in the city of Sarcelles. He would be my broker: he would be responsible to transfer the cash out of the country.

I had a phone number to call and a delivery « from his Swiss cousin. »

We met on a late windy day on the parking lot of a Total

petrol station on the A1 north-bound highway; the rush hour had sprung its usual trap to thousands of motorists, who struggled by, leaving Paris. I parked in the truck area, pretty much hidden from the shop and the traffic.

He arrived late; I had been waiting for him for thirty minutes, which had made me conspicuous, forced me to look under the hood and pretend to have some kind of engine trouble. Needless to say that my mood was not the most welcoming.

He did not apologize and asked me for my « credentials » : a half teared eight of spike, that Ibrahim had given me back in Lausanne. He huffed and puffed, smoking a foul smelling cigarette, some cheap Turkish import.

« *What you want?* » he said.

« *You heard about Kamaal?* »

« *Hmm…* »

« *Well, I am the new Kamaal and I want to organize how we will be working together!* »

« *You don't organize, I do! I tell you where, how, when; you come and give me the kebab. Then you go…* »

This was going right in the wrong direction: I was in the position I hated the most, dependent on someone with no immediate alternative… But, fuck it, I was not going to be jerked around so easily. I smiled.

* * *

« Listen vieux[47], you've got a system in place, I respect that, but don't push it too far because if I lose confidence in you, you not only will lose my business, but I'll make sure that you have a hard time explaining to your community why you got caught on tape fucking your wife's eleven year old cousin… »

He paled.

I went on: *« Are we ok then? You don't like me, I don't like you. I don't give a shit! Let's get down to work! »*

So we did: agree on how to communicate, a Telegram account on a new burner phone; when to communicate, only dates ending by 3 or 7; agree on how to request a removal of cash, as he and I surely did not want to interact; how to make sure that the transporter would not screw us…

The general idea was to get cash in the Hawala[48] brokerage system: he had a contact somewhere, probably Turkey; He would communicate to him the amount that I had delivered, minus his commission, and the broker would pay that amount to someone send by the brothers; no bank, no transfer information to hack; absolute trust, for the penalty for trespassing was death to the broker and his close family, usually at the hand of his own clan.

Fazil owned various businesses, including a small dilapidated kebab fast-food chain; this made it easier to

---

[47] French: old man

[48] Hawala is an informal money transfer system based not on the movement of cash but on the performance and honor of a network of money brokers

transfer the cash… It had the down side of me eating in his, at best, lackluster joints once in a while…

*   *   *

Ok, money taken care of, let's move to the most dangerous issue: the mole…

Ibrahim had given me a contact: some guy working at the French Police Paris HQ.

« *Careful with him* », he had said, « *the guy's half crazy, with ego issues the size of the Eiffel Tower.* »

He had not mentioned that the guy was half-deaf, had a limp and an absolute disregard for any kind of operational security…

I approached him one afternoon, as he was going home after work; I had been waiting, seated at a café terrace, enjoying the warm sun, eying behind dark sunglasses the summer dresses and short skirts passing by…

« *Bonjour Jean-Pierre* » I started walking next to him

« *Who are you? Do I know you? Leave me alone!* »

« *A friend of mine has told me about you, that you could help me with a little problem…* »

« *Yeah right, don't give a shit about your friend. No one helps me; why should I bother helping anyone?* » He turned his back on me and crossed the street.

* * *

« Let me buy you a beer or a coffee, come on! I've got stuff for you »
It wasn't too difficult to follow him and he knew it…

« Ok, ok, who's your friend? »

« Let's sit first, ok? Here, the café round the corner, is that all right with you? »

I entered the café and directed him to a table, away from the street and possible onlookers. I sat against the wall, facing the entrance. I ordered a demi[49] for me, he shrugged and asked for one as well.

We took our time, the tension slowly easing away as the beers were drunk…

He sighed: *« Who's your friend? »*

« Oscar from Switzerland… »

He looked at me.

« Oscar's always getting me in trouble, asking for information that is difficult to find, very dangerous for me… »

He was smelling the cash and not doing a very good job of hiding it…

I ordered two extra beers.

« There is an informant ratting for the Police; he is the one who gave the name Kamaal Musa to the counter terrorist unit at Quai

---

[49] French: half pint of beer

des Orfèvres[50]*… I want to know who he is! »*

« No, no, this is very protected information; almost impossible to find without being noticed. It's hidden behind firewalls and codes… »

« Good for me that you're their IT specialist, no? »

« No, you don't understand: there are random checks, connection passwords, even only specific computers who can access that kind of… »

« And those computers never have maintenance issues? » I gently interrupted him… *« I mean, should one have a problem, you would be the guy in charge of correcting it, no? »*

« Yes but, what you're asking is impossible… They would notice the intrusion… »

« Well, that's disappointing, » I said, *« Oscar told me that you were really good, the best, he actually said, and his bosses are too stupid to realize that they have a cador*[51] *in their team… »*

He frowned: *« Yes, they are stupid but you know their real problem? Their real problem is that they are just full blown racists; I'm black so I'm stupid… They smile at me like they… They don't even realize what I can do, what I know… »*

He finished his beer

« Hmmm, maybe I could do it, but it is dangerous, so

____

[50] Street name: Paris Police HQ
[51] French: heavyweight

dangerous… »

Back to the money…

« Are you taking some vacation this summer? » I asked, *« Are you going back home? »*

Home was an island in the Indian Ocean, twelve hours flying from Paris…

« Are you crazy? Do you know the prices of the plane tickets? »

I did…

« How about I help you with those? I understand Business class is a total bliss… I know a travel agency that can get you really great deals… And imagine when them bosses smile at you, who will have the bigger laugh? »

That nailed it!

« Let me think about it. »

« Let's have another beer here, next Monday; You'll get a call from the agency very soon, ok? »

« Ok »

« Good, take care my friend! »

He left the café, oblivious of the people around him. I followed at a distance until he arrived home.

Meeting him again was a security issue for me but I was

certainly not going to initiate a digital trail with that walking disaster…

*   *   *

I also needed to reorganize my network: there was simply not enough time to visit the associates and keep tab on my guys: I had to delegate that to someone and Chuppa was the obvious candidate.

I had groomed him for months now; his gangsta stance was slowly morphing into a more casual, inconspicuous style that helped him blend in the environment. In a sense, he was getting more dangerous and his faith had gotten stronger, listening to preaches and watching videos of fighters in Iraq or Syria. We were training sometimes in discreet parks and he was always eager to learn new hand to hand combat skills: I made sure to kick his ass regularly to remind him who was the top dog…

Over the following days, I introduced him to my four guys and the various safety measures I had in place with them.

« *Have you done all this to me too?* » he asked as we walked away from a meeting.

« *What do you mean?* »

« *You know everything about those guys: where they live, where they work, who they fuck…* »

« *What do you think Chuppa? Would I delegate this job to any jerk?* »

* * *

He moaned: « *argh man, everything?* »

« *Well* », I grinned, « *I'm actually impressed that you haven't cheated on Sabrina too much yet…* »

I burst out laughing, seeing him redden.

« *Forget about this Chuppa: I trust you and we are doing good work to help the brothers and our Jihad. This is what counts!* »

*　　　*　　　*

It was quickly time to get back to my miserable IT specialist…

I was waiting for him at the same café, a dozen yards from the Métro exit; as for the previous time, he did not see me and jumped when I appeared at his side.

« *Do you have time for a beer?* »

« *Ah, it's you… Hm, yes, yes, one beer is fine.* »

We went to the same place and ordered beers.

« *Did you get a call from the agency?* » I asked.

« *Yes, it's incredible: they said that I had won an all expense paid trip to the Réunion Island for me and my family…* »

« *What did I tell you? I can make things happen… But can you make things happen?* »

He looked around and, looking very much the conspirator, whispered: « *I can and I have…* »

* * *

« Do you have a name for me? » He did…

« You know, » he said, *« in his file, there was his browsing history on the computer they seized when they arrested and turned him; there were many links to dark net websites explaining how white men had screwed us… »* The whispers were gone leaving room to a growing rage… *« Are you making them pay for this? How? »*

« Yes », I said, *« but that's not your fight; you'll give us great service where you are… »*

« Yes, yes, but with my wife, we look at those videos; she is happy because I am praying more with her… » He grinned. *« She better not know that I drink beers… »*

« Have you told her about me? »

« No, this is a secret, no? »

« Yes! » Time for him to spill the beans, I remained silent.

« Mustapha Alloum » he said. *« he was caught smuggling some weed and agreed on becoming an informant in exchange for some leniency and his brother's shortened jail term. »*

« Thanks, » I rose and left some money on the table. *« Enjoy your vacation! »*

« Wait », he said, *« How do I contact you if I can have more information? »*

« I'll find you if I need you. »

* * *

I left, having no intention whatsoever of seeing him again. This proved to be the right call when, several months later, he went berserk on a killing rampage[52] in his office at the Police HQ, getting shot dead in the action…

*   *   *

I now had a name and needed to think of a strategy to get rid of him: the obvious solution was to not do anything: Ibrahim had been adamant that he did not know the other members of the group and it made sense as none of them had been picked up by the DGSI or the anti-terrorist police.

But I had a credibility problem: first, would Ibrahim understand that I do nothing, and more importantly perhaps, could punishing the rat ostensibly have a 'positive' impact on the others and inspire a proper and sane rule abiding fear?

I had gotten away with one murder but that was pure self-defense and was well within my personal ROEs[53]; this, on the other hand, would be premeditated and attract some media coverage, which was the goal, and a major Police investigation…

I needed to think of it.

On the Métro[54] home, I decided to make a detour and visit Louise, the masseuse I was seeing once in a while.

The massage parlor was located on a quiet street of the 14th

---

[52] https://www.bbc.com/news/world-europe-49997776
[53] Rules of engagement
[54] subway

arrondissement, in the south of Paris. The parlor window was obscured by massage ads and price list, acupuncture body maps and the regulation boards so favored by the French administration.

The air inside was smelling of incense and fried noodles. A waving good luck cat had been positioned next to a makeshift altar on the small bench by the window; Louise was seated behind a desk looking at some Youtube video. She was petite, a third generation-Chinese French citizen, with shoulder long black hair and a bland face.

She looked as I entered and said something in Mandarin towards the back of the room; another Asian girl walked in, this one I had never seen, and smiled at me; I removed my shoes and put them in a locker on the side. Louise signaled me to follow her and we walked along a narrow corridor sided by a couple massage rooms. Those were dedicated to the massage-only customers…

 At the end of the corridor, we took the stairs going down into a dingy basement; there was the room on the side that I was used to frequent.

Louise closed the door and turned towards me; she removed my jacket and dropped it on a chair. She unbuttoned my shirt, vaguely caressing my abs, opened my belt, pulled down my trousers and dropped to her knees.

She stroked my dick through the fabric of my boxer short and, once satisfied by its hardness, pulled it out and started sucking it.

I stopped her: she looked at me and nodded. She stood and,

in a swift move, removed her dress. She was fully naked underneath.

I took a condom from a box resting on a small dresser, unwrapped it and put it on. Louise had now moved to the bed and was positioned on her hands and knees: she knew that I liked it doggystyle.

I grabbed her waist and entered her slowly; she was quite wet, which would have been comforting had I not seen the bottle of lubricant close to the bed. I moved faster to her weak cries of encouragement.

It was all over quite quickly…

As I was seated by her side on the bed, she lit up a cigarette and asked me: « What's going on? »

Those were the first words that we had exchanged since I had arrived.

« I have a problem… »

It was nice to express it out loud, even if I did not give her too many details…

*   *   *

In the end, I found a different albeit efficient way: I let it known discreetly around his block that Mustapha was a Stup[55] informer. The drug dealers quickly took it in their own hands to settle the issue; Mustapha was found dead in a

----

[55] French slang: drug squad

dilapidated building, his last hours having clearly been dreadful; his brother was stabbed a few days later in the jail showers and died in the prison infirmary.

Once the mole was removed, it was several months before I had a reasonable grasp on the network; the workload was overwhelming, even with Chuppa's help. I had to hire officially an extra accountant for my small company: he would do the actual work while I was 'developing the business'…

Depending on Fasil for the cash transfer was not satisfying and I started thinking of ways to industrialize that part of the business; fortunately I had help and some computer genius came up with an idea: use an AI to create accounts and manage transfers between the many professional and private bank accounts, in a way that would evade TRACFIN[56] and other financial auditing services. It started nicely on a small scale, once Ibrahim had given me the receiving bank accounts details.

---

[56] French financial intelligence service

CHAPTER 9

Washington DC,

June 2nd, 2014

John took a Uber ride for his first day of work in several years; the car dropped him in front of Georgetown Park mall; he checked the address but it was the right one. There was a brown, nondescript door once inside the mall entrance, on the right, with a sign that read 'Westfry Consulting & Programs'. He rang the bell.

« *Yes?* » Answered a feminine voice.

« *John Quirston, I have an appointment with… * »

« *Come in!* » She interrupted.

The door unlocked with a buzzing sound; John pushed it and was surprised by its weight. He entered and found himself in an empty grayish waiting room, facing an elevator. Its doors were opened, there were no buttons inside. He walked in and turned to see the doors closing on him. He felt the lift move up, then a stop. The doors opened silently.

* * *

He was facing an empty reception room and some double doors. The elevator doors shut behind him; a buzz in front of him; a muscular man carrying an AR15 appeared, pushing the right door opened.

« *Good morning sir, please come in!* »

A sixtyish old woman was waiting behind the muscle.

« *Mr Quirston, my name is Amanda Jones; I am the office manager at WC&P. Mike told me that I would see you this morning. Welcome to the Red House!* »

« *Morning,* » he muttered, a little impressed.

« *Please follow me: we have a bit of an admin tunnel to go through, I'm afraid, before you get to meet the team.* » She led him to a room facing the canal, the only one with a window he learned later, and was offered a coffee.

The tunnel turned out to be three hours of indiscriminate paperwork to fill, non-disclosure agreements to sign, detailed federal punishments in case of a breach of confidentiality to understand and a polygraph test… John's head was spinning with the load of information. Amanda had also placed his phone in a code secured locker for him to use: « *nothing digital gets any further,* » had she said.

Finally, Mike Willow appeared: « *Hi John, how are you doing? Sorry I couldn't make it earlier…* »

« *I'm fine.* »

* * *

« *A bit of hassle this admin right? You don't know it but you are actually lucky: at Langley, this would have taken you a month… Now, I think that Amanda's happy with you; follow me!* »

They went through yet another heavy door after ringing a bell.

« *Notice how heavy they are? They are all opened only by an operator from the security office. If the operator doesn't recognize you on the video feed or a member of your party, you don't get in; in case of an emergency lockdown, you'd need a powerful breaching charge to break in, at each door… On top of that, the elevator is equipped with the latest Xray and sniffing tech: you carry a gun, you don't get out; you carry various types of explosives, chemicals, you stay stuck in it… And the operators have the ability to gas you from a distance…* »

He grinned like a kid facing a candy.

« *Yet they did opened the door to me.* »

« *What do you think? They've had your picture, hand prints and a vocal signature for a week…* »

They had entered a large windowless office, several thousand square meters big, with quite a few cubicles. There were some twenty people staring at him.

« *Folks, this is John!* »

« *John, this is the Red Team! The best out-of-the-box thinkers you'll find anywhere and especially not in the administration! Aaannnd where is Bubba? Ah there you are! John, Bubba's going to show you around, how we work, the tools we use, What we do and don't do... »*

A giant red-haired, bushy bearded guy appeared from behind a desk and extended his hand; he was wearing a very cheeky Hawaiian shirt and pink flip-flops...

« Hey, nice to meet you! Come on, let me show you your work station, then I'll introduce you to the team... »

His cubicle was in the far left corner, a thirty square feet space, filled by an impressive display of large screens and several computers, empty shelves and the most complex office chair he had ever seen.

« Yeah, this is a piece of art, that chair, John; you can sit on it in more than ten different ways; pretty comfortable to sleep on it too... »

The look on John's face must have been telling...

« Let me get you a feeling of how we work in here: the house's opened 24/7; people work when they want or need to; there are a couple of us who actually live permanently in a different time zone; notice the various clocks up there? »

Clocks were displaying time in various locations: DC, Kabul, Baghdad, and others, including the Zulu time indication for each.

« There is no dress code here: some like it formal, some less... » He smiled, ironing his flamboyant shirt with his hands.

« Bring your food with you: it's a bit of a hassle to go down through all the security just for a pizza... Amanda has told you about where

to park, right? Oh and yeah, if someone asks you what you do and what we do, basically, we are a think tank doing consulting for the government on auditing matters. You'll need to get familiarized with the full charade: it's waiting in your House inbox… »

« Now, let's get you aware of the system. »

He powered the main frame and asked him to set his index on a print reader and read a sentence that had appeared on the main screen.

« The system asks for a different random finger and a difference set of words each time. I'll take you through the various databases this afternoon, but let me show you the cool stuff… »

He launched a program called DIGA, for Digital Intelligence Gathering Aggregator.

« So, let's diga you… John Quirston »

« Two hundred and forty eight entries only… Of course, not a very usual name; hmmmm, not a birth place, too easy… Missing a leg maybe? »

John's life appeared on the screen!

Birth place, Yale grades, phone numbers - including an old one, long discarded - bank accounts, Marine files, browsing history, pictures of his wife and Josh, potential friends, even sports club membership…

The look on John's face must have been telling… Bubba laughed: *« This is why I love introducing the new guys to DIGA; how cool is that, hu? On my first try, I actually found a membership that I had forgotten to cancel and was still paying… »*

« Now, keep in mind that the system records everything you do and keeps an eye on you all the time: it checks your queries against your DIGA; no stalking an old girlfriend or you'll get Amanda in your face pretty quickly! »

That sounded like something that you didn't want to happen to you!

« We got DIGA quite recently: an IT genius fed up with Oracle; Mike managed to steer him our way before our big sister screwed him up… Xavi built it on top of ICREACH[57] and, to be honest, it's a massive improvement!»

« Who? What?» said John who was slowly recovering from seeing the picture of a two-years old Josh, a smiling little man…

« Langley… Our big sister, obnoxious, overbearing and loud! » He sighed. *« We don't go there, unless we have been really, really smart or really, really bad… Mike's pretty good at covering for us. »*

« Have you been? »

« Yep, first time I put a suit in a long time, let me tell you… And I didn't like it: briefing the DCI[58] and the DDO[59] ain't for me, but man, did we nail it! » He smiled. *« No need to ask, you have no*

---

[57] NSA-built 'Google-like' search engine created to share billions of records about phone calls, emails, cellphone locations, and internet chats

[58] Director of the CIA

[59] Deputy Director for Operations

need to know! But you were a Marine, so you're familiar with all that OPSEC[60] *stuff. »*

John spent the rest of the day learning the ropes of the system and meeting the team: it was a mix of youth and age, professors and hipsters, scientists and laymen. There was a former cop, a journalist, a musician, a botanist, a pastor... It felt like the Encyclopædia Universalis in personae; even the muscle were part of the team: « *Mike has tasked them with knowing everything about every infantry weapon on the planet, make, use, sound... Everything; got a question? Ask them and they don't know? They get to buy you a bottle of whatever you drink... Only caught them once... »* chuckled Bubba, « *That was a niiiice bottle of Machir Bay whisky... »*

The cubicle themselves were an extraordinary mix of order and complete mess, from the maniac Cistercian emptiness to the exuberance of books, plants, sports memorabilia and, for a few, military life.

He left at 6pm to meet a real estate agent who had been recommended by Uncle Williams, a not so subtle « get out of my house » hint. It was time for him to move in his own place!

Money was not an issue and he instructed the agent to find a house within a twenty five minute drive, starting by Palisades; it should have three or four bedrooms: that Katie and Josh came back at some point was a somewhat foggy goal; the house was the first step back to a normal life...

*   *   *

---

[60] Operational security

* * *

The following weeks were an intense slide into a high paced life: work from 8am to 6pm and in the evening: lessons with Asal, exhausting rehab sessions with Will. Diner with Uncle William were rarer now; yet, he was happy to discuss intelligence methodologies and investigation successes or failures with John, thus helping him get a sound knowledge of his business environment. « *War stories from boring old blokes are useful, you know, as they help the newbies get a grip faster on what awaits them* ».

Saturdays were buddying time with the guys at the pool; they had celebrated John's new job with a lunch at their usual place; Phil, the ultimate conservative, had gently raged against yet another big government job before being subdued by his friends' positive energy. Several beers made it hard for a wobbly John to get home late in the afternoon…

His onboarding culminated with the purchase of a house in Palisades, on Potomac Avenue NW, a nice three bedroom craftsman-style house, located on a quiet and green road close to the Potomac River and the Capital Crescent Trail; in its particular way, it reminded John of his family home, back in Rhode Island. The negotiation was swift: the seller was eager to retire in Florida and John's ability to pay cash for the house made it a quick deal.

John went back to Middletown for a few days, long enough to work out the transfer of most of the furniture to DC, the rest, including a lot of Kate's stuff, going into a local storage to be forgotten; he did not have the time, nor the envy, to review every piece of his past and decide on it. Once the house was empty, he put it on the market at a reasonable price: it was sold within a month to a family John never met.

* * *

The workout with Will and Jenna was transforming him painstakingly : he was now reasonably confident with his prosthesis and was able to walk longer distances on the treadmill; as his health improved, so did his competitive streak; this was not missed on by Jenna, who started pushing him harder. After a session that had had the others cringing and moaning on the side, John had come out of the swimming pool, exhausted and breathless, and, lying on the wet floor, had looked up to see a radiant Jenna.

« So, looks like the Marine is back in you; I like you better like that! »

« You mean, helpless crawling on the floor in front of you? » He almost belched.

She smiled and winked.

« Exactly! »

She turned and went yelling at John's poor buddies…

He couldn't help but get an eyeful of a perky ass.

*　　　　*　　　*

Sleep came easily enough, thanks to the exercise with Will and Jenna, but he was still having nightmares regularly; he would wake up, drenched in sweat, his heart beating at a frantic pace. Though the circumstances changed, he would always end up locked up in some inescapable run for his life, trailing behind, slowed by his absent leg, the glued crutches, the crazy head winds…

* * *

Booze in the evening was out of the equation: that had been clear by Uncle William; John was holding to this mantra like a man overboard to a floating jacket. But sleeping pills could not do much harm and quickly became part of his sleeping routine.

His arrival in the neighborhood had been noticed; after a couple days, a lady rang the bell on a Saturday. She was blonde, in her late forties, a walking caricature of the traditional house wife.

He opened the door clumsily, encumbered with his crutches, not having had the time to put his prosthesis on. The right leg stump clearly unsettled her.

« *Good, good morning, my name is Mrs Kopf; you can call me Isabel; my husband and I live next door. I thought that it'd be nice to welcome you in the community. I've brought you some cookies I made this morning. And don't worry: they're gluten-free…* »

« *Good morning, I'm John, John Quirston.* »

« *I wanted to let you know that if you were in need of some help, we have been living here for some twenty years, our two boys were borne here actually, and so we know the local scene quite well; oh and also there's a church down the road, Father Heeney always has donuts and coffee after mass on Sunday at 11am: you should come; it's a great way to meet all the nice people who live in the street…* »

« *Hm, thank you, I'll think about it… And thanks for the cookies!* »

He grabbed both crutches in the left hand and took the box in the right; he turned back clumsily and managed to push the door closed with some dignity. Mrs Kopf turned awkwardly and walked down the porch back to the yellow house next door.

That was the classical neighborhood test. He had failed it!

*   *   *

Getting amazed by DIGA was easy: working it, understanding the various ways to formulate queries, how the different databases interacted, how to request assistance from a different entity, what the numerous acronyms meant was something else… The jargon was especially daunting, as it seems that each government body had its own mysterious way of calling the same things: from the mundane, toilets would become heads in the Navy, to the more complex: CAP could be a Combat Air Patrol in the Air Force, a Community Assistance Program at FEMA, a Criminal Alien Program at DHS; a targeter could be a laser designator device or a CIA analyst tasked with finding a specific person…

And add to that need to know, codenames, aliases and sanitization, entire blacked out paragraphs…

Bubba, the House's Chief analyst, and Xavi, the in-house DIGA genius, walked him patiently through the various technical tools at his disposal, getting him to learn their bias and limits; a former LAPD Criminal investigator spent an entire week explaining the basics of a criminal investigation. The Pastor tested his knowledge of Quran and walked him through a map of the latest Sunni-Shiites rivalries, local sects and tribes in the Muslim world. A lawyer came to the office to train him on the different legal coercion tools at the disposal of the Government, from the casual queries to the powerful

National Security Letter.

The team was welcoming but remained a bit distant; John slowly realized that each were living within their own bubbles, often oblivious of the world around them. A few worked terror-related stuff, some kept an eye on Russia or China; one monitored water-related conflicts…

One morning in August, Mike Willow arrived at John's desk and asked him to grab a coffee and follow him to his office.

« *How are you doing John?* »

« *I am fine… I mean, I'm still learning but, err… »*

« *Getting a bit bored, aren't you?* » He smiled. « *Ah, don't say anything: I would be too… »*

He grabbed a folder from his desk and handed it out to him.

« *Look into this, will you? ISIS is getting a lot of traction*[61] *and we need to look at this in a different way. I am not looking for anything specific: just be curious and tell me in a month what you would like to do with it.* »

---

[61] On 29 June 2014, ISIL announced the establishment of a worldwide caliphate. Abu Bakr al-Baghdadi was named its caliph and the Islamic State of Iraq and the Levant was renamed the Islamic State.

CHAPTER 10

Paris, France

August 27th, 2014

The blast took me by surprise; it shouldn't have: I had been building that bomb for ages. It's just that I couldn't help shaking when I inserted the detonator in the Semtex block; that was stupid: Semtex is inert until it is activated by electricity… And yet, it blew up!

I saw in slow motion both my hands being ripped off my arms; there was no pain, just an obsession: « *My hands, what am I going to do without my hands? Where are my hands?* » I started crying as I looked around me; the scenery was lovely: I was seated at a wood table by a large lake or was it the sea? The sun was blazing and the heat was uncomfortable…

A seagull flew away close to the ground, snickering at me and holding one hand in its beak… I yelled!

And woke up seated in my bed, drenched in sweat!

I had not had nightmares for a long time, at least not since my fighting days in Afghanistan and Baghdad. The mission was taking its toll on me and the regular exercise and yoga sessions were barely helping me cope with stress: I was wondering more and more whether this had any sense; praying didn't help either; there was no one I could confide in apart from Louise and, even with her, I had to remain watchful. I had a discussion with Ibrahim the week before. He had noticed it as well.

« You look tired my friend. »

« No, it's ok; it was a long day coming to Geneva yesterday… »

He looked at me deeply.

« You're a fighter Alain; Afghanistan, Iraq… You might have what Americans call PTSD[62]… »

« What? No, I am strong, not like these kafir[63] who have no courage and no faith… »

We were seated inside a café close to the lake. The music was quite loud, filled with laughters from a group of Chinese tourists enjoying a drink before dinner; at least three or four different languages could be overheard.

« Be careful Alain, your mission is an important one and you are doing a very, very good job; I understand even the Caliph[64] has taken notice of your work! Your country is an important one for us: it sends to the cause many, many fighters, money; it is weak and

---

[62] Post traumatic stress disorder
[63] Arabic: infidel
[64] Abu Bakr al-Baghdadi

ripe for us to take... »

I was tense, sweating and nodded: *« It's just that I wish I could do more than just collecting money... »*

« My friend, money is the blood that will undo the infidels! As I said, we have many fighters, from all the countries of the world: they fight and die for Allah, may they be blessed! What we need from you is a different fight; the infidel journalists like to depict us as a disorganized, ragtag army: they are so wrong! You should see how well Mosul, Raqqa, our land, once freed, are run, how efficient and unstoppable the Caliphate is! »

His eyes were fixed into mine.

« We need the same from you: ruthless efficiency! The money that you are sending is making the cause stronger everyday; we are fighting against the world's most powerful armies and scaring them! Have faith my friend, have faith! »

He stopped and took a sip of Coke, cooling down before anyone noticed how tense he had become...

« This computer system of yours, do you think that it would work in other countries? »

« I think so, provided that the banks accept remote digital orders... Why? »

« It could help us a lot; could you take some vacations in the next weeks? Let's test it. »

*　　　　*　　*

* * *

Back in Paris, I started preparing my trip: I would travel to Asia and play the perfect tourist; first a plane to Vietnam, a few days in Ho Chi Minh City, the former Saigon, a visit at the Dien Bien Phu[65] battle site, then a flight to Siem Reap in Cambodia to visit the world famous Angkor Wat temples; from there I would drive to Thailand, crossing the border at Poipet, sleeping at a casino-hotel located on the no mans land between Thailand and Cambodia. The final part of the journey would take me to Bangkok and finally Koh Samui, a tropical tourist hell full of sun and sex seekers…

I met with Chuppa and told him that I would take a few weeks off; I reminded him of our emergency contact procedure.

« I have something to tell you, » he said, a little worried.

« What? »

« I took the liberty to give some money to a guy I know, Saïd; he is a good man; his brother and him have been to Yemen and are close to our cause. They are looking to avenge our sons and daughters of Islam killed in Syria, Iraq, Afghanistan… »

It made my hair stand up on the back of my neck!

« What? What are they planning to do? How much did you give away? »

The questions came out aggressively and I couldn't stop it!

* * *

---

[65] Famous battle won by the Viet Minh communist revolutionaries against the French army

« Do you realize how dangerous it is? If they get caught, they know who you are! It endangers the entire operation… »

« They won't rat and we met by chance: I was coming back from a collection; I don't even have their phone number: we hadn't seen each other for years! They are true believers… And it's only three thousand euros. »

« Yeah right, just like Mustapha Alloum… »

« What? Who? The guy in La Courneuve? He was working for you? Did he… Did you… ? »

« Chuppa, don't ever do again that without my approval! You got it? »

« Shit man, ok, but still, How can I not help a brother? »

« Chuppa, you don't know how high the stakes are… Don't! Period! »

He was still clearly sulking when I left him; I hadn't calmed down much: I had now an operation being prepared on my turf, of which I knew nothing and, with a potential link back to us, it could compromise my entire mission…

On the 11th of September, I boarded an Air France Airbus heading for Ho Chi Minh City; the flight was going to take over twelve hours. Once in the air, I felt somewhat relieved, as if the absence of physical link to the ground had temporarily removed part of my ever present stress.

As we were flying smoothly above Croatia, I started to slightly doze off; I woke up thinking about Afghanistan, the place where I had truly become a fighter; I remembered the first shots I fired at someone, the first time that I was shot at... The first time was disconcerting:

« *Someone's shooting at us,* » I yelled stupidly, having heard several shots.

« *Yes, the shooter's on that ridge,* » smirked the old-timer next to me, showing a hill some six hundred yards away...

« *Are you sure? I heard the shot coming from there...* » and I showed him a building on the right side, much, much closer...

« *Nah, he's there; you got a sound distortion. Did you notice the lag between the first shot and the second? Well, it's actually only one shot and the noise of the bullet flying by... The good news is that we didn't hear the whizz, so the guy's not aiming at us... Let's move!* »

Apparently bullets cracked, thumped and whizzed when you were getting shot at! This was one of the many things I would learn during the six months I spent in Afghanistan... I had also, out of necessity, managed to learn some Pashto; surprisingly, though I had never been too keen at school, I belatedly took a liking to learning language. Arabic would come a few years later.

If Afghanistan was my awakening at war, Baghdad was my entrance in hell, driving across a city to the sounds of gun fire, helicopter engines, muffled explosions.

I had managed to enter the country from Jordan. The Al Karamah crossing had been a non-event: the border guards were clearly more concerned by who might enter in Jordan;

on the Iraqi side, the Traibeel control area was swarmed by trucks transporting an incredible variety of equipments, food, even animals. Our NGO[66] logoed Toyota Land Cruiser was of absolutely no interest to the guard, as soon as he had found the hundred US dollar bills folded in our passports!

The rest of the drive took us close to twelve hours, because of the various check points and, incredibly, of a few good old-fashioned traffic jams…

There was four of us, all French but the driver, an Iraqi national; he was supposed to help us find an accommodation in the city, introduce us to the people we had come to see and find the guy we had come to kill…

*   *   *

I was able to sleep for the rest of the flight and was awakened when the lights were brutally turned on, forty-five minutes from landing… The Ho Chi Minh Tân Sơn Nhât International Airport was the usual hive of lost tourists, focused travelers, airline workers and the multitude of informal jobbers. The air was damp, smelling of fresh rain, and in the high eighties, a welcome thirty degree improvement from Paris.

I had booked a private transport from the airport to my hotel, located close to the eccentric Notre Dame de Saigon cathedral; finding the driver was easy and the drive was expectedly slow, burdened by the morning rush. The hotel was small and some sort of upscale guesthouse recommended by the famous French 'le Routard' travel guide; I dropped my luggage, changed into running gear and

---

[66] Non-governemental agency

went for a relaxed run along the river.

Playing the tourist was actually fun: touring the city must-see spots, tasting strange food in of the street restaurants, getting lost in the maze of a market… Ibrahim had been right: I had needed some time off; I hadn't felt this calm for quite some time, away from the real world! I took the habit of spending some time in the cathedral before going out to diner: the cool temperature was a nice addition to the silence and the smell of incense; it had been a long time since I had entered a church back in my youth!

Choosing a hotel close to the cathedral had another purpose: it was a quick trip to the business district and the local subsidiary of the International Bank of Indochina…

I entered the Bank on a Friday morning; it had rained heavily during the night and it was a shock to enter a frigid air-conditioned hall. I had chosen this bank because it was big enough to have an international coverage, being headquartered in HongKong, foreign customers and digital access; it was also small enough that I could maintain some discretion; the account set up was eased by a nice bonus to the clerk who appropriately forgot that I had no permanent address in Vietnam apart from the guesthouse next door and who did not ask for any Id. I made the required five hundred thousand Dong[67] deposit on the various new accounts and left the bank within thirty minutes, a spring in my step. Happiness is a job well done…

It was soon time to hop on another flight to Hanoi in order to visit the Dien Bien Phu battle site; the contrast was stark

---

[67] Slightly more than twenty US Dollars

between the French colonial Ho Chi Minh and the more severe communist city; the day trip to the battle memorial was, as expected, full of rather justified bravado and the Vietminh victory over the colonialist invader.

Siem Reap followed the next day; the city was the entrance to Angkor Vat but, apart from marveling at the banyan trees growing within the broken down temples, I wan't impressed by the site, maybe because I could never be alone, always surrounded by a loud, obnoxious crowd…

From the hotel desk, I hired a cab to drive me to Poipet, a city at the border with Thailand. I had booked a room at the Blue Temple hotel in order to catch the first bus to Bangkok the next morning.

The hotel was a casino, which probably made sense for tax reasons, as it stood on the no man's land between Cambodia and Thailand; there were bedrooms on the first two floors, a casino, bars and a restaurant on the third, karaoke and massage rooms on the top floor; the masseuses in the lift next to me, as I was going up to grab a quick diner, left little to the imagination…

The whole place was noisy, dirty and cheap; I ordered a hamburger, fries and a coke and ate my meal without any pleasure. I then went to the bar, sat in a corner and asked for an Angkor beer. There were several groups of raucous Asians guys, hardly any Europeans and some bored looking bartenders. A few masseuses took half-hearted rounds offering me a massage but quickly forgot about me when a new loud group arrived.

I was halfway across my beer when a middle-aged Asian

man walked up to my table:

« Excuse me, are you Mister Jones? »

« No. »

« Ha? Sorry, sorry... »

He made some kind of a bow and left...

I looked bored, which was easy, and finished my beer. I stood up and discreetly picked up the paper that the guy had dropped next to me on the bench. Back in my room, I unfolded it and found the banking coordinates of several Middle East and Asian accounts. Time to develop my system on a bigger scale, but not here where I had absolutely zero confidence on the anonymity on the wifi access...

The following week was best to forget: I just couldn't stand the crowds in Koh Samui. I woke up very early and went for long swims, took some sun and spent time looking for some quiet places where to run... Evenings were spent in my room, away from the crazy bars raging outside; I tried to make up for the many prayers days that I had missed, not trusting the absence of cameras in the various hotels: Cambodia and Vietnam's ruling authoritarian parties liked to find goodies on international travelers, a nice inheritance from their communist days...

It was almost a relief when I came back to a cold Paris: it was time to really launch the AI and test it across different continents and banks. From what the guy had told me, the idea was to move funds around accounts, with no logic, across jurisdictions, via offshore banks and various tax havens, with amounts remaining below understood scrutiny levels; it would made the funds untraceable and would unable authorities to find patterns; some banks even allowed for accounts to be created and terminated digitally…

The Ai would juggle between accounts in order to create an inscrutable maze and protect the destination accounts used by the purchasers in Mosul or Raqqa. It was even able to buy cryptocurrencies, access the main money transfer systems like Western Union.

And it could ultimately rid me of Fasil who I was having a hard time supporting, not counting his twenty per cent commission…

I had agreed with Ibrahim to start slow and increase the amounts once the system was thought to be safe. It would then require the creation of more accounts, especially in offshore banking havens; I would need to find a way to travel more. Some were easy to set up discreetly and rapidly: after all, if Liechtenstein, Jersey or the Isle of Man were just a few hours driving away, the Cayman Islands were a different story!

I planned to officially subscribed to a reputable university online program in September: it was focused on international banking and provided me with a reasonable explanation for my sudden interest in banks around the world. Unsurprisingly, my end of year paper would focus on offshore tax havens…

All this didn't prevent me from doing my normal collecting job and visiting the various intermediates, roughing up one of them here or there. The AI was supposed to help me by identifying the drop outs or the unusual variations of delivery… And it did, getting some in big, big troubles!

Roughing up people was getting easier by the day and it was inevitable that I ended up killing remorselessly in the following year!

International Bank of Indochina
Account Number: 7011114642
Balance: US$ 21.00

CHAPTER 11

Washington DC,
  The Red House,

September 10th, 2014

John maneuvered his Cherokee into his designated parking spot below Georgetown Park mall; he was starting to get a liking to the sturdy vehicle that he had purchased out of necessity a few weeks earlier: he had sold his old Camry after the convenient store incident and a daily use of Ubers and cabs was getting both impractical and expensive. The car had been retrofitted with a left foot accelerator to give room to his new prosthesis and John, after a few hard accelerating and braking scares, was now quite happy in control.

The drive from his place to the office had taken some fifteen minutes; the side window rolled down, he had enjoyed the cool promise of a nice day. There was some comfort into having a routine: wake up at 6:30 am, exercise, leave home at 7:30, arrive at the office before 8, work until 6 pm and then more exercise with Will or some reading; no work was allowed from home for security reasons but John wanted to have an in-depth knowledge of his work region: middle eastern and « stan » countries geography, demographics, economy, agriculture, history were an endless provider of books and academic essays for the bookshelves in his study. Diner was at eight, except on Saturdays at Uncle Will's. Amalia came on Mondays to tidy up the house and would bake a generous amount of meals that went right into the freezer; she had given up on fighting the microwave oven…

A few minutes later, he arrived to his cubicle and powered the system; he briefly talked to Bubba in the cafeteria while the expensive espresso machine poured a small cup of rich smelling coffee. Bubba was his usual self, sporting an eye raising electric blue poppy seeds sleeveless shirt!

Back in his cubicle, he reviewed the night's worth of news alerts: he had set up a few daily digas - DIGA queries - on topics of interest and reading them while drinking a burning espresso was his quiet work build-up.

« *Good morning John.* » said Mike, appearing in his ever-perfect suit. « *Can you come to my office?* »

« *Sure.* »

Mike closed the door; there was a soft instrumental jazz music in the background.

« *So, what have you being up to?* »

« *Well, I have reviewed the file you gave me on ISIS and there is something I would like to follow upon…* »

« *Oh? Good, tell me!* »

* * *

« Right, how familiar are you with ISIS? I mean, err… »

Mike smiled: *« Rather familiar, I should think… But do indulge me, go on! »*

« Ok, err, where to start? Err, yeah, what is the main difference between Al Qaeda and Isis? AQ is a mess! »

Mike raised an eye brow.

« No really, they know how to wage some guerrilla against us in Afghanistan, they know how to inspire fanatics, but what is their organization? What is their goal? UBL[68] was a preacher; he only escaped us in Tora Bora because of our own stupidity and our reliance on local Afghan commanders who looked the other way with a nice check in hand to let him escape… We had so many warnings before September 11, I mean, we screwed up badly! »

« I tend to agree with you John, though you might want to tone it down a little if you ever get to Langley[69] or to the J. Edgar Hoover Building[70]… Inter-service cooperation and appreciation and all that… » He smiled. *« Ok, ISIS? »*

« ISIS is something else entirely; when you look at its founders, where they come from, what their occupation was… It all goes back to the second Iraq war and the absolute disaster that it was… »

He looked at Mike and cringed: *« Sorry, inter service chmukthing again? »*

* * *

---

[68] Usama Bin laden
[69] CIA headquarters
[70] FBI headquarters

« *No, no, much worse, politics…* »

« *Right, the biggest fuckup, err, dysfunctional and unfortunate event,* » *Mike nodded,* « *was the Iraqi Prime Minister's nomination: Nouri al-Maliki. He is a Shiite and, though he was nominated with the approval of the Quds[71] commander at the time, he was evaluated by the CIA as being sufficiently independent from Iran; yet, he has run the country for the past years, especially since 2010, with a sectarian vengeance against Sunnis and the former Baath Party[72]* »

« *So ISIS was borne from this: the disbanding of both the Baath Party and the purge in the Iraqi national Army; it let out loose a number of trained and highly motivated people with a grudge against the government and its backer, the US… Abu Musab al-Zarqawi capitalized on that before he was killed in 2006; some of his successors and their ideologues originate from the Iraqi Army; they don't really care about religion: it's only a tool to gain power and keep it… They want to run an efficient organization and that's why they are so effective at the moment: they gain territories and have set up a real government: all the information that we have from Mosul and Syria point to that…* »

« *Ok; that might be a bit more complicated but I understand the short cuts… Where are you heading to?* »

« *Money… They need a lot of it if they want to balance their budget: a government needs to raise taxes, pay civil servants and soldiers, buy equipment… They got a head start in Mosul with the raid on the banks there, even if I don't think that they actually got the four hundred million plus US dollars that people speak of… But they'll need money and, in order to run that budget, they need*

---

[71] Iran's paramilitary and intelligence force
[72] Saddam Hussein's authoritarian party

people: qualified collectors to raise the money, purchasers, auditors to control the waste, etc... A complete administration »

John was getting energized and it showed in his speech.

« Remove these people and you remove the administration, the ability to have a state... Remove the state and you remove the longterm threat and they are back to some troubling, yes, but still basic insurgency! »

Mike remained silent, gazing at the antic Samurai sword displayed on the wall right next to a quaint picture of the planet...

« Fair enough, keep digging, I like the idea; come back to me when you have something that's actionable! Good work. »

John left the office and, for the first time in many days, there was a spring in his steps...

ISIS made money through various means: raids on the conquered city riches, donations from individuals, NGOs, or even states; there was also the proceeds of smuggling: archeological treasures and, of course, the elephant in the room, oil... Most of it was in cash, some in gold bullions. Intercept the cash and you remove the group's strength. Remove the people who handle the cash and you cause major disruption.

The major Western nations engaged in the fight against terror were all looking for suspicious banking transactions; he decided to look for the people behind those...

Defining them was not easy; yet, defining what they were

not, that was an idea he wanted to pursue: they wouldn't be fighters; fighters were living a very dangerous life, with a low life expectancy; by nature, they were loud: visible on films, hearable on audios; they were admired, therefore discussed by the crowds; they had ranks: chief of that patrol, founder of this brigade; they needed the exposure in order to recruits combatants… They had experience and had fought western armies in the past across countries, multiplying the encounters with potential future prisoners, who would eventually talk; they all talked…

The CIA, DIA[73], SOCOM[74] and the likes went for the warlords and the flashy headlines…

John started looking for the unsung, discreet, overlooked, boring people; the people whose names might appear in some investigations, but always on the fringe of operations, as side notes; he went looking for the professional experience, for the former shop owners, the accountants and bankers.

It was tedious; even with the amazing help of DIGA, it implied reviewing hundreds of profiles, a grinding process of iterative steps; he had DIGA spent weeks in vain looking for what graduates of Iraq's business schools were doing those days, which tribe they belonged to, who had died, who had left the country, who was in jail, who had gone missing. Those who had disappeared would be the interesting ones, or not… Most promising leads ended up in cemeteries: A study in the *PLOS Medicine*[75] journal had estimated the previous

---

[73] Defense Intelligence Agency

[74] US Special Operation Command: unified command supervising all US special forces

[75] PLOS Medicine is a peer-reviewed weekly medical journal

year that 461,000 Iraqis died as a result of the Iraq War…

His first break arrived five weeks later: a guy was named in an intercepted conversation between a broker and a mechanic in Jordan… The mechanic, known for his close ties to ISIS, wanted to buy spare tires for his trucks and the specs of the tires had attracted John's attention: they were fitted mostly on oil trucks… The broker had refused adamantly to be paid in gas; the mechanic had finally said that « *he would have to speak to Abdallah about it as, only he could release some cash!* » Monitoring his cellphone and the garage's landline was easy but it took four long days, thanks to some administrative snafu[76], before he finally got a phone number, then a name: Abdallah Wassem.

He had a thread to pull…

*   *   *

And weekends to look forward to…

Will had started training him on an exercise bike for a few weeks at the rehab centre. Then, one Wednesday evening, he said:

« *John, you lived in Palisades right?* »

« *Yes* »

« *How far from your work again?* »

« *Fifteen, twenty minutes, depending on traffic. Why?* »

---

[76] Acronym: Situation Normal, All Fucked Up

* * *

« That would be, what, five miles? »

« Yes, more or less… Why ? »

« I think its time that you ride a bike to work… »

« Oh, hmmm, wow… »

« You need to practice your balance; can you shower at work? »

He could; they agreed on a mountain bike and Will ordered the specific prosthesis that John could set on the right pedal and block his stub in. The first trial was actually fun, if not awkward: they had met on the Canoe club parking near the end of the Capital Crescent Trail and set up John's bike. Will had run a few hundred yards next to him until he had found his balance. They then had gone for a few exhilarating miles…

The toughest was to get organize alone : find the balance to remove the prosthesis, bag it, insert his stub in the bike adaptor, secure it tightly… and not lose his equilibrium on his right!

Fortunately the Crescent Trail flowed past his home, just a hundred yards away; there was a hole in the fence and a path that neighbors used regularly. He was thus able to test and trial his new bicycle away from car traffic. That did not prevent him from arriving once in the office dirty and bloodied, with the muscles raising the alarm, going in badass mode and Amanda full motherly on him once he had explained the accident: having swerved brutally to avoid a stray dog, he had ended up tangled in a bush on his back.

Some horrified onlookers had jumped to his rescue, helped him unsecure the adaptor, remove the bike, then climb back on it and ride away. John had a foolish grin telling the accident around a beer the following Saturday…

Rides to work increased slowly to longer rides on the weekend to the rehab center on Saturdays and along the Trail all the way to Bethesda or towards Cedar Island and Carderock. The original stiffness of his joints and the abrasions on the stub's skin left way to real pleasure and a sense of freedom…

His rehab sessions with Will were taking a different turn now, twice a month only, and were more focused on building his ability to run; Will had asked the in-house prosthetist to find the most appropriate running appendage for John; they had settled on a futuristic looking blade model that was made by the same Icelandic company that already made his daily walk possible.

Saturday mornings had changed as well as his DGSquare - « damaged goods group » - as they called themselves were ending their rehab sessions; they had met for lunch after their last training with Jenna and agreed to keep on swimming together weekly at a local indoor swimming center. Jenna had been there as well: she had told them, for the first time, how proud she was of their progress… It had been a subdued but quite emotional moment. John had felt affected in an odd way; on a whim, he had discreetly asked Jenna whether she would like to go biking on a weekend « *one of these days* » : his clumsy request was met by a surprised, then striking, smile and a cell phone number…

Two weeks later, they met at the Southern entrance of the

Gateway Park on a Sunday morning; the air was crisp and the sun bright. John had biked in and arrived early… Jenna arrived, radiant as ever in a full pro-looking, very fitting cycling gear, hugged him gently and took out of her car a nasty looking racing bike…

« *Hey,* » said John, recovering from the smoothness of their first contact, « *You said that you biked once in a while…* »

« *Did I? Well, didn't want to scare you…* »

Eighteen mostly flat miles later, John was relieved to learn that they had reached the end of the trail, facing Mount Vermont Estate. There was no way that he would have confessed it but Jenna's pace had been right at his limits… Once seated at an out-door table of a bar for some drinks, she had suggested that he switched to a lighter bike but the sparkle in her eyes was not lost on John. They chatted and laughed for an hour before heading back north at a cool pace.

« *That was nice!* » an elated John said as he was climbing off his bike.

« *Just nice? I'd have hoped for more! You're the first patient I ever meet outside of work.* »

John felt suddenly hot… Jenna laughed.

« *Relax, I'm teasing you! Though not on the first patient thing… We should do that again, next week?* »

John nodded enthusiastically earning himself a beautiful laugh and a quick kiss on the cheeks.

* * *

« See you next week! »

The ride home was perfect, all fatigue erased for a humming John.

Two days later, in the evening, his wife called…

INTERLUDE

Forward, forward, forward, forward,
Without ever retreating, never surrender,
Forward, forward, forward, forward,
Undefeated Warrior, sword in hand, kill them!

Kill the apostates that the devil has led astray,
With the fool's people war is declared,
No more controversy or philosophy,
Either you kill them, or they kill you, only claimed.

Anyone who opposes Sharia law is lost,
Even when he claims to practice virtue,
So cut off the heads of ignorance,
Cut off the heads of wandering soldiers!

Forward, forward, forward, forward,
Without ever retreating, never surrender,
Forward, forward, forward, forward,
Undefeated Warrior, sword in hand kill them!

CHAPTER 12

Paris, France

October 25th, 2014

My flat had been visited…

I had no savvy safety measures such as a sticky hair across a drawer: that was appropriate for 007 in the good old days! What I had were perfectly hidden cameras filming most of my living room and my bedroom, linked to a mobile app on a burner phone. Each sequence of movements generated an email to a gmail address that I checked once a week.

My visitors had been careful: two Arabic looking men in their early thirties; they had searched the apartment, finding the Glock I kept well hidden as a decoy: the real cache was below it, like the treasures in the Egyptians tombs! I had counted on the satisfaction of anyone finding hidden stuff to overlook the real deal: money, guns and ids… It had worked like a charm: the guy had been excited to find the gun, put it carefully back where he had found it and closed the cache. They had also found the prayer mat and the worn Quran in my bedroom: the Holy Book was treated with profound respect: That was the clue I needed to understand Ibrahim and I were playing by the same playbook!

I had now nine different identities… All were legit and I was using them to open accounts at the various banks that Ibrahim had deemed safe. I could be either a French, Belgian or Swiss citizen but only used three of them, the strongest legends[77], to travel; the rest were presented to the various lawyers and clerks creating the shell corporations that would hide me away from the prying eyes…

Ibrahim had provided me with the Swiss one as we had met near Konstanz, Germany, right across the Swiss border. He had requested an emergency meeting via Telegram the week before. I had boarded a small white cruiser in Konstanz and had enjoyed the smooth sailing on the lake until I had seen him board the ship at Mainau; There were few people onboard and no other ship on the quiet lake. Once cleared from the land, we met inside.

« Hello my friend, » said Ibrahim, *« How are you? »*

« I am well, Alhamdulillah[78]! » No one was near enough to hear me speak in Arabic.

« You must wonder why I asked you to come? I have good news for you! The Caliph likes your program and would like you to expand it: the State needs to increase its revenues and we think that Hawala brokers are increasingly under surveillance from our enemies… We need to connect more accounts to the system: some already exists

---

[77] A spy's claimed background or biography, usually supported by documents and memorized details
[78] Arabic: Thank God

and I will give them to you! »

« Ok, I'll need to create some accounts in more bank havens; the IA requires them in order to maintain the discretion of the transfers. I have been to Jersey and the Isle of Man and have created several companies; I will use the opportunity this week to travel to Liechtenstein to do so as well... »

« How do you travel? »

« By train or cars that I rent. »

« I worry my friend that the DGSI[79] could become suspicious to see all those travels! »

« Yes, I understand but I use a couple identities that I was able to get thanks to some brothers, and it's Europe: the agents at custom, they don't even ask for id... »

« Good, good, for the next international trip, I want you to use a different one, Europe is quite safe indeed, but if you travel to the Middle East, it would raise suspicion; I have here a Swiss passport and documents to explain who you will be... »

« The Middle East? »

« Yes, we would like you to visit the State!

« The State? »

« Yes, come to Mosul and meet out people! »
* * *

---

[79] French FBI

My heart stopped. « *The Caliph?* »

Ibrahim laughed: « *No, my brother, no… It would be too dangerous for him: very few approach him. We are expendable, not him… But still, there are people in the organization who want to speak to you!* »

« *Wow…* »

We agreed on a date of visit in January and a point of entry in Turkey; from there on, I would be cared for until I was brought back. In the meantime, I needed to go to the Caribbean and Central America…

Ibrahim walked off the ship at Meersburg and left me in deep thoughts: traveling to Iraq had been expected at some point but still, the news was incredible and fantastic!

Lindau was my final destination; I spent the night there, playing the tourist and came back the next morning to Konstanz. Two hours later, I was in Vaduz, Liechtenstein, in the quiet posh office of a lawyer; by the end of the day, I was the untraceable founder of yet another trust…

Talking about company, I had to take care of mine: the frequent travels were having a toll on my work and even friendly partners could not but notice the trend. I had to hire someone to help out with the daily consulting business… That also meant having an office. Beginning of November, I rented a room in a shared office building located on the métro[80] 14 line; it was close enough to be convenient, yet far enough to allow me for privacy: I was not looking for a

---

[80] French: subway

chance encounter with my employee or an office neighbor close to my place. I also hired a young guy, Nicolas, strait out of accounting school and tasked him with the most tedious and time-consuming part of the job; I was going to focus on 'developing the business and recruit customers'.

The first territory to 'develop' was the Martinique Island, a French gem in the Caribbean Sea; I flew there beginning of December under an alias and hopped on quick flights to the US Virgin Islands and Barbados, both well-known offshore banking paradise. In Bridgeton, Barbados, I met a lawyer who had flown in from Panama to finalize a trust with bank accounts in the Cayman Islands. The simplicity of the set-up was dizzying, provided that you came up with the five figure lawyer fee…

And what's sixty-seven thousand US dollars these days? Well, not so much anymore!

The amounts handled by the AI were increasing regularly; I had 'entree' accounts where money would appear from my providers and many other sources unknown to me, the numerous 'mulling about' ones whose goal were to mix the trails and make following them impossible, and the 'exit' accounts drained upon locally by the 'users', the State's purchasers… An allocation to the various exit accounts was agreed upon with Ibrahim. A maximum amount per 'exit' account was also fixed in order to avoid detection in case a user went 'off grid', voluntarily or not…

The whole total had gone up to a staggering million US dollars transiting automatically through more than fifty accounts per month!

* * *

Beginning of January, I told Nicolas that I had a family emergency and that I would be unreachable for a week. I drove to Munich, Germany and flew away to Antalya, Turkey, under my Swiss personae; after an uneven flight, I went across the border patrol checks without problem, just another tourist coming in to visit the city and enjoy some better weather. I took a cab from the airport and asked him to drop me of near Hadrian's Gate. Almost noon, it was a beautiful day with fresh temperatures. I walked for five minutes in the neighborhood towards the North-East before a small truck stopped next to me.

« *Come in,* » said the driver, « *no, no here, in the back,* » as I was opening the passenger door. I walked around, pulled up the dirty canvass and climbed in the dark body of the truck. We drove for an hour before stopping.

« *Out!* » Said a different voice; I pushed the canopy and jumped off. The truck drove away in a cloud of dust and dirty smoke. I was in some sort of a garage, a dilapidated industrial building with few windows, all broken. A man stood in front of me; his face hidden under some cheiche, he was 1.70m, muscular, dressed in jeans and a Chelsea FC teeshirt.

« *Strip!* »

« *What?* »

« *Strip!* » He said again, with a very strong accent.

I was tempted to play the smart ass but heard behind me the distinct noise of a gun being cocked…

* * *

So I stripped!

He indicated that I was to remove it all, including my watch, and pulled a hand held metal detector from a bench; so there I was, stark naked in the middle of God knows where being screened by a beeping wand: not my usual fantasy…

He threw a bag at me; it was full of reasonably clean clothes, more or less my size. There was an eyeless balaclava; he made a sign for me to put it on. A vehicle arrived and I was helped on. I was obviously in the back of yet another truck, this one reeking of some animals; we drove for a long time, probably east as it was the direction of the border, some fifteen hours away from Antalya, and I somehow managed to fall asleep. We only paused once: I was given water and some bread and dates to eat; I peed in a plastic bottle that was carelessly thrown out of the truck by my handler.

After several hours, the truck stopped and a guy climbed in to help me out. We walked a few yards before I was allowed to remove the balaclava. I was inside a house, in a dark bare room: in a corner a poor bed, a bottle of water; opposite, behind a plastic curtain, a sink and some foul toilets. The shutters were closed but it was obviously dark outside.

« You rest now… »

« When do we go across the border? »

« You don't ask, you do what we tell you! »

He left and, after five minutes, the only light bulb went dark. The air was cold and smelled of dust and disuse. I wrapped myself in the brownish blanket and lay down on the bed.

Sleep came fast.

I was awaken by a dog barking; life was arising around me: I could hear people speak, some children laugh, some chickens here, a goat or a sheep there… I had slept surprisingly well considering the circumstances. My handler entered the room with some food on a plate: bread, white cheese, boiled eggs and an apple.

« *Eat!* » He left.

It was a long boring day…

Then, several hours later, the guy came back:

« *Toilet now, later no time!* »

He handed me a jacket and asked me to done the balaclava on again.

« *Here we go for the serious stuff,* » I thought, climbing awkwardly in the back of yet another truck. I had probably been driven an hour or two from the border and my new friends now needed to get closer to cross it at some point in the night. We drove and were stopped at what sounded like a checkpoint; no one inspected the back. The road was now rough and I had to block myself in a corner not to be tossed about. We stopped again.

« *Come out; remove the mask.* » Said my handler; I pushed the canvass of the canopy on the side and jumped off. It was pitch dark. My eyes had been in the dark for a while so I was able to make out a few people in the darkness.

* * *

« *You come with me now.* » said a guy in Arabic. « *Understand?* »

« *Yeah.* »

« *You do like me: I walk, you walk; I stop, you stop, I crouch, you crouch… ok? And no talking…* »

I only nodded, which seemed to satisfy him. He walking away without looking whether I followed.

I heard the truck leave behind us but we were quickly engulfed in silence; there was only the sound of our breathing, short and hissing for my guide, long and deep for me. We were walking in a ditch, a dried up river, with few bush, and making good time. After a kilometer or so, my guide turned left and climbed out of the river bed. There was more wind now and I could make out some lights far in the distance. Some time later, headlights appeared on our right; we stopped and crouched behind a bunch of shrubs. A car drove by. We waited several minutes before crossing the road and walked on, following a small path. After what seemed like a hour, we finally arrived in a small opening; two men were smoking cigarettes next to a pick up. My guide asked for one and left in the darkness.

« *Good morning brother,* » said the older one in Arabic. « *It's been a long trip for you; two more hours and you can rest. I am Mohammad and this is Abdul.* »

The dim light of the car interior allowed me to see them: Mohammad, fortyish, rather dignified, and Abdul, the expected young thug.

* * *

I nodded: « *Yes, rest would be fine, thank you.* »

We drove away and, it was to be expected, I was again in the back, with no view of my surroundings. Overtime, the roads gradually improved; traffic became more present. We entered a city: that was clear, from the honking, the many motorbikes passing by, the frequent stops. I heard a distant muezzin call for the morning prayer.

We finally stopped and I heard gates closing in a scraping sound. Mohammad called me out. I jumped and landed in the large empty yard of a big house. Some poor bushes were the only threads of an ancient but long gone garden, lost to the absence of care and water.

« *Come my friend, we are late for the prayer!* »

We entered the house: it was warm and smelled of incense; he took me to a side room, obviously meant for communal prayer. There was a sink on the side. He looked at me expectingly. I removed my shoes and socks, set them on the side and went through the appropriate Wudu[81]. He silently joined me and together, we said the morning prayer.

« *Now, we can enjoy a meal together at last; we had been waiting for you for several days.* »

We walked to an adjacent room: a woman draped in a full burka was busy preparing a meal that had me salivating. She quickly retreated when we arrived.

We ate in silence.

---

[81] Islamic procedure for cleaning oneself before prayer

* * *

« You will stay in this house while you are in Mosul. Your bedroom is right above us; please do not go out and do not open the window! Your identity is very precious to us and there might be kafir spies in the streets around us. There's also the danger of spying satellites and drones. With your white face, you would stand out immediately! »

« Some people will come to see you this afternoon, I would suggest to be very honest with them; they have no sense of humor and little time! »

With that warning, he left.

I suddenly felt very tired from the harassing journey; I walked up the stairs and found my room: I undressed and fell asleep in a breath.

I jolted awake as someone was gently knocking on the door: it was the same woman who told me through the door that lunch was ready.

As I was finishing lunch, three guys arrived, dressed up in military garb; they yelled the trembling woman out of the room and told me to sit.

They didn't introduced themselves; two were obviously guards and remained by the door, the third one, a mean looking weasel, was the interrogator.

« Where are you from? Where were you borne? Name the five prayers! How much money do you have on your bank account? Where did you go to school? Who was the last woman you fucked? Tell us your favorite Sura from the Quran! When did you get

committed to Jihad? What was your occupation before Jihad? Which Sheik inspired you? »

An endless flood of questions fell upon me, my life, my war in Afghanistan, who I was spying for… He would fill a questionnaire thoroughly after each answer;

Counter intelligence, I suddenly realized: these guys were making sure that I was not sent by a Western agency or worse, Israel… But still, fuck them, I started to get angry: I hadn't gone through Afghanistan and Baghdad to be messed with by some myopic bean counter asshole.

It turned into a shouting match when they asked me to fill in a form; a fucking form like at the Sécu[82]!!! What better way to ruin my cover: fill in some document that will go into computer, ready to be hacked by the fucking NSA… Not counting my picture, my prints on the document… Little did I know at the time that such an event[83] would happen the following year!

The two guards had moved closer to us and I was seriously considering kicking their asses off, regardless of the consequences, when a new guy arrived.

If the guards were tense before, they suddenly got very nervous…

« What is going on? » Said the guy gently…

* * *

---

[82] French national social security administration

[83] https://www.theguardian.com/world/2015/may/17/syria-raid-isis-leader-killed-congress-intelligence

Followed a long explanation by the weasel that I had to fill the proper forms and that my identity was not confirmed and the…

« Out! » The guy said, looking at me.

« But the… »

The guy looked at him: the weasel left dragging along two relieved thugs!

The man smiled:

« Hello my brother, I apologize for this; the people from Amni[84] are very dedicated and, when they hear that a foreigner has arrived, they move quickly and in a way that, while often efficient, was not appropriate with you. You would not be here today if people had not proofed you many times! Including my friend Ibrahim… »

I was slowly calming down.

« But I haven't introduced my self: my name is Kazem; I made you come here to discuss your system; Ibrahim described it to me and I found it very, very smart; maybe we could expand it to other parts of our organization? »

« Nice to meet you. »

In those meetings, there would be no last names and no small talks for security reasons: what if a spy learned that a French guy, fan of the PSG[85] and living close to Chinatown in Paris,

---

[84] ISIS counter-intelligence service
[85] PSG for Paris Saint Germain: Paris main pro soccer team

had been there?

« Explain it to me! »

« So, the general idea is hide financial trails from the security agencies by multiplying the trails, through different banks, countries, tax havens, etc. Even if they identify a deposit, they will lose it in the maze. So, maybe they can cut one source, but cannot go downstream. One function also is to make sure that there is no pattern in the transfers: we are creatures of habits, only a computer can create uncertainty in the amounts, the detention of accounts, the destinations… To that end, I use aliases and entities that must remain on Good Guy[86] lists of the various banks»

We spent the following hour going into more details, security failsafes, VPNs, etc. He was, in a different but much more effective way, prodding me and digging into my life and my work. He was just as ruthless, as I discovered that evening.

« Grab your jacket and put this cheiche on! » He said.

I had learned not to ask questions!

For the first time in several days, I was out in the daylight; we climbed into an old dusty Toyota. He sat next to the driver and I went in the back seat.

« I leave the fancy BMWs to the stupid fighters who arrive from Europe. » He grinned. *« Americans like to target those with their drones: they associate nice cars to big bosses! In Vietnam, the*

---

[86] List of customers who supposedly present a low risk of illicit transactions – are permitted transactions without any or limited screening

American officers, they removed the ranks from they uniforms in the jungle...»

I noticed though that there was a discreet group of bikers that seemed to advance at our speed.

We drove through dusty streets littered with debris; many buildings wore the scars of war; people were mulling about in a severe atmosphere; armed men were seen everywhere: the city was in permanent stage of war.

We reached a checkpoint; I expected that we would go through quickly but we remained stuck in the traffic jam just like any other cars. Kazem smiled behind his cheiche: *« I never stand out... »*

Well, looking at the sudden stress on the guards face, he was clearly known to them!

The car entered an underground parking. We got out of the Toyota and walked out on the other side of the building; we were in a football stadium; in the large empty grassless space, there was a silent crowd waiting, facing a group of soldiers and what looked like dignitaries, standing next to a truck.

We walked across the crowd and joined the small group. Kazem nodded at their leader. He yelled and the soldiers half pushed, half carried a bloodied naked man out of the truck right in front of me.

« Kill him! » said Kazem as he handed me a worn handgun, an old Makarov 9 mm.

« What did he do? »

* * *

« He spies for the government in Baghdad! » His voice had taken a somber tone. *« Kill him! »*

I looked down at the guy; on his knees, he had one eye swollen closed; one hand no longer had nails. He was breathing in quick raspy mouthfuls and his whole body was trembling… I looked around and realized that I was standing on an execution grounds: flies were buzzing around dark stains on the sand…

« Why do I have to cope with this shit? Don't you trust me? Fuck! »

I looked at Kazem… and shot the prisoner in the head; he fell on the ground; I leaned in and shot him a second time in the head. As I did that, my cheiche slipped and I felt a cool breeze on my face.

« Happy now? Don't we have anything more to do? Can we get back to business?»

Kazem nodded; we walked through the crowd again. The people parted away silently as we neared them. There had been not one sound from them since I had arrived!

We drove back to the house.

« Tonight, we celebrate! » said Kazem.

« What? Killing this guy? »

« No, we celebrate the courage of your fellow French fighters! »
* * *

« Oh, we have French guys here? What have they done? »

« Not here, in Paris, some of your brothers have attacked a jewish shop and a miscreant newspaper[87]*! You know, the newspaper that published those blasphemous images of our Prophet! »*

« Charlie Hebdo? » I said stunned.

« Yes, they killed those journalists and many jews… »

« Were they caught? Will they fight again? »

« Alas no, the two brothers and their friend died fighting like true soldiers of the Faith… »

« One of the brothers' name was Saïd, no? » My head was spinning.

« Yes, why? »

I recovered from the surprise: *« One of my men gave them money for a hit… »*

« Aaaah my friend, then, you are responsible for making this happen! One more reason to celebrate! »

We had a quick diner together working out the future steps for the system; towards the end, Kazem pulled out of a cupboard a bottle of whisky and poured me a generous glass.

____

[87] January 7th-9th, 2015: Paris was the scene of two attacks, one on a casher supermarket, the other on the satyrical newspaper that had published caricatures of the prophet; all terrorists were killed by police after killing 17 people.

He raised his glass and we toasted to the death of our enemies…

As the woman was tidying up the table, he told me: « *If you want to fuck her, go ahead; no need to ask!* »

I pleaded that, unused to drinking and very tired from the day, I needed to sleep.

« *As you like it my friend; time for me to say goodbye anyway. You leave tonight!* »

Mohammad, the guy who had driven me into Mosul shook me out of a troubled sleep and I started the long journey back to Antalya; I spent two boring days in a guesthouse where my rucksack and my clothes had been waiting for me, compulsively watching the news from the Paris attacks, before catching a plane back home.

*   *   *

That trip had been exhausting: the long uncomfortable travels, the permanent stress of being arrested, the brutality of the treatments I had witnessed, the man I had murdered; the nightmares had been more frequent. I felt heavy inside. I longed for company, any company… I called Louise.

*   *   *

The weather was miserable: cold and wet with a permanent

drizzle that belied the beauty of Haussmannian[88] streets. A man was seated on a sofa in a small apartment rue Ordener in the eighteenth arrondissement[89]; in his fifties, bald, wearing a black sweater and chinos, there was nothing special about him. A bell rang. He opened the door.

« Hello Louise, come in! It seems that we have much to discuss… »

« Yes, Jean, much… »

The door closed.

---

[88] 19th century Architectural style (from the Baron Haussmann who carried out a massive urban renewal program of new boulevards, parks and public works in Paris)
[89] District: Paris is made up of twenty administrative districts

CHAPTER 13

The Red House, Georgetown, Washington DC

January the 25th, 2015

The sound of the video was poor, the definition wasn't much better. The video appeared to be shot on a mobile phone with an unsteady hand.

There were six men standing in front of a brownish wall; they were, for four of them, probably Iraqis; the last two however wore cheiches which completely hid their faces. A seventh man was dragged in and dropped in front of them; he was obviously in a bad shape and remained crouched on the ground. There was a quick discussion between the two masked men and, unceremoniously, one grabbed an offered hand gun and shot the prisoner dead. The scene was shocking by its brutal indifference! The shooter leaned in and casually shot the guy a second time. The video stopped.

It was labelled '*Spy executed by the vigilant protectors of the Caliphate*' and had been delivered in John's daily digas to review. It had been highlighted by the system because of a small slip of the shooter's face cover; yet, the poor quality of the video, even enhanced, prevented the identification of the fucker…

John sighed and deleted it: Nothing actionable there, apart being a reminder of the daily horror show that was ISIS…

Abdallah Wassem, on the other hand, was more promising!

John had been monitoring the guy's phone line for more than a week and was getting a pretty good picture of the perp; he was clearly a smalltime player in the system, an accountant trying to buy stuff at a cheap price, bargaining all the time, almost whining when talking to unidentified higher ups, bragging and being an ass with the few below him. He didn't even hand the cash: he would always « *have the cash delivered* » by a third party.

Climbing Abdallah's food chain was John's priority; the calls upwards were too few to account for the guy's activity; he had to have another phone, mobile or landline to work from… The land line was inexistent according to the records: it had to be another mobile phone. Though the local cell tower had been hacked by the NSA, it was somehow not possible to know who Abdallah was calling…

Having boots on the ground was pretty much excluded, the only way was an ISMI catcher[90], either onboard a plane or a drone. This was cutting eye tech and not yet officially acknowledged. The idea was to have a plane or drone fly above Abdallah's location, the ISMI catcher acting like a cell tower, identifying all mobile phones in the area and inserting

---

[90] An international mobile subscriber identity-catcher, or IMSI-catcher, is a telephone eavesdropping device

itself between Abdallah and his boss; After receiving a request for payment, Abdallah visibly needed someone's agreement; it was a logical leap to expect him to call right after a request...

The problem was to have the tech in the air, close enough, at that specific time. Abdallah seemed to receive most requests in the hour before lunch; John had heard him once yelling at some poor guy who had called him before 11am: Abdallah has apparently « *been in a very important meeting!* » So, the target hour would be 11am till 1pm.

The real problem, John learned quickly, was being last in the picking order of security services... The CIA, NSA, DIA, local military intel guys, even the SEAL teams came before him! And, on top of that, the administrative steps to process his requests were absurd to the point of laughable: there were up to five different forms to fill, from the tech required to the legal implications - '*no American should be intercepted unless in the following...*' followed by five paragraphs and extra procedures - and the flying hours interdepartmental billing allocation...

Two weeks went by waiting for an authorization; the target hour was proving the right one: Abdallah clearly had most of his calls during the target hour. John grew more and more restless.

On the 26th of February, ISIS released a video of destructions of the museum in Mosul. Absurdly, it enraged John: the sight of the men in their white thobes or janitor garb pushing the statues down, breaking them with sledgehammers were the tipping point.

* * *

He rushed into Mike's office without so much as a polite knock; Mike was on the phone and looked up.

« Martin, I've got something to handle right now; do you mind if I call you back later in the day? »

« … »

« Good, 1100, that's settled then, good bye! » He hung up.

« That was the Chairman[91] *of the Joint Chief of Staff Committee… Speak! »*

John suddenly felt like a jerk; he had certainly acted like one!

« The intercept request I made? Regarding the accountant in Mosul…»

« Yes, what with it? »

« It's been more than two weeks; I can't get any traction on it, I don't even know whether someone's actually working on it; I got a real feeling this could lead to something but… »

« It was easier to have a target you could shoot yourself, do everything on your own! »

« Well, I mean, I know there's a lot of admin but I didn't imagine that… » He sighed.

« Right, two things now: one, I'm going to make sure that your

---

[91] Highest-ranking and most senior military officer in the United States Armed Forces; at the time General Martin Dempsey

request gets a proper green light; two, you throw a tantrum like that again, you'll be back crying at that Subway shop in Middletown faster that you can say fuck! Clear? »

Reddening, John stood to attention.

« Yessir! »

« Out! »

The outlash was not missed on in the office; Bubba came to his cubicle an hour later.

« I suggest now is a good time for coffee… »

He followed the big man to the cafeteria.

« What's going on John? » He handed him a burning espresso.

« Well, it's just, I have the lead that I want to pursue; And I can't get the guys on the ground to actually do it… »

« In Iraq? »

« Mosul. »

Bubba nodded.

« John, you've got to understand: Iraq is the biggest clusterfuck of our history; we are pouring billions into this and every single branch of government wants to be part of it… Hell, I even saw a report from the ATF requesting an office there… There are one hundred times more fucking guns here in the US and those idiots want to send some teams there… Everyone is pushing its weight

around! And we, at the Red House, are the small people... yes, we are with the CIA, but not quite; and the boys at Langley, they would like to pull the curtain on us; makes them look bad when we find something they didn't! So, your request, even Langley doesn't give a shit... »

« But, then, how do you... »

« Very, very patiently! And certainly not by jumping on Mike's arse like that! » He chuckled. *« You gonna be the talk of the day... It's been a long time since anyone did that! Who was on the phone?»*

« General Dempsey, shit man. »

Buba patted him on the shoulder and left, laughing out loud...

It turned out that Mike and General Dempsey were friends and had been planning a golf round at the Army Navy Country Club, and that Mike, true to his word, had moved things around. John received a notice that an intercept would be attempted on the 6th of March, 1100 local time, eight long days later.

*   *   *

The message had arrived on his phone one Sunday afternoon, after John's first biking session with Jenna!

« Err, hello John, this is Kate. Uncle William has given me your new phone number. He has told me that you had moved to Washington... »

* * *

There was a silence.

« Well, I'm coming to DC end of May for a real estate trade show; I think, err, do you think that it would be a good time to see each other? Well, call me; my number hasn't changed. »

Hearing Kate's voice was a shock! John realized that he had somehow been living in an alternate reality for more than a year and that, inevitably, both worlds had to collide... With Kate came Josh; on a whim, John opened an email account that he had long forgotten: in the middle of the hundreds of spam, dozens of emails from his father-in-law waited patiently: they were wordless and just contained pictures of a little boy he did not know anymore.

John sat on the floor with his laptops on his knees and spent the next half hour scrawling the pictures, seeing Josh smiling, running, hugging, playing, laughing... The more he looked at his little man, the more excruciating the grief became; John started crying inconsolably.

It took him a long walk on the adjacent trail to get his act together; the fresh air, the commuters on their bikes, the buzzing lives all around brought him some peace and a resolution: he would call back Kate and see her.

The call was awkward for both were prudent and hesitant: Kate had seemed relieved that he had called back and had told him that Uncle William had called some weeks before to give her some news about him; they agreed to see each other when she came.

*   *   *

* * *

The 6th of March was a Friday; John had been waiting for what felt like ages: he would finally get his intercept on Abdallah's phone.

He arrived at four am at the office; the main room was quiet, in the dark with a couple cubicles alight; there was one guy John had never seen and who was nicknamed « the owl » as he apparently worked only at night; he did not respond when John waved a hand, a usual behavior apparently.

Double espresso in hand, John started looking at the various screens and, yes, saw in the workload of the day, a planned MQ1 Predator flight; it was a secret variant of the original drone, while armament had been replaced by a SIGINT[92] and intercept payload.

Predictably, when Bubba arrived at eight am, John was pacing back and forth like a first time father-to-be in a maternity ward!

« Hey John, whassup? Ho, right, your very first intercept... What time did you get up this morning?

« Three... »

« OPS jitters, hu? »

John shrugged.

« Well, you should have asked me; they need some time to process whatever they get; don't expect anything before noon... »

---

[92] SIGnals INTelligence is intelligence-gathering by interception of signals

* * *

Bubba was right: the data came in at one pm; John high-fived himself mentally: the number called by Abdallah Wassem was identified, a cell phone in Raqqa, the unofficial capital of ISIS! Though no name was given, it was a significant step upward. John forgot his hunger and jumped on it.

A couple hours later, Mike Willow asked him to come in his office.

« It appears that you've put your finger on something that's of interest to Langley: they've just called me to ask why we had specifically requested that intercept. They didn't get into details but it seems that the number belongs to a person of interest, a local tribe leader, that they've been trying to tie to the ISIS organization. The link between him and the oil business is significant because of the control exerted by Daesh over oil. And also, ISIS has banned satellite and cell phones; his usage of one highlights his importance. Well done! »

« What will they do about it? »

« They didn't say but I would expect that that guy's life expectancy has suddenly been shortened... »

« No, they mustn't, I need time to learn who's above that guy; that's the only way I'll be able to do real damage... »

« I get it. Work on it, don't lose that number, but again, that's probably not going to last! I'll see what I can do but it's a team based in Baghdad that's working that lead and those guys are pretty pushy...»

John felt both elated and frustrated: what was the point of

finding a guy if that person was going to be neutralized quickly? And yet, finally he had put a target on someone's back and some payback was on the way…

Working the following days, he quickly recognized that, without a source on the ground, it was nigh-on impossible to go any further: ISIS leaders, for fear of interception and localization didn't communicate by electronic means. Therefore, the tribe leader would probably visit them. Following him was not possible without a full team, that John doubted they had deep inside those fucker's lines…

Then a week later, on a Friday, John got in his daily digga deliveries a memo highlighting a predator strike in West Raqqa, that had killed four men and caused some local tribal uproar: John sat back, breathed deeply and smiled: a good day was getting better, one fucker less…

He had come in the office dressed up in a white shirt, chinos and a slim fit dark blue jacket. Amanda had raised an eyebrow, the muscle had whistled, and a death metal t-shirted Bubba had snickered: « *Getting some action tonight?* »

He was having dinner with Jenna and looking forward to it…

She had been, well, herself after one ride the previous weekend:

« *How many more miles are we going to bike before I get invited to a dinner?* »

John's brain had bugged.

« *What do you mean? I … Erm, What?* »

* * *

Jenna sighed, rolling her eyes.

« You, me, good time biking; you, me, good time dinner! Capice? »

« Oooh… »

« Yes, oooh… »

« Err, sure… This Friday night, eight? »

« Yes, perfect; just send me the address and I'll meet you there! »

She kissed him good bye and left, leaving behind her a very confused and increasingly jubilant rider…

*　　　　*　　*

The restaurant was hard to find: after all, he had been living like a monk for the past months and had not bothered going any further than the occasional local shop. In the end, after a lot of soul searching, he had asked Judy! He had become a regular at the steakhouse as it was close to the office and had gone the following day for lunch.

« Judy, I need some help. » as she was serving him a salmon à l'unilatérale[93], *« I need a nice restaurant for Friday night, not something too fancy, but not something too casual, you know… »*

« For a date? » Her eyes sparkled. *« Hmmm, let's see, not uptight but still she must feel special, right? »*

---

[93] French recipe: fish is fried on one side until it is heated all the way through

* * *

John nodded, feeling suddenly hot…

« Hmm, oh yes, how about the Black Sky? It's pretty close and I heard it was really nice, with a roof top and a great view, very romantic! »

« Err, thanks Judy! »

« My pleasure, let me know how it went! » She winked and left.

There was a table available that Friday night, a *« lucky late cancellation »* had said the Maitre d.

*   *   *

There was a mishap in John's brain: it had stopped working the instant Jenna entered the restaurant; up to that moment, everything had looked fine: the place was as expected, a spot-on advice, energetic yet not loud, classy but not stuffed-up, their table on a side window allowing for a nice view and privacy, and a joyful crowd of diners.

It was all Jenna's fault: under a fancy grey coat, she wore a naughty little black dress that, on the obligatory second look, was more modest than it advertised; her blond hair was raised in a casual bun that highlighted her slender neck. Black high heels shoes and a light make-up completed the model look.

« Good evening John »

She frowned.

* * *

« *You know, I like it standing like that but may I, at some point, be invited to sit?* »

Her glittering eyes belied her fake anger; John finally got his brain to work.

« *Sure, sure, please…* » as he rose. « *Wow, you are stunning.* »

« *I noticed!* » She smiled…

The diner was perfect: the Champagne for starters, the food, the wine, the light banter along the conversation…

« *You never talk about your work John; is it that boring? You don't look to me like the kind of man who has a nine to five tedious job…* »

« *It's just…* » John hesitated. « *The think tank I work for deals with Government projects and most of them are classified; so, it's complicated for me to… Let's just say that, today, was a great day at work, I scored my first, err, success!* »

« *Hm, playing the sexy mystery man are we? I like that; let's drink to your success then!* »

So they celebrated a man's death…

« *Wait, did she say sexy?* » John's mind went on overdrive…

*   *   *

She lived in Belle Haven, close to the river; John had offered the customary ride home, that had been accepted with a wry smile.

* * *

The first kiss was electric!

The second was frantic!

They ended up tangled on her bed, kissing, caressing, groping, undressing each other as in a race; the moment that John had dreaded, nightmared on for months, the removal of his prosthesis, his naked stub, was lost in the frenzy.

There was heavy breathing, moaning, grunting, sweating, softness, hardness, and in the end, a perfect crescendo…

CHAPTER 14

Paris, France

September 2015

My life was crazy, absolute madness! I was losing weight, needed pills to sleep at night, energy boosts to wake up in the morning; my runs were becoming more sparse.

I was juggling with several live grenades: keep the French network in order, travel to various destinations to open still more accounts and create more shell companies and trusts, maintain a proper legend in France via my company and manage my ISIS bosses…

My legit business was stable but was becoming unmanageable by the day: Nicolas, my employee, one day told me that I was never there and that he was wondering why he was doing everything while I was having a good time abroad! The fact that he imagined me dancing on the beaches of Ibiza was quite good for my reputation as a former dedicated muslim and would keep the DGSI[94] people away

---

[94] French FBI

from me, though it could attract the French IRS… I had to let him go with a reasonable severance package, high enough that he was happy, low enough that he did not become suspicious…

I got in touch with my clients at the end of June 2015, letting them know that I wished to terminate our contracts; I think that both were relieved: they had kept me on their books pretty much only out of fear… They could not report me without compromising their companies for fiscal reasons and potentially their personal freedom if they got convinced of financing[95] a terrorist organization, a French wide ranging legal web; I was safe on that front…

I had kept my company, better not to raise any extra scrutiny, but had altered its business model: I would be doing some consulting over French accounting and fiscal procedures with a few foreign clients, entities that I had created myself and that, being empty shells, would require no time from me apart from a contract and a few invoices once in a while. I had kept my yearly wages at the median amounts of a French consultant in my field: enough to pay my bills and a few perks yet below the level that would make me an attractive target for a zealous IRS inspector…

I had also kept my office which, apart from been a legitimate front, was also where I kept the server I used to host my system; it was always on and would transmit orders at random hours, hidden behind an accumulation of VPNs and shared servers; the guy who had set it up had told me that not even the NSA could find it! I wasn't sure of that but had

---

[95] Liable to prosecution under French law (art. 421-2-2 of the French « code pénal »)

to trust him! I had a back-up stored in a safe house that would be updated once a week.

Working for these companies had the additional bonus of allowing for some legit travels two or three times a year; I needed them as Ibrahim was asking me to increase the number of accounts that would be managed by the software, and for five 'entree' accounts, I would probably need to create one or two exit 'muddling' ones…

I would travel under my real identity to places where I had my customers: Vietnam, Liechtenstein and the Channel Islands; my legends were in play when I needed to go to more 'exotic' places such as Panama or HongKong: I always flew out from different European airports: German security wouldn't fret about a Swiss national flying to Panama, Spanish immigration wouldn't mind a French citizen flying away to Hong Kong…

Once in the tax havens countries, I used a different set of identity to present myself in the various lawyers' offices or banks.

It went smoothly most of the time; I did have some rare and awkward moments when I had a memory lapse and couldn't remember who I was supposed to be…

The first time it happened to me was in a lawyer's office in Panama: he needed me to fill in and sign some documents; I suddenly froze and thought: « Fuck, who did I say I was? » I just couldn't remember and couldn't open my passport in front of the guy to check: how credible would that be!

There was a silence…

* * *

I was dealing with a real pro; he cleared his throat and said: *« Erm, I might have forgotten a document for you to review; I'm sorry, I need to go and check with my secretary! »*

I frantically retrieved my id and filled in the required documents; all my aliases were following the few same rules: they had the same initials and sounded reasonably like my real name; my fake signatures were composed of my two initials followed by a stylized second letter of my alias' last name.

He came back: *« Sorry, I was mistaken; I think all the forms I need are here… Oh, good, you're done; fantastic! »*

After that incident, I made it a forceful habit to incorporate in my routine a 'pre-ops identity check': I would take five minutes reviewing my identity before entering an office or an airport; for airports, I would spend that time hidden away in the toilets, both before security and before boarding. As a final precaution, I would always have in hand a document with my current working name clearly visible on it.

I also had a close call in Germany once when I got flagged for an reinforced control at customs: the officer came inches from finding two passports hidden in the cover of a large book… It was clearly a random check but still, it made me think about it and alter my process: I established safe boxes in various countries under my legends: the additional aliases identification documents and credit cards would either be kept permanently there or sent to them by DHL and the likes. The safe boxes were paid out quarterly from one account, separated from the system, which had enough cash to pay for the following decade…

* * *

Entering Syria discreetly in 2015 did not require any identification but: one, a very compelling reason, two, a very good guide!

The compelling reason was simple: Ibrahim had disappeared… We had a meeting scheduled in July and he never showed up! I travelled by train to Gruyère, the alternate location we had agreed on in case of a security hiccup: I visited the magnificent castle, enjoyed the strawberries and crème double in a local restaurant, in short, the perfect tourist; once I had waited as much as I could, I had to ride the train back, increasingly worried.

Back in Lausanne, I went to an internet café and scanned the local news for a dead Ibrahim; there it was: « *Un banquier genevois tué dans un dramatique accident de la route,* » a Geneva banker killed in a dreadful car accident! It seemed that, for an unknown reason, Ibrahim Kellerman's car, that was the first time I learned his name, had swerved and plunged into a deep ravine; there was no witness and the car had only been found because of hikers walking up the river one Sunday morning… Single, his disappearance had not been noticed quickly…

I drove back to Paris, confused and worried: could this be a trivial road accident due to a nasty wet road or was there something most sinister and dangerous, to it? Had Ibrahim been identified by some security services? The Swiss wouldn't have killed him, the Americans? Or had it been ISIS but what for?

The fact that the Swiss hadn't stopped me meant nothing: they would pass the bucket to the French if, thanks to

Ibrahim, they had identified me… I needed to be even more cautious driving back to Paris!

I had never logged on the emergency website, but that week, after driving back to Paris, I did. There, in the comment section of an obscure rock group: « *We did it.* »

I sighed, relieved, but impressed at the audacity, the risk taken…

Three weeks later, I received a travel newspaper by mail; it had been posted in Germany and advertised Antalya! I bought a plane ticket to Antalya and booked a room for the first two weeks of September in the guesthouse were I had spent a few days the previous year.

The weather was wonderful, sunny, with temperatures in the low nineties; I played the tourist and visited the old town, the aqueduct; I had a lazy afternoon on Lara Beach, a nice seafood diner near the old harbor. Then it all changed…

It was perfect déjà-vu: a truck stopped by me as I was walking home; the driver signaled that I should climb in the back and off we went!

The first part of the trip, striptease included, was eventless in a scorching heat: we stopped at the same place in the evening; I got to sleep a few hours in a very hot room, before being woken up and, blinded, being helped on board another vehicle. The drive was shorter it seemed.

We stopped; I was brought out and the vehicle left me seating on the ground with the balaclava covering my eyes… It was a little windy and I was getting cold. After a while in complete silence, I removed the hood and dropped it: from what I could see in the moonless night, I was on a dirt road, in the middle of some kind of field; there were some weak lights in the distance on my left, a village, and some more ahead of me.

I felt, more than I heard, a movement on my right; a shadow appeared and waved me up.

« *Follow me!* » said the man in heavy accented Arabic.

We walked for more than a mile; first, we followed the road, but, quickly, we turned on a path following the contours of fields. There was little noise, the occasional insects buzzing, a night animal yelping, the only man-made sound, the quiet roar of a jetliner flying high above us.

We crossed a dirt road without a pause and, after another hour of careful walking, reached an abandoned village; we stopped there for a short while. We were close to a border, that was obvious: I could see a lighted portion of barrier a few hundred yards away. The guide was seated, his back against a wall still warm from the day's high temperatures.

« *We wait!* »

That was the second time he had spoken since we had met.

« *Iraq?* » I said, showing the border.

« *Syria* » He shrugged.

I sat next to him.

* * *

Some time later, I heard a heavy vehicle come from one side of the border; it drove alongside the wall, past us without stopping; a patrol I realized.

As soon as it had left, the guide stood and motioned me to follow. We walked swiftly across light bush towards the barrier; it stood some ten feet tall, topped by thick razor wires and light every twenty yards.

Some thirty yards, away, the guide suddenly crouched and disappeared!

I followed carefully; there was a natural depression, some six feet deep, hidden by the bush. The guide wasn't there anymore and, hearing some scratching noises, I quickly realized that there was an opening on the side: a three feet wide water conduit. I crouched, then crawled into it.

If I had been cold outside, I quickly started to sweat as I made my way along the drain; it was warm, very dusty, the air filled with a foul smell as if some animal had come to die there… I was suddenly thankful to my guide who might have to cope first with whatever could live in there and who, by grunting, gave me a sense of direction, not that I could go anywhere else than straight ahead!

After what felt like ages, I exited the pipe and enjoyed a long breath of fresh air. We were yet in another ditch; we followed it for a while then climbed out. A hundred yard away stood a dilapidated house; the guide signaled that I should go there and disappeared back in the ditch. I reached the ruin, had a pee and waited again…

A guy appeared from nowhere and asked me to come with

him. We walked an extra mile before reaching a car; he told me to get into the trunk and gave me a bottle of water.

« *Putain*[96], *ca va jamais se terminer ce truc!* » I sighed climbing in and trying to get comfortable; the water was warm and stale but welcomed after that trek.

We drove for ages before stopping abruptly: the hood opened and I was roughed out of the trunk. Bathed in a weak light, I was facing some soldiers at a checkpoint; on one side of the blockade, there was the black flag, emblem of ISIS. I had arrived but they didn't seem to know that I was a good guy: they were pointing their AKs[97] at me and asking what the fuck I was doing here… My driver seemed upset and scared, showing a dirty paper that they didn't care about.

I blew up, I mean, I lost it! After getting through all that shit, I wasn't going to be fucked around by some idiots who barely knew how to speak Arabic! They were French fighters who obviously thought highly of themselves, a couple seemed high.

I started insulting them in Arabic: they, their mothers, their families for generations gone and to come… I had been a soldier for the cause before they had ever fucked a goat, I had killed fakirs with my own bare hands, I had been an imam in Afghanistan! My driver had been a safeguard and they had blown up my cover. I must have been a sight: a dirty, rambling mad man!

Surprised by my outburst, they took a step back, unsure. I

---

[96] French: « Fuck, this is never going to end… »
[97] Kalachnikov assault rifle

climbed in the passenger seat, told my driver to start the engine and yelled at the assholes to get out of my way, which they did as we drove away…

My driver kept glancing nervously at me, visibly wondering whether I was a warlord or a maniac.

« I need to cover my face » I told him. *« Do you have something? »*

He nodded and showed me a scarf in the back; I took it and wrapped it around my head.

After two hours, we arrived in a small city, Aïn Issa, according to my driver. All the buildings were a brownish grey, some were badly destroyed. We stopped outside the city and prayed quickly. An hour and a half later, we arrived in Raqqa.

Raqqa was displaying the attacks of the Western forces: there were more destroyed buildings here; I could see impact of bombs or missiles at nearly every block.

We entered a courtyard of a small house; a guard closed the portal behind us. I walked out of the car in the morning heat and entered the house; Kazem was waiting for me and embraced me.

« My friend, such a joy to see you; you must be exhausted after such a long journey; come, come and have tea. »

A tall veiled woman brought some tea and biscuits; she seemed cute, very, very nervous and relieved to be asked away.

* * *

« Such a sad thing, our friend Ibrahim... » he said. *« He was very efficient and served our cause well. »*

« Yes, I was worried when he didn't show up at our meeting and sad when I saw on the internet that he had died. »

« We need to discuss your system; this is why I asked you to come, knowing the risks... I will come back this afternoon once you have rested and we will also celebrate your wedding! »

« What? » I was so tired I probably didn't hear right...

« This is your house; this is your woman! She's Yazid filth but she has come back to the Pure Faith; you'll make her a better woman and restore some honor by bedding her... »

He left.

The woman came back and asked me softly if I wanted to clean; I realized how filthy I was, covered in sweat, dust and reeking of the drain smell... She took me to my bedroom where there was a small shower. I was so tired that I undressed before her like a robot; the meager water jet was lukewarm but felt like a blessing. Clean, I lied down on the bed and fell instantly asleep.

She woke me up for the midday prayer; I had some food and fell asleep again.

This time, I heard the muezzin call for the late afternoon prayer; I got up and worshiped again. Once done, I walked out of the room and entered the living room; here I found the woman - my wife? - preparing tea and some food. When I thanked her, she jumped...

* * *

« Don't be afraid, you have nothing to fear from me. »

She didn't reply.

« What's your name? »

« Layla, » she whispered, not looking me in the eyes.

« I'm… Mourad » resorting to my name from my Baghdad fights. *« Thank you for the tea, it's good. »*

She shied away.

There was nothing to do; I remembered Kazem's advice regarding going out and spent the remaining of the day watching Al Jazeera on a poor television. It seemed that France was about to attack Syria… *« Wonderful, »* I thought, *« Now, I'm gonna get whacked by a French bomb! »* The dark irony was not lost on me…

With sunset came the muezzin call and the prayer; it felt right to get back into this religious routine; I was careful not to do it in Europe and not even at home; I couldn't be sure that at some point cameras would be hidden in my flat and I had to maintain a perfect front; I even drank some alcohol once in a while and kept a few bottles at home.

Kazem didn't come that evening and I performed Salat Al Isha quietly in my bedroom.

I tried to take a quick shower but there was no water. I went to bed and fell asleep quickly.

* * *

I was jolted awake as someone lay by my side; it was Layla. She came close to me and I realized that she was naked!

« *Wait, stop!* » I gently removed a hand that had gotten very personal…

« *No, we must, I'm your wife…* » as she curled up against me. I could feel the heat from her body.

« *But, no, it's not right; you don't have to…* »

She interrupted me!

« *Yes, we have to; they will check if we don't, if I haven't… Please, please, let me have sex with you! If you don't take me, they will sell me on the slave market… If you take me, if I become truly your wife, they can't; you're an important man to have a house just for you… Please, please…* »

Her pleading got more desperate: she was close to crying. Her hands were now all over me; I let go!

She kissed me with desperate energy; a leg came in between mine; her heavy breasts brushed my torso and I felt a brutal arousal. I turned her on her back and started kissing her voraciously. I tested the salty sweat off her smooth skin. I grabbed a handful of her long hair and kissed her neck, then came kissing down to her tits; as I licked, sucked, bit her erected nipples, her hands caressed my short hair, her fingers dug in my shoulders. I could hear her breath hasten. Ravenous, I slid down to her navel and batted her hands away.

« *No* » she said; I was ravenous: I didn't give a damn…

* * *

Her pussy had a clean smell and I enjoyed discovering it, kissing and licking.

« *No, no,* » she said again, in a subdued voice.

She arched when I found her clit, giving out a long hiss. Sighs gave way to moan; then she tensed, trembled and abandoned herself back, breathing rapidly.

I climbed back to her lips, kissing and caressing her along the way; she turned her head and started crying.

I fucked her, as hard as I could, mercilessly, and came in a burst of rage…

I lay on the side and felt her move away.

« *Stay!* » I grabbed her wrist. « *You're my wife now!* »

She lay back on the bed.

I fell asleep only to wake up to quiet sobs.

I turned and took her in my arms gently; she tensed, then after a long moment let herself go. We woke up in the morning still entangled with one another, her naked skin against mine. My dick was resting against her thigh: I became very obviously aroused…

To my surprise, she stared stroking my dick hard, then straddled me; there was enough light now for me to see her. And what a sight! She had a beautiful body, heavy yet firm breasts, a slim waist and a dark alluring skin. She must have been in her middle twenties.

Her hands on my chest, She slowly, ever slowly, lowered herself on me, started rolling her hips; her mouth was half opened, her eyes lost somewhere, her tits moving hypnotically. My hands went to her hips; she conducted them to her breasts. I couldn't resist long and came into her. Without a kiss, she rolled off me and left the room.

There was some water that morning and I was able to wash quickly before the morning prayer. Layla brought me some breakfast; I tried to talk to her but she left the room without a sound.

It must have been eight or nine when a petulant Kazem came back.

« Hello my brother, I've heard that you enjoyed your wife! Good, good, a warrior needs his rest! » He winked. Yet there was something more sinister in his eyes: I had some how passed a test, my loyalty was never assured…

« Now, let's talk business! You need to give us your system! »

« What? You don't trust me? I can assure you that I am absolutely loyal to the cause. »

« Yes, yes, my friend Alain »

I glanced toward the kitchen: Layla was nowhere in sight.

« Your loyalty is not in question but you must understand that we want to control it… It works very well: the security seems very efficient, the transfers are fast and the hawala brokers are unhappy,

which is great because we don't have to rely so much on them! Yet, we must keep it under our control in the State. »

I was not going to let go easily…

« Ok, I understand but keep in mind that the system needs a broadband connection, a VPN, a server that is always on, no electricity cuts… You cannot move it around easily! And the Americans, they certainly monitor all internet connections in Syria, Iraq; in Europe, there are so many they can't! »

« Yes my friend, we do not think that having it here is appropriate; we want you to bring it to Jordan where it will be safe and the technology that you need will be available… »

He was not going to be swayed: we agreed on a timeline and a way to contact his people in Jordan in the following six months. Meanwhile, I was going to increase the system's capacity: I had a long list of new 'entree' accounts to factor in. It would be sent to me in different draft messages on a new email address, 'entree' and destination accounts information cut in pieces and hidden in pictures. Little did I know that tens of millions of dollars were quickly going to flow through the system…

We were interrupted once, by a not so distant explosion: Western warplanes and drones killing brothers!

Kazem frowned: *« it's not safe here anymore, you will leave tonight; this time, you will travel with a group of refugees: it's less discreet but you were noticed by your compatriots and we think that you will be safer in a group! »*

« They really are a pain these assholes, aren't they? »

* * *

He rolled his eyes: « *You have no idea; they know nothing; they think themselves great fighters but shit their pants as soon as they get fired at. They want bigger houses, more women, drugs... And when they don't get it, they complain as if on a vacation! A few of them, though, are ruthless and very, very dedicated; you'll certainly hear about them in the future!* »

On that cryptic note, he kissed me, wished me a safe return and left.

I did not say goodbye to Layla that day; she remained cloistered in her bedroom and only came out to bring some food in the main room. When I left the house at night, I only saw a dark figure and moving shades at a window.

The journey back to Turkey was hot, uncomfortable, packed in a truck with fifteen of so scared migrants, men, women and wailing children; once across the border, I was whisked away back to the guesthouse in Antalya.

In France, it was business as usual; the French network was now completely under Chuppa's direction; while he still respected me, Chuppa did not view me as a boss anymore, a bit confused and maybe suspicious by my withdrawal from operations, and went about his daily collections with belief; he still worked with Fasil.

And some of my French brothers were ruthless indeed...

The first bombing from French Rafale fighter jets came on

Raqqa a few months later after the Bataclan[98] attacks…

---

[98] On 13 November 2015, 130 people were killed in a coordinated terrorist attack in the Bataclan theatre and various places in Paris

International Bank of Indochina
Account Number: 7011114642
Balance: US$ 35,788.21

CHAPTER 15

Washington DC,

November 20th, 2015

« Bastards, fucking bastards! »

John was fuming at the television, watching an endless replay of the terror attacks in Paris: more than a hundred people killed at a concert hall or shot randomly at café tables in the street! He knew those streets from his student days; he had been to concerts at the Bataclan[99]; he had drunk wine with friends late in the summer evenings, redesigning the world until the morning lights chased them to bed; he had chatted up cute girls and seduced a few, his American accent an obvious help…

At least, a majority of those scumbags had been killed but some were on the run!

* * *

---

[99] Paris concert hall attacked on November 13th, 2015; 90 persons were killed, several hundred injured

And he had nothing to work on… Since that local guy had been killed, Abdallah Wassem had gone dark; the guy was probably scarred to death, and rightly so. He was probably stuck between Western bombs and Amni, ISIS' secret service, that was certainly looking for the informant who might have given out the sheik. After dragging their feet as usual, the French had arrived in a furry and their Rafale fighter jets were dropping tons of bombs on Raqqa, hoping to kill the French 'citizens' who had turned up in support of ISIS…

Yet, the organization was still able to maintain spendings; the troops on the ground did not complain of any ammunition shortage. The antiterror coalition was now eagerly targeting the oil trucks, destroying them by the dozens, as they did not want to damage the production facilities - business is business… - and therefore reducing starkly oil generated cash. There had to be something else…

He had seen something intriguing one morning: DIGA had highlighted, as usual, some money related activity of the previous day; in the long list of reports, analysis, intercepts, pictures stood a small comment by a Turkish guy complaining about a drop of activity in his business. What was interesting was that, if officially the guy sold textile to Europe, his business was cash transfer! He was one of those hawala brokers, transferring money around with a nice interest rate for his work.

A drop in hawala money transfer meant two things: either a drop of support from European muslim crowds to the communities back home, which did not play with the past trends, or some of the cash was going elsewhere… « *Where?* » was the million dollar question!

* * *

He shared his thoughts with Mike one afternoon; his boss had never spoken about his outburst months ago and John still felt a bit awkward in his presence.

« So, there's money flowing somewhere according to you? You know most analysts don't seem to think that; the current consensus is that, with the four hundred millions stolen in the Bank of Mosul and the cash from the looting of the various museums, ISI seats on over one billion US dollars, a quite substantial amount, sufficient for many months of fighting... »

« Yeah, I've seen those reports but they're crap; I mean, there was never four hundred millions in the Mosul bank, maybe one fourth of that only; you've got to look at it in a practical way: there were no real transport out of the bank when they arrived; a lot of small details hint at both national and local management helping themselves in the months prior; one of the Mosul junior managers was arrested with a bag of cash as he was trying to sneak in Turkey: he had three hundred fifty thousand dollars in Franklins[100], and the banknote serial numbers were in a sequence! »

« And you're saying that money is still flowing in? »

« Yes, and if it isn't oil, archeological artifacts and the local taxes, it has to come from outside! »

« Right, let me talk to someone: keep digging, I'll let you know what. »

One afternoon a few days later, he came up to John's cubicle: *« You've got a meeting tomorrow at Fort Meade[101], with a guy*

---

[100] US$100 notes carry Benjamin Franklin on one side
[101] National Security Agency (NSA) HQ

called Henry O'Connor; he'll brief you on INGOT, an operation that they have been running quite recently. The meeting's at 11 am. Let me know how it went. »

A DIGA query a few minutes later left John intrigued: there was no such operation according to DIGA! That was weird. He went to Bubba and asked him whether he had ever heard about it.

« Nope, and you say that you digaed it and found nothing? Well, it's not your usual stuff then: undigable, code-worded and NSA usually implies deep black stuff... » He stopped and smiled, *« Well, should be an interesting morning! Don't tell me what you found... »*

The drive from home to Fort Meade took an eventless forty-five minutes; he exited the Baltimore-Washington parkway at the MD-32 E exit and accessed the NSA grounds; being late in the day, he had to park hundreds of yards away from the visitor center in the visitor parking lot and walk in the rain up to the small two-story building. He was asked for an id and the name of the person he was visiting. He handed out his blue military id. A « VISITOR » badge was issued to him with a stern lecture on security and access; having opted to leave his phone in the car got him a nod of approval and proved the right option when he had to go through the metal detectors: his prosthesis was enough of a hassle... His temper got a little more challenged when he was asked whether he needed a transport to the main entrance. Grumbling, he just grabbed his rucksack and walked briskly in the rain towards the main entrance.

It was an extra ten minutes before this O'Connor guy arrived and allowed him in through the second set of barriers. They chatted about the latest football game while walking down bland corridors and finally entered a windowless room. His host closed the door and handed some forms.

« *What's this?* » asked John.

« *Confidentiality procedure...* »

« *But I already have a TS[102] clearance!* »

« *Yeah I know but still, we do things a little differently from you guys at Langley or wherever you come from...* » He didn't seem so happy about the meeting.

« *Man, this better be good,* » muttered John as he filled and signed the documents.

« *I think that we are good,* » said Henry; « *Please wait,* » He left and locked the door.

Fifteen minutes later, a guy walked in; he had the typical look of an accountant: white, middle-aged, a receding hairline... He didn't introduce himself!

« *What we will discuss here is one of the agency's most guarded secret; I am very surprised that you were brought into this and, frankly, I don't like it...* »

If John's eyes could kill... The guy was totally oblivious !

* * *

---

[102] Top Secret

« *So, we have quite recently found a way to access the SWIFT*[103] *network; it's something that we are very proud of as the level of cryptology is very secure.* » He scoffed; « *well maybe not so anymore…* »

« *I'm aware of your efforts with VISA and SWIFT thanks to your buddy Snowden* » smirked an irritated John to the guy's dismay. « *But it didn't seem to be very deep!* »

« *Not anymore, we have now total access to the SWIFT network! I'll spare you the technical details: they are classified like out of your league, besides you wouldn't understand anything…* »

John let the jab pass: « *When you say access all, you mean all transactions? From end to end? Realtime? Can you actually work the data or do you only monitor it?* »

« *Theoretically, we could work the entire data but, with dozens of millions of transactions a day, the computing volume remains too high, even for us but, focus on a bank, an account and we can deliver it to you!* » The pride was evident and, in John's eyes, well justified.

« *This is incredible! Can you map a network? Can you analyze patterns? How would we work?* »

The tension in the room was gone. John was now in hunter mode.

* * *

---

[103] The Society for Worldwide Interbank Financial Telecommunication (SWIFT) provides a network that enables financial institutions worldwide to send financial transactions in a secure, standardized and reliable environment

« You give us a thread and we'll send you the raw data; you do whatever you want with it... But you need to know that we are talking thousands of lines probably... Even with a simple account! So if you start asking about whole banks... »

« And I can target anyone, any bank, anywhere in the world? »

« Yes! » Let ACLU[104] lawyers go berserk at that!

They worked out the details: how John would ask for the info, an anonymous governmental email address - John still had no name for the guy facing him, ACLU be damned - and when it would be delivered on a secure USB device, always the same, that would be returned wiped out...

On his drive back, John's brain was buzzing: a thread, he needed a thread... Then, suddenly, somewhere near Mount Vernon Triangle, he realized that he had one: Abdallah! The mediocre accountant buying tires had to be skimming some cash for himself; that was a logical heap from his attitude on the calls. He probably got some cash back from the suppliers; identify his bank account and you identify all the suppliers; identify the suppliers and you may identify one or more accounts used by ISIS... Not everything could be in cash!

That was his focus for the following days... along with Kate's visit to come.

*   *   *

---

[104] The American Civil Liberties Union (ACLU) is a nonprofit organization founded to defend and preserve the individual rights and liberties guaranteed to every person in the USA by the Constitution and laws of the United States.

* * *

Back in May, they had met for the first time in a bar facing the Walter E. Washington Convention center; she was fifteen minutes late because of an unexpected meeting and had arrived in a frenzy; he had been sat there for a while, drinking a whisky, not knowing what to expect... The fact that he had slept with Jenna the night before made the whole rendezvous all the more uncomfortable.

She was more beautiful than he remembered, a tall brunette with black eyes, smartly dressed in a dark pantsuit, every bit the successful professional. There was an assurance about her, a certain weight as if the past rough years had armored her...

She had ordered a Perrier with a slice lemon. An awkward silence had followed.

« *You have a new leg.* » She grimaced: it probably had not come out as she intended.

« *Yes, err, it's a Norwegian model, quite modern.* » He dabbled on, like a poor salesman...

« *It's interesting... * »

A silence.

« *This couldn't be worse could it?* » she said. John raised his eyes and chuckled.

« *No, I, err, You probably wouldn't want to buy a prosthesis from me... * »

* * *

Kate smiled for the first time, a subdued, mocking smile:
« Probably not… »

« How was your meeting? »

« Good actually; I'm sorry I was late but the guy I was meeting is the president of a pretty big real estate company and he wouldn't… I just couldn't… »

« Don't worry, I can understand that he would make the meeting last a bit longer: you look wonderful! »

She smiled, a first bright smile…

« Thank you, you look great too… »

« That's easy; I wasn't my best last time… » Her eyes darkened then eased.

« Can you walk for me? » She said. *« I want to see that fantastic prosthesis in action before I buy one! »*

So John played the fashion model, attempting a catwalk to Kate's laugh and applause.

They spend two hours together, she explaining her new career, him telling her about selling the house in Middletown, getting a job in DC, the rehab… John asked softly about Josh: how he was, was he a good boy, did he like sports? Kate showed him pictures and video…

« He misses you, you know? I mean, he doesn't remember you, but I have never stopped telling him about you, showing pictures of you; his favorite teddy bear has a broken leg… »

* * *

« *I miss him too; I…* » John sighed and stopped; Kate put her hand onto his.

« *You know, maybe next time I come to DC in December, he could come with me? Your Uncle William has often complained of not seeing him…* »

They left the bar, the night had fallen and the air was getting fresher.

« *It was good to see you John! Let's talk more often ok?* »

« *Yes, we should.* »

She caressed his cheek lightly and walked away.

*   * *

John was wet, dirty and cold and hadn't felt so happy for a long time; he was lost in the woods in the middle of God knows where Western Virginia and loved every minute of it…

« *Hurry up John!* » said toe-less Phil, « *We gonna lose the trail!* »

« *You know, maybe we should slow down a bit: this is a bit obvious no?* »

« *Come on, I'm gonna nail Anton's ass for once…* »

So they hurried… and died in a glorious cloud of paint ball explosions and cheers from Anton's team!

* * *

« Argh fuck, next time listen to me, ok? » Said a vexed John.

« Reconnnn, » laughed Anton, approaching with a couple of beers.

John grinned and took a sip: *« That was recon shit for sure; raiders would have nailed your ass! »*

Anton raised an eyebrow: *« bit late for a rematch, we are expected for dinner but happy to see you in action next time! »*

Phil had called John two weeks ago and had offered to go visit his buddies in West Virginia: they were members of the Wild Westerners, an outdoor club that gathered its members, mostly West Virginians, every other week for some hunting, paintball or football games. West Virginia being what it is, most wore camo jackets, carried a handgun more or less openly, a couple would even bring their AR15s to show them off…

A local Pastor said Grace before diner and it was then a full-out assault on the barbecue. John, a wounded decorated Marine, had been quickly adopted by the gang; there were few other vets in the group and his combat experience was visibly highly respected. As beers emptied, discussions turned political, the lot being unsurprisingly rather conservative and rooting for Trump in the coming primaries…

On the drive home, Phil said: *« The guys liked you; they don't open up like this often… »*

« Yeah, well, they're nice and it was fun, even though you're a crap platoon leader… »

* * *

« You know, missing fingers makes it actually easier to hit people: I don't have to worry about dislocating one if I hit too hard… »

They laughed their way back to DC.

Being late thanks to some guy who had managed to flip over on the US-48, John asked Phil to drop him of at Uncle William's house where he was expected for dinner.

When he arrived, muddy and reeking of smoke, Amalia opened the door and ran away, fretting about the dinner; Uncle William was his usual self, reading a report, a glass of Caol Ila pure malt whisky in hand.

« Good evening John, I see that you've been out? »

« Yes, a weekend in the woods in West Virginia, good fun! »

« Nice, funny how a grueling exercise imposed on oneself in the Marines becomes an entertainment years later, isn't it? Oh, by the way, General Dempsey sends his regards… »

John reddened: *« He didn't! Err, you've heard of… »*

Uncle William burst out laughing: *« No, and yes, It's the greatest laugh Mike and I had in months… »*

John grimaced: *« That wasn't very wise… »*

« No, but Mike likes your intensity! »

That, and the news from Kate, set the mood for a quiet, happy dinner.

CHAPTER 16

Unspecified location,

January 2016

Alain was never discussed on the phone ; nor were emails or anything remotely digital used. No names would ever be used and no one would ever admit knowing him. The two men would meet at a changing discreet location; it would be proofed in advance of their meeting for eavesdropping devices in the improbable event that enemies would have found it.

« *What's going on?* » Said the first man; he was, as usual, dressed formally, the way the men in his function were in his country.

« *I am worried,* » replied the second one, shrewd, an albeit inferior yet respected warrior.

« *The pressure?* »

« *Yes, the danger and also the absence of results: he wishes he could do more and doesn't see us succeeding in the long term... »*

* * *

« Obviously… Yet he knew that it would be a long journey! »

There was a silence. The first man lit up a cigar, the only vice of a life-long servant.

« Is he still loyal? »

« I think so: the system is working well and the volumes are increasing daily! Should we ask for some proof of loyalty? »

« No, he has done enough. If we ask for more, he'll become wary. Keep an eye on him; if I were him, I would start preparing my exit plan… »

« Money? »

« Yes and identities… Keep close contact and work on a plan to protect him and the system: I am worried that the Americans find him. »

« If they do… »

« Then we'll have lost a good man… »

CHAPTER 17

Paris, France

June 2016

I woke up in a frenzy, my heart beating like a mad drum.

I hardly had a night without a nightmare: people would try to catch me, people would shoot at me; I would be locked up in doorless dark rooms; spiderwebs would grow all around me and choke me…

They had become worse after the Bataclan attacks; I remember returning to Paris and being stuck in front of my television, looking at the 24/7 news.

I didn't have anything to fear from the Police: I wasn't connected to anyone involved. Or so I thought…

A stressed Chuppa asked to meet me one morning, just a few weeks after the events. We met in a busy café on the Bastille place. He looked harried and worried.

« *I have something to tell you: I think that I know one of the guys who was at the Bataclan! »*

« *Shit,* » I thought, my heart skipping a beat.

« *Tell me!"*

« *There's this guy, Yassine: he asked me for some money and accommodation some months ago. He had some friends coming over from Belgium*[105]. »

I didn't say anything, yet was starting to boil inside!

« *So I found an apartment in the neuf trois*[106]; *I know the landlord: he doesn't give a shit who rents the place and takes cash. I called him and asked him if the apartment was available for a few months. He said yes, so I called Yassine and gave him the guy's phone number and some cash.* »

« *Do you still have the phone you called from?* » I had turned in a robot and Chuppa was clearly worried, and rightly so.

« *No. I… »*

« *Was it a burner?* »

« *Well, I… »*

« *It was registered under your name!* » That was deadly evident… « *So, the cops, when they find the location, will get your*

---

[105] Most of the Bataclan terrorists came from Belgium
[106] French: 93, area code number for the Paris Northern department, with the highest rate of immigrants in France, high unemployment and poverty

name from the landlord… And when they catch Yassine, they'll know that you gave him money… »

« We're not sure that they will catch him and I know him, he won't talk… »

I laughed bitterly: *« C'est pas vrai*[107]*! How can you be so fucking stupid, Chuppa? It's the biggest terrorist attack of all times in France! Of course, they will catch everyone! And they will talk, all of them! And I can tell you that, if they can't catch them, they'll kill them! Wherever they are! »*

His own guilt conveniently forgotten, Chuppa was getting mad and clearly didn't believe me. I sighed.

« Ok Chuppa, this is what we're gonna do: we'll never meet anymore, ever; I will destroy the phone that you use to contact me; keep working with Fasil and collect the funds for the fight. May God be with you Brother!»

« What? You're quitting? Running away like a coward? » Chuppa was yelling and people started looking at us.

I rose, dropped some cash on the table and left without a word.

Walking away on a sunny rue Saint-Antoine, I was fuming: Chuppa was becoming a liability and could endanger the whole mission: good thing that he did not know where I lived.

I only had one thing to do; I just wasn't sure that I wanted to.

---

[107] French: literally « it can't be true, I can't believe what I hear »

He was, in an odd and pathetic way, my only friend…

*   *   *

Kazem had asked me to open a more frequent line of communications: we agreed on a list of future email addresses that would be discarded after use, just like a burner phone. I had hidden it in the thesis that I was writing, well, copying and pasting, on international banking: I would quote various economists in my paper, yet some would not exist and be used in a sequence.

The logic was simple: once an address had been used, it would be erased and we would both monitor the next one. An email was never sent and remained in the draft box until it was read and the whole address cancelled. I also monitored an instagram account that told of the daily difficult life of a lone Mosul journalist: we had agreed on a casual message in case of an emergency.

With the destruction of the oil financial lifeline, the state needed money more than ever; traditional supporters in Saudi Arabia or the UAE were getting warry of sending money directly and had been very discreetly advised to use my system.

I was traveling more than ever now; arguing that I was working both in Israel and in Arab countries, I was able to receive a second French passport[108] under my real name; it helped me avoid scrutiny from border officials in the various European countries I would leave from.

---

[108] States like Iran or Lebanon may cause trouble at entry for visitors who have been to Israel

* * *

Thanks to Ibrahim and various contacts, I had now some fifteen identities allocated in the various safe boxes that I had established in Europe, the Caribbeans and the middle-East and South-East Asia. Each had opened between fifteen and twenty accounts in various banks.

Dozens of accounts entered money in the system, dozens retrieved cash…

The emergencies occurred when an account was compromised at entry or exit level; the way the system was designed made it impossible hopefully, to climb up beyond the next level of accounts; the identities of the account holders were also well protected, either by local law or by unfortunate events…

One of the accounts that I wanted to protect the most was hosted in a bank in Panama City; the holder, a shell corporation, had its business and principals represented like many others by a local law firm, located in a colonial building standing on its own in Casco Viejo. As a customer, I had inquired about the safety and confidentiality of my informations; a zealous young lawyer had impressed on me how secured their servers and archives were and reminded me how protective of banking secret their local laws were. As a matter of fact, he hinted at the fact that even a US District Attorney had not been yet able to access their informations to the satisfaction of some unfortunately very unsavory customers…

That wasn't enough for me, even if it was ok for local drug lords, even if my corporation was one amongst hundreds hosted there…

* * *

I had noticed that the room, where I was invited to review documents and where, when I asked for a favor, I could work for a few hours, was located near their archives; on top of that, both rooms seem to share a ventilation vent. I carefully looked around the study and decided that there were no hidden cameras. Standing on a chair, I was able to see that the vent dropped slightly towards the Archive room: After taking some pictures of the exhaust, I had a draft of a plan; I needed time and help to make it work.

Four weeks later, I entered Panama and got in a taxi to my hotel downtown; the same day, after a routine surveillance detection walk around Casco Antiguo, playing the tourist, I met with an unhappy looking forty-years old French guy in a back alley close to Independence Square: walking up to me, he quickly handed me a rucksack without a word and walked away. Back in my hotel, I checked the content and nodded: I had everything I needed.

The next morning, I entered the law firm premises where I had booked the room to review a contract before signature. I asked for the contract to be printed and gave the clerk a USB drive. Then, requesting some privacy, I waited for the lawyer to leave me alone; I put some gloves on, removed my shoes, dragged a chair close to the wall and climbed on it; I carefully and discreetly unscrewed the ventilation cover. I removed from my computer bag two black boxes I had received the day before: they were the size of an A4 document, nineteen centimeters thick and several kilos heavy. I pushed them as far as I could down the vent in a sequence, then screwed the cover back on.

I pushed the chair back to the table, put my shoes back on,

hid my gloves in the bag and, after half an hour, called the lawyer, made some minor adjustments to the contract and signed it.

Eight days later on a Saturday, at one AM Panama time, as I was enjoying a late drink in a bar in Pointe-à-Pitre, Guadeloupe, I turned on a burner phone, called a US cellphone number and waited for the first ring; On my way to the hotel, finding a dark street, I broke the SIM card in two, stepped on the phone and threw away the pieces in a street garbage can.

In Panama City, thousands of kilometers away, a spark lit up the vent on one side of the highest box; it quickly grew in a flame. The plastic bag that occupied most of the box melted suddenly and released a burning liquid that flowed along the second box, itself also filled of liquid, igniting its shell.

A burning thread fell from the vent inside the archive room and seemed to jump at the paper archives; within seconds, the room was a raging inferno of smoke and white sparkling light. The firemen, when they arrived fifteen minutes later, battled the blaze with several hoses, but were only able to contain the fire and make sure that it would not spread to the nearest buildings. The whole colonial wooden structure collapsed after less than an hour.

That's what mixing white phosphorous, turpentine oil and papers does to a fire!

I had also asked the geek who had built my system for a killer USB drive; It contained an undetectable virus that roamed the various servers and that randomly reallocated or deleted data, but would only be activated by a 'main server down alert'; the whole building burning and crashing on the main server was the trigger... And the contract printing my access point to the network!

No paper trail, no prints, no security videos and an absolute digital mess: let them identify me! Besides, the whole event would probably be attributed to those smugglers that a, now very frustrated, US District Attorney was targeting!

*   *   *

It had been a while since I had seen Louise; she called one evening!

We had an odd relationship: I was obviously a customer and would pay every time I visited her; yet, I had given her my telephone number, the real one!

« *I haven't seen you lately. Have you met someone?* »

I wasn't going to tell her about my 'wife'...

« *Come over, this one will be on me.* » She chuckled.

We had sex and we talked...

My brutal need for a confidant surprised me. I'm afraid that I said too much that day. The look in her eyes made me shiver: what was she seeing? Had she understood what I was, what I was doing? Did she know how conflicted I was? How I was wondering whether all these sacrifices were worth it?

CHAPTER 18

New York City,

September 2016,
   6 am

It was a quiet, rather narrow street, going from Broadway Avenue to Water Street; on both sides rose high buildings, old and new. There were few people walking around as most of the working crowds had not yet joined their offices to make corporate America, if not them, richer.

The first sign that this was going to be a different day went mostly unnoticed by the few who worked: internet connections were quietly shut down in most of the street!

Suddenly, a convoy of black cars appeared at one end of the street: a string of black Chevy Suburbans drove down the street and stopped in front an ordinary looking seven-floor building. A lonely plaque on the side displayed a name: '*PIBB - Pakistan Inter Business Bank*'.

A cavalcade of dark-suited men and women exited the cars and entered the building. The leading member of the group, a forty years old stern looking woman walked up to the welcome desk and showed her badge to a bewildered janitor:

« *Special Agent Walker, FBI. I am executing a search warrant; do not call anyone!* »

The agents moved up quickly into two groups, to the fourth and fifth floor. On the fifth floor, Special Agent Walker entered a plush reception, introduced herself to the first person she met as her agents moved alongside her.

The few people working in both floors were routed up in one meeting room after submitting their smartphones. A dark-skinned man in his fifties, apparently the duty desk manager, was showed a copy of the warrant.

A long day had started for both FBI agents and PIBB employees…

*   *   *

The feeling was great, no, better than great, fantastic: John was breathing heavily; down below the sheets, she was giving him a memorable blowjob!

« *Stop, slow down, you're, you're… argh, man… *»

She enjoyed being in total control and wasn't going to let him off the hook: she accelerated until he came in a grunt.

Breathless, it took him a minute to recover and smile: « *Thank you, that was… Wow!* »

Kate smiled and kissed him gently.

* * *

Sex between them had come back almost by surprise, back in May, during a visit he had made in Providence; it had been the first time he had gone up north since selling his house in Rhode Island. He had spent the day with Josh playing ball, visiting the Roger Williams Park Zoo, making faces at the macaws and marveling at the mighty elephants enjoying the spring sun. The December reunion awkwardness was behind them now and the little man liked to laugh with his 'bionic Da'.

On the drive back to Kate's place, an exhausted Josh quickly fell asleep; a light diner barely woke him up and he was in bed before eight.

When Kate walked in the living room, she offered John a glass of red wine and sat besides him on the couch.

« *It's good for Josh that you are here…* »

« *Yeah, he's a great kid…* »

They chatted and laughed for a while, slowly drinking the bottle away; then Kate stood, looked at him - « *Come,* » she said - and walked away to her bedroom.

*   *   *

Every Monday, John received a special delivery from Fort Meade; a black drive containing data from bank transfers and account identification was brought to him by the same stern agent. As per procedure, the drive was first proofed by the office IT girl, a thick glasses average looking black girl who reigned on IT safety; once assured that there were no virus -

« *Can't trust those NSA jerks…* » she had said - the drive was given back to him for data uploading.

Facing tons of data - the NSA guy had been right - John had gone to see Xavi, the DIGA guy, and presented him with his problem: was there a way to identify patterns, relationships between the various accounts, transfers?

« *Let's take this transfer,* » John said, « *US$ 34,987. It is sent from a family account in Saudi Arabia to a bank in Nassau in the Bahamas; From then on, it's a dead end: I don't have the destination account because of local laws. Would there be a way to link that wire to other transfers exiting the bank, even not knowing the intermediary bank account?* »

« *Right, I suppose there's no following transfer of the same amount?* »

« *Nah, that'd be too easy…* » He had checked, though.

« *And there are thousands of exit transfers…* »

Xavi nodded.

« *So, I would need to reconstruct amounts from different exiting transfers to sum up to 34 something dollars… But the account might have, probably, argh, certainly has a balance before that original wire… So maybe, we could… How many banks did you say you have?* »

« *Right now, seventeen, and a couple hundred accounts each!* »

« *Hmmm, I need to think about it!* »
* * *

He dragged a folding screen to close his cubicle away: the interview was over! John had gotten used to the strange habits of his coworkers: one would walk barefoot; one never removed his noise canceling earphones, even when talking to you or going to the toilets; one alternated between eating raw fish and burning incense, his desk having been moved right below a ventilation suction port, to the relief of the entire floor… And then, there was Bubba's shirts, the most memorable of which, a pinkish Barbie girl engaged in rather explicit adult activities had raised a record two eyebrows from a rather stoic Amanda!

The past months had been tough on ISIS: the US were getting better at identifying and killing the men in charge of financing the terrorist movement; regularly, John would hear of HVTs[109] being sought and, more often than not, killed[110] by a predator strike. Once in a while, he had been the one identifying the target thanks to some banking mishap. He actually took a perverted pleasure at watching the graphic videos of the strikes or of the harsh interrogations of those who had been arrested and lost away to some black site…

And yet, it still managed to access cash, buy weapons and fight another day!

Then, one afternoon, Mike called him: « *You need to go to Fort Meade; they have something for you… The meeting's tomorrow morning at eight!* »

After a short night, an elated John exited Jenna's apartment in

---

[109] High Value Target
[110] Dec 15, 2015: Isis 'financial minister' killed, says US (ft.com)

Belle Haven before seven in the morning; the evening had been fun with a diner in a local wine bar and followed by a short walk to her place and a wild night in the sack!

« *Life's good.* » smiled John on his way to the NSA headquarters, « *If only they can get me some more shit I can use…* » Fucking both Jenna and his wife was pretty cool too: no worries as both lived hundred of miles apart and the sex was great and different: the energetic athletic blonde and the tall sensual brunette…

Arriving before eight got him a closer parking spot and the usual security hassle went smoothly. It was seven fifty when he got seated in the same anonymous room.

« *Morning,* » said the same man with no name, « *we've been looking at stuff since you last came and we recently put our hands on data retrieved from a FBI raid on a bank in New York City. You might want to have a look at it: one of my guys flagged it to me.* »

« *Why? What did he find?* »

« *Well, nothing really, but…* » he raised a calming hand, « *my guy has a funny feeling about the whole stash; he's a bit of a nerd…* »

John couldn't help but smirk.

« *Yeah right, as I said…* » continued the guy, « *he's been looking at it and trying to find links between what you ask for and the inside data we got from New York; he thinks… How to say it? He thinks that some of the data's too clean; I know it doesn't make sense but let me give you an example: are you familiar with Benford's law*[111] ? »

« *No* » said John.

« *Well, very basically, it's the way digits appear in big sets of numbers: there's a mathematical model for that; so you can take a batch of data, let's say bank transfer amounts and if your sample's big enough, you can expect to see a specific amount of one, twos, etc. appear as the first digit of the amounts... »*

« *And here it doesn't? »*

« *Oh no, it does, and very well! »*

« *I don't get it: if that's what the model expects, what's the problem? »*

The guy sighed: « *It works perfectly in agreement with the model, with a ridicule deviation... As if... »*

John suddenly got it: « *As if there was someone behind all that data it making sure that it seemed normal... »*

No-name man nodded: « *that what thinks my guy, but again, he's a bit... »*

« *Nerdy,* » smiled John.

« *Yeah, personally, I don't think there's anything there, but I heard you guys at the Red House liked to walk strange ways... »*

* * *

---

[111] Benford's law is an observation about the frequency distribution of leading digits in many real-life sets of numerical data.

John did not know whether to feel flattered or insulted!

The guy made a face: « *Anyway, that's all I have for you; and by the way, we're not legally entitled to have that New York data... »*

« *Which is why you asked me come in person! I get it. »*

On his drive back home, John couldn't help wondering whether there was something to this or whether that was just a nerd gone mad from too much exposure to computer screens... To be honest, he liked the idea that some guy would be behind the flow of cash to ISIS, a global mastermind, hidden, and that no-one even knew existed.

« *How cool would that be that this man exists and that I can find him... »* he was thinking, « *a guy financing those bastards, like a banker... »*

The image popped in his mind, all those headlines: « *ISIS master banker arrested thanks to an unnamed governmental agency... No, not flashy enough, the devil's banker! Yes, that's it: on the front page, devil's banker arrested, judged and toasted on the chair... »*

John grinned maniacally all the way back to the office! He was going to find the bastard and make him pay...

*   *   *

As he arrived to work, he discreetly went to the bathroom and popped a Vicodin: it seemed that his missing limb was hurting every day a little more. Will Jones, the physio that he had stopped seeing a couple years back, had warned him that it might happen and if so, that John would need to get professional help…

« A shrink, Jesus, he wanted me to see a shrink… Who does he think I am, a weak, mommy-crying liberal? Come on! It'll pass anyway » John remember thinking.

That was two years ago and, though the medication helped, the pain had never gone away… He knew that, at some point, if it got out of hand, he should discuss it with the company, but right now, he was cool and in control…

What had almost disappeared on the contrary were the daunting nightmares that he had suffered from back in Middletown: they were just few and weeks apart…

And now, he had a guy to find; the more he thought about it, the more he liked the idea: the devil's banker was somewhere and he was going to get the world rid of it!

But first some work to understand the data he had been given - maybe a visit to Xavi's cubicle - and then, a fun week-end in the woods with the boys…

*   *   *

Not far away, in a rather stern government building, Uncle William was frowning while reading a document; it was titled: *'FBI internal bulletin - restricted'*. Thanks to an inside informant, it detailed the worrying development of a Western Virginia militia, the Wild Westerners; it seemed that the group, on top of piling up AR15s and the likes, had been successful in attracting former law enforcement officers and even one former Special Forces Marine; military-like trainings were held twice a month and the political discussions went quite far-reaching…

Uncle William poured himself a glass of sixteen year old Lagavulin single malt whisky and walked to the window.

« Oh John, » sighed his uncle, looking at the traffic below, *« What have you gotten yourself into again? »*

CHAPTER 19

Amman, Jordan

November 2016

The early day was hazy with temperatures in the low twenty centigrade; I had just walked out of King Hussein Airport in Aqaba; the private flight from Frankfurt, just over four hours, had been quiet.

I had rented a car and a driver via a shell company to take me to Petra. Once there, I had waited for him to drive away and had walked to the tourist center. As expected, a bus was leaving thirty minutes later. The trip to the center of Amman took well over three hours in the afternoon traffic. I then hailed a yellow cab to get to the Marriot.

Entering the hotel grounds felt like entering an army base: telescopic anti-ram bollards that were lowered only upon inspection of the car, metal detectors before the entrance of the main lobby, armed guards everywhere… Such places, like other international ones in the region, were always at risk of terror attacks! After all, three international hotels had been attacked in 2005 in the Jordanian capital city, dozens had died…

Once inside though, nothing really differed from main international hotels around the world: business men and the usual expat crowd strolled about the bars and the restaurants.

I opened my suitcase on the bed and put away my clothes in a closet. I powered my pc and, having connected it to the local network, pretended to work for a while; I was officially on a tourist trip for just four days and would quickly visit the Citadel, the local roman ruins overlooking the city, the Jordan museum and would of course make the obligatory visits to the forgotten city of Petra and the Dead Sea.

In the midst of all this, I was expected to meet with Kazem's envoy and hand him over the drive on which ran my system: after updating it with the latest transactions in the hotel, it would be, until then, carefully locked up in my room safe… Now, hopefully unbeknown to them, it was only a mirror image of the real deal that would remain under my control in Paris: I wasn't going to let myself be let redundant and lose control of it! The transfer that had been agreed six months earlier with Kazem was getting more urgent: on one draft email, he had explained to me that the State's resources were slowly dwindling and that my system was getting more crucial every day!

The first two days in Jordan were dedicated to Petra and the Dead Sea; both trips were booked via the hotel; in a minibus with other tourists, I daydreamed the whole three hour drive to Petra; the visit was amazing and I couldn't help but marvel at the lost city; a powerful civilization wiped out, with only ruins remaining: I could hear some echos of my fight amongst these standing stones… If Petra was more than what I expected, the Dead Sea was a major disappointment: rows of modern buildings, tourists vaguely covered with mud posing for their friends' cameras and or testing the floating bath…

It was a relief to come back to the hotel and prepare for the handover the next day.

The next morning, I went for an early swim in the hotel pool; I lost myself in the water, forgotten memories coming back to me: the visits to the beach with my parents, my buddy encouraging me for an extra lap, the vertigo from a deep dive… When I stopped, a little out of breath, I realized that I had been swimming non-stop for more than forty minutes.

« You're in very good shape! »

A woman was in the water, not far. Close to forty, she struck a nice figure in her one piece swim suit.

« Sorry? »

« You've been swimming since I arrived; I thought that I was pretty good; you're putting me to shame… »

She didn't seem very troubled at that and was eyeing me quite frankly, her hands bringing her wet hair in order, a wedding ring shining in the sun.

« I come here every morning to swim and I haven't seen you before; here for business or pleasure? »

The way she said it was an explicit invitation: an expat wife looking to escape the boredom of her life and what was there not to like with a quick tryst with a passing stranger in his hotel room…

I swam close to her and, looking in her eyes, said: « *I'm in room 817.* »

Surprised, she breathed in quickly then smiled.

I dried up, put my bathrobe and went back to my room.

Five minutes later, there was knock at the door. I opened the door: she was wearing the same white hotel robe and stood confidently.

« *Come in!* »

She entered the room and I closed the door behind her.

« *My name's Diana. What's your…*»

« *Strip!* » I barked.

« *What? This is not…* » she blurted, her confidence suddenly gone.

« *You want to get fucked? Strip or get the hell out of here!* »

She opened her mouth to protest. I raised a hand: « *Last chance, strip or fuck off!* »

Her eyes down, her hands slightly shaking, she slowly released the cord of her robe and let it fall on the floor. She looked at me valiantly but could find no empathy in my burning eyes. She sighed and slipped awkwardly out of her suit. She finally stood naked in from of me, breathing quickly, her hands hiding what they could.

« Hands behind your head! »

She complied, not daring to look at me. She had a great body: large round breasts that probably owed to her husband's wallet, a thin waist and long legs; her daily swims did pay off!

I removed my robe and stood in front of her fully naked: *« Come and suck me! »*

She walked up to me and kneeled; the blowjob she gave me was great, almost as good as that of a pro; at that thought, Louise coming to my mind, I felt a burst of anger.

« Stop! » I barked again, *« on the bed, on your knees… »*

Again, she obeyed nicely and, once on the bed, presented me with a fine ass. She cried when I entered her violently but the wetness of her cunt betrayed her excitement… The sex was brutal, a slap on her ass here, a squeeze of a breast there, a bite on a shoulder that she was going to have to explain; the more she moaned *« no, »* the rougher I got… She came suddenly, her whole body shaking, bent heavily on the bed. I kept pounding her for a few minutes until I came into her. She suddenly realized that I hadn't bothered with a condom…

« Out! » I said.

« But err, » she was still breathing quickly, *« I need to clean and… »*

* * *

« Out! » and I went for the door handle.

She grabbed her swim suit and clumsily slid into it. I threw her robe at her and opened the door… She quickly closed the kimono around her and left without a word, tears in her eyes. She was probably not going to come for a swim the next day, but would certainly not talk to anyone about it: married, going up with a stranger in his room, wearing only a swim suit…

Just before eleven am, I was ready to leave my room; I had the perfect tourist attire: red Nike cap, dark sun glasses, a backpack with a visible Routard[112] travel guide, water, a big camera and some stupid sun screen. I also had a black box stuck in a small pouch underneath my shirt: the drive.

I walked out of the hotel lobby and walked to the first cab waiting; there was no way it would be expecting me: observing from above in my room, I had made sure that the line moved swiftly at each departure. I asked the driver to take me to the Roman Theater via Istiqlal Street, a bit of a detour but faster roads.

The drive was smooth; the driver spent the whole time on the phone with a friend, explaining that *« he had another stupid French tourist in his car who thought he knew the city better and that he would make me pay double the fare. At least I wasn't American: had I been, the fare would have tripled !»* There was still, many years later, a lingering Chirac[113] effect in the

---

[112] Famous French tourist guide

[113] In 2003, Jacques Chirac, President of France, vetoed a United Nations resolution threatening war against Iraq, thus becoming very popular in the Arab world

country… Little did he know that I understood! I always made sure that no one knew that I spoke Arabic…

The cab dropped me at a parking near the folklore museum and asked for an outrageous fare that I paid, thanking him heartily for the ride: just another forgettable, gullible tourist! I spent the next thirty minutes visiting the theater, taking pictures after pictures, repeatedly checking them out and taking some more; besides playing the tourist, it also helped me check for potential tails; there were few people on the plaza facing the theater and I was able to get a good grip of who was where: a few tourists, some cops and the usual bunch of locals hoping to make a euro out of tourists.

I suddenly heard the call for Dhur, the midday prayer; from the many minarets around me, the muezzins started their slow, hypnotic recitations, overlapping each others in their call to believers. That was my cue: I had a meeting scheduled in the Raja Souk, some twenty minutes walking away.

I exited the Theater via the main plaza and turned left on Al-Hashemi Street; I followed the road along the gardens. Thanks to the prayer, traffic had trickled down and there were much less people in the street. I followed Quraysh Street, facing the few cars still driving and turned right into Khalil As-Saoud Street. I had there a counter surveillance checkpoint, some Roman ruins, the Nymphaeum[114]: it provided me with the perfect opportunity to pause and gawk at my surroundings. Walking in against the traffic had removed the possibility of a potential tail from a vehicle and left only foot soldiers, who would have a harder time hiding

---

[114] Ruins of a Roman public fountain (middle of the second century ad)

thanks to the prayer lull. Indeed, most of the stalls were partially closed and what should have been a busy street was, for a short time, rather quiet.

And indeed, there were few pedestrians.

Suddenly, for no reason, my inner radar went off: not a blaring alarm but something was amiss! I took a couple more pictures... Hmmm, the guy with a camo jacket and dirty jeans! I checked the pictures I had taken on the theater plaza and, there he was, talking with another guy wearing a black jacket with a golden shield on the back.

It wasn't time to go into full emergency mode yet, but it called for some clear and immediate action: I conspicuously packed away my camera in my back pack and discreetly removed a black bonnet that I hid in a pocket of my jacket. I then took off again and turned into King Talal Street; « *Merde*[115] *!* » I muttered in my breath as I saw the black jacket guy, standing idly on the opposite pavement ahead of me. One observation was coincidence, two meant purpose...

I stayed on the left side of the road. The prayer was ending and there was a crowd of worshippers already exiting the Grand Husseini Mosque. I moved behind a group and slipped behind a cleaning booth; I quickly abandoned my cap and my bag, donned the black bonnet, turned my reversible jacket inside out and, keeping my head low, left mingling with another group. It was probably not going to work but was worth a try and, at least was going to create a need for the opposition to communicate and add some confusion. I quickly crossed the three-lane boulevard and took off in a

---

[115] French: shit!

small street facing the mosque.

Crossing the street was getting me closer to 'black jacket' but further away from 'camo'; if they were with the GID[116], I was probably screwed: there were very efficient on their own turf; the country being surrounded by Israel, the West Bank, Syria, Iraq and Saudi Arabia, they had plenty of experience with foreign operators… But it didn't make sense: they could have picked me up at anytime since I had arrived in the country. It wasn't the Americans either, as they worked hand in hand with the GID…

So, Kazem's guys or someone else? That Kazem had me followed didn't make sense either, I was coming to see his representative and the final part of the journey in the Souk was enough to identify and evade potential tails. So, it had to be someone else!

I turned left into Abu As-Sun Street and kept walking quickly on the right side pavement; I had prepared the walk the day before and had a rough evasion plan. I turned right into Al-Kabariti Street and, once out of sight, started running as fast as I could up hill; forty yards later, I quickly turned left, then made a mad dash up the long flights of stairs to reach Othman Ben Affan Street.

As I reached the top of the stairs breathless, several gun shots shook the quiet neighborhood from below me: 'black jacket' was randomly shooting at me from the bottom of the steps! I moved away a few yards to the left, then, out of his sight, ran to the right up Othman Ben Affan Street. Fifty yards later, there was a two-story coffee house on the side: I pushed the

---

[116] General Intelligence Directorate (Jordanian intelligence agency)

door and entered, trying to recover from the run; it was rather busy and I moved unnoticed to the second floor. There was a table close to the window with a view to both the street and the stairs. I sat in the shadow and waited for the waitress.

'Black jacket' appeared on the opposite pavement, obviously out of breath from the sudden run. He looked up the street then around, and took his phone. Several minutes later, 'camo' arrived: they talked quickly and left in the opposite direction.

I could now enjoy a coffee and let the Jordanian security services remove the threat from me: gun fire in Amman insured a powerful response!

I breathed in slowly and tried to calm down; my hands were shaking and I had to hide them under the table when the waitress came. It was too close a call and I couldn't help thinking that Kazem had doubled me: getting the system and killing me would be tempting…

The hand-over was off now and I had only one thing to do: get the fuck out of the country asap… and alive!

Sirens were heard and several police cars sped by the coffee house.

After forty-five minutes and a light lunch, I asked the waitress to call me a taxi; I had to get back to the hotel and hole up there until my flight the next day: hotel security was high and the thugs who had tried to jump me were not going to get in. I was also reasonably confident that the local police wouldn't identify me as being part of the pursuit.

* * *

The dusty yellow cab arrived and stopped in front of the café: I walked out, climbed in, shut the door and let myself lie low; on the way down the hill, we crossed several police checkpoints and heavily armed officers. The ride was tense and short, just over fifteen minutes, to get to my next destination: the King Abdullah I Mosque. During the ride, I took a burner phone, powered it and called the emergency Turkish number that Kazem had given me.

« Hello, is Fayçal here? » I said in English.

A woman answered: *« No, do you have a message for him? »*

« Tell him that I can't come to his birthday: the bus was too crowded; I had to go home… »

I powered off the phone, removed the SIM card and, my left arm hanging casually out of the window, dropped the chip in the middle of the traffic.

The driver stopped in front of the Mosque and I walked for a few minutes; being surrounded by official buildings, close to Parliament and various ministries, guaranteed my safety thanks to a healthy police presence; the draw back was the numerous security cameras. I kneeled, tightened the laces of my left shoe and dropped the burner in a drain hole; I then quickly hailed a passing cab and asked to be driven to the Marriot.

I was only able to let go when I closed the door of my hotel room. I undressed quickly and spent the next thirty minutes seated on the floor, under a brutal hot shower. Away from the real world, in the warm mist, I was distraught, shaking and heaving; I might have cried a bit…

* * *

I was still shaking when I dried up: the adrenaline toll, the possible betrayal, the weeks and months and years of hiding, the tension of wearing a mask at all times were slowly killing me. I poured myself a generous glass of whisky, popped a couple antidepressant pills and fell on the couch. I had to admit that I was slowly becoming an addict: prayers when not at risk to be uncovered, some yoga and a nice run every day used to be enough to keep a straight head, but not anymore; the nightmares were so frequent that I had to get some medication to sleep; I had even tried cocaine in the morning to get myself going…

The rest of the day went in a stupor; I don't remember doing much and slept badly. My plane was at eleven the next morning but I left the hotel at six am, after ordering a cab for an eight o'clock departure for Petra at the desk the previous evening: I wanted, first, to be unpredictable and, second, to be in the safety of the Amman Civil Airport VIP lounge, beyond security controls as soon as possible.

The flight was eventless; I was even able to sleep a little before arriving in Germany. My fake French passport worked its charm at the local TSA checks; I then had to recover the rental car that I had parked near the airport and suffer though a long boring six hour drive back to Paris.

As I had expected, I had a draft message from Kazem waiting for me on the temporary email account: « *Those unexpected rude guest were not invited to the wedding; they are distant cousins that we do not talk to anymore; it was a wise decision not to talk to them and to come back home. You'll find another time to bring the wedding present because we must find first who invited them… »*

* * *

I checked the news: there had been a gunfight downtown Amman between police officers and some terrorists; one had been killed and one had escaped. The story was short: officers were called in after shots had been fired; as they searched the area, they came under fire from two individuals. The two men were apparently linked to another incident at an army base, earlier in the month, that had led to the death of an American soldier and that was rumored to be related to Al-Qaeda…

« Ok, so the organization's got a mole… And there's an additional bunch of assholes who want a shot - ha! - at the money! » I sighed: at least, Kazem did not seem to be behind this mess…

The next day, after yet another rough night, I visited Louise; it had been several weeks since our last encounter. When I entered the parlor, she looked up from the table where she was reading a magazine and her eyes widened:

« Oh my god, you're so pale… Are you ok? Come, come downstairs, I'll take good care of you! » She locked the outside door and led me down.

That evening, for the first time in my life, I was unable to have sex…

*   *   *

« What are you doing? » yelled my dad; *« Are you crazy? »* He kept ranting and ranting, my mother crying at his side until their corpses decayed and crumbled into dust…

Just another nightmare…

CHAPTER 20

Washington DC,

January 2017

In the end, it was down to pure luck: the combination of a high level US foreign department visit and a tuna melt sandwich...

The Under Secretary for Civilian Security, Democracy and Human Rights had been in town for some official, and not so official, discussions with the Jordanian Government; refugees and counter-terrorism obviously high on the agenda; he had taken residence in the Marriot hotel in Amman with his team of assistants and DSS[117] bodyguards. During his stay, as was per procedure, the NSA had sent in a small team of counter-surveillance experts; it would not have been the first time that a foreign power, or even the host, would try to listen in on private communications...

So, a day in advance, the NSA guys, after physically

---

[117] The United States Diplomatic Security Service is the federal law enforcement and security arm of the U.S. Department of State

connecting to a wireless router on the top floor, had launched a discreet cyber attack on the hotel network, bypassing its security: they would now be analyzing all traffic, incoming and outgoing, until the departure of the delegation.

More than two thousand miles away, the tuna melt sandwich had disgorged some mayonnaise and tuna on the lap of an IT guy in Amsterdam; in the swearing and fracas that followed, the guy accidentally saved his partial maintenance work on the main frame, rather than on a shadow partition. The immediate consequence was to create a protocol conflict that the server couldn't handle; automatic safeties powered it off and alerted the duty technician, who was busy swearing and cleaning his chinos in the toilets...

 By the time he came back, realized his mistake and corrected it in a frenzy, the server had a downtime of five and a half minutes; it was early in the day in the Netherlands so the glitch went mostly unnoticed by most customers, one of which was a local VPN provider...

The NSA team leader, once back in Fort Meade, had brought back the gigabytes of information that they had stored during their routine monitoring. Nothing had attracted their attention and the whole trip had been rather boring...

Yet, deep down in the gigantic basements, the robots routinely analyzing the data highlighted a particular set that met a specific permanent query; an alert was then sent to an analyst who, shrugging, copied it onto a black portable drive...

*   *   *
* * *

John couldn't believe his eyes: he had a match between a transaction and a physical location! The transaction involved an account, that had been under scrutiny for a while as it belonged to a wealthy Saudi who was believed to be friendly with radicals, a middle-man bank in the Bahamas and a recipient in Iraq known for its links with jihadists; the previous transfers made from the original account had fallen in a digital black hole…

The location was a high end hotel in Amman.

« *Time to pinpoint the room and get an idea on the perp!* » thought John. « *I need a guest list and an access to video feeds in the hotel; once I get a face and an id, the guy won't get far… * »

The time for analysis was over: he needed to get on the ground and get the ball rolling. He sent a message to his boss asking for an urgent meeting: no more rushing in, lesson learnt!

« *Now!* », answered Mike five minutes later.

« *What do you got?* »

John went through his reasoning and stopped.

« *So you need to go there?* »

« *Yes, we can probably hack the hotel video feed and network, but it'll be faster and more efficient if I'm there with some help with the Amman CIA station or, even better, the locals; can we make an official request?* »

« *Ok, you might be onto something; I'll organize a call with the*

Amman Station Chief: we'll see how he feels about this. How big was the transfer? »

« One hundred fifty thousand US dollars… »

« Ok, let's make it one million; the Chief's not going to move on something smaller than that, even with me in the loop… »

« You mean, we'll lie to him? » said John eyes wide opened.

« Of course, how do you want to get your stuff done otherwise? » grinned Mike. Then he frowned: *« don't even think of ever doing that to me, clear? »*

« Clear! »

The video call took place three days later; Patrick Foston, the Station Chief didn't seem too excited by the whole story, but Mike evidently carried some weight: he agreed to a visit a few days later; *« by then »* he said, *« I'll have talked to my guy in the GID[118]; he'll probably be willing to help. »*

*   *   *

John flew in under a fake identity; he had fantasized about using a fake one since entering the Red House, but Amanda had rebuked him and explained that *« he was not paid to play spy but to think… »* Yet, before his trip to Jordan, she had come in his cubicle with a brand new passport and a short legend under the name John Jesper; *« JJ »* had smirked Bubba; looking fiery at him, she had reminded John that she was nice enough already to have booked a business class ticket for him!

---

[118] General Intelligence Directorate (Jordanian intelligence agency)

* * *

A smiling guy in his forties was waiting for him at the international arrivals exit: he had walked up to John, introducing himself as Terry Williams *« from the Embassy ! »* They climbed in the back of a beige SUV that was waiting in a no-parking area, with a serious looking American driver; once under way, Terry said: *« ok, we've booked you at the Marriot; seemed easier to be on the spot where the shit happened; plus they got top notch security… »*

« What's the threat level at the moment? » John had read the office threat assessment but - former grunt oblige - would rather rely on the legs on the ground.

« It's ok right now, though the shit hit the fan a while back, following the attack at the King Faisal base[119]; we biffed up security a notch but nothing that really gets in the way of business. The Jordanians really got mad when it happened and they've been trying to stay on our good side since… »

They drove straight to the Embassy; there, in a basement office, John was introduced to Patrick Foston, a weary looking guy in his fifties. *« Have a seat! »* He had said without looking up from his desk. After a few minutes reviewing a document, he sighed, swore softly and signed it. Looking up, he sat back in his chair.

« So, Mister Jesper, to what do I owe the pleasure of your visit? » He raised a hand before John could speak: *« Or no, let me rephrase: why should I use whatever credit I have with the*

---

[119] A shooting occurred on 4 November 2016 at King Faisal Air Base, a Jordanian air force installation near Al-Jafr: three U.S. trainers were deliberately killed by a Jordanian soldier.

authorities in this country to look for some guy transferring a stupid million? »

Yet again, Mike had been right…

So John explained his work of the past months again, carefully staying away from using the Banker's nickname. Once he had finished, Patrick Foston looked at Terry who shrugged, then turned towards John.

« Where did you lose the leg? »

« Baghdad, 2013 »

He nodded: *« with whom? »*

« Marine Raiders »

There was a silence; Patrick turned and pulled out a bottle of Bourbon and three glasses out a small cabinet.

« Now John, in all honesty, I don't buy your story but, put aside the fact that I'm making a friend with a Director back home, at least I owe you your service! Terry here is going to take you to a meeting tomorrow morning with Colonel Ahmad Saleh, directly at the Marriot; he's with the GID and will help finding your guy. »

They discussed the upcoming Super Bowl, both spooks being fans of the Falcons; John was a Patriot at heart since his early days in Rhode Island and enjoyed his favorite status…

The same guy dove him to the Marriot; as John was exiting the SUV, he noticed another one stopping behind them; he looked at Terry: *« security »* he said, *« we wouldn't want anything to happen to you… »* He frowned: *« or to me… See you tomorrow! »*

John quickly checked in and settled in his room; it was already seven pm and the long day was taking its toll. He took the elevator down to the restaurant; he noticed a bar on the right and, on a whim, decided to have a drink first. He sat on a stool at the counter and ordered a Scottish pure malt whisky. There was a lull in the action and the Jordanian bartender seemed eager for a conversation: they quickly discovered that they were both fans of the Patriots, a surprising coincidence which rewarded John with a generous refill of his glass. As John was looking at a good looking woman who was passing by, the bartender asked him: *« single? »*

« It's… complicated. » answered John *« and I'm not looking for any action tonight; got to look intelligent tomorrow… »*

The bartender laughed: *« I'm sure you'll be fine; besides, sometimes looking for some action gets you too much of it! »*

John raised an eyebrow.

« Well, you see: expats living in Amman, sometimes, they come to the Marriot to have some fun; a couple weeks ago, one of them got a little too much of it! » He smirked. *« She was seen by a hotel maid, half naked, exiting a room upstairs… »*

« Well, » said John *« I raise my glass to the adventuress! Thanks for the conversation! Good night! »*

« Good night, Sir! »

* * *

Diner was quick and unabashedly American: t-bone Steack, French fries and a Bud; an exhausted and slightly drunk John dropped on his bed and fell asleep immediately.

Terry called John at nine the next morning: « we're in the bar; ready to come down? »

John had slept like a baby: like a stone until two, then the jet lag kicked in and he couldn't close an eye! A scalding shower and three espressos had put some life back into him.

When he entered the bar, he saw Terry raising a hand from one corner; he was seated with a distinguished looking fifty years old Jordanian: Ahmad Saleh, the DSS guy.

« *Good morning Terry, Sir!* »

« *John, let me introduce Colonel Saleh; he's one of the sharpest minds in the GID…* »

The Colonel smiled: « *Terry has been flattering me for almost ten years now; another decade like this and I'll start believing him…* » His English was flawless, with an Ivy League accent.

They shook hands.

« *John here is a fellow soldier, with a distinguished career, though unsavorily with the Marines…* » Terry was an unabashed Army brat!

« *Well, someone has to do the jobs you won't take! An honor to meet you Colonel.* »

They chatted over a coffee until Terry said: « *I think it's time we get to business: we've got an appointment with the Head of Security of the hotel at ten thirty. »*

They met a very nervous man in the lobby: Colonel Saleh clearly carried a heavy clout. The Head of Security took them to his office.

« We have looked at the information that you gave us: the IP address was wrong. My technician thinks that an IP spoofer was used; he was only able to pinpoint the location down to the eighth floor. So, on that night, we had twenty seven guests on that floor; here's the list, with the details of their passports. »

« Would you have a video feed that day so that we can have a visual on each? » asked John.

The guy freaked out: *« Err, well, we keep the records for fourteen days and it was seventeen days ago… So we have some footage for the guests who have remained until last Friday. »*

« I thought that we had mandated that records be kept for three months, » asked Colonel Saleh softly.

John thought that the Security guy was going to have a heart attack.

« We'll talk about that later: I wouldn't want to use my friends' valuable time. Did you gather the staff working the eight floor like I asked? »

The guy nodded nervously: *« they are next door in the meeting room. »*

Three maids were waiting there; the interviews in broken

English went quickly: no guest had stood out; they had been the usual mix of lonely businessmen and tourists, usually in a couple.

As they were about to leave, John noticed two maids exchanging a glance.

« Wait; do you have something else to say? »

« Well, there was this woman; I saw her walking out of a room… Err… » Her English was poor but this wasn't what was blocking her.

John clicked: *« And it wasn't her room? »* The story was familiar.

« No, she does not have a room in the hotel. »

« A hooker? »

She didn't understand at first then was offended: *« No, We don't have that here… No, she comes everyday to use the spa… »*

« What was the room number? »

« 817 »

« A Belgian national » said Terry, shuffling through the guest list, *« Henry Gilbert ».*

A very relieved Head of Security walked them back to the lobby.

Terry and John parted with Colonel Saleh with the agreement

to touch base in the afternoon, once the GID will have reviewed the guest list.

« What do you think? Will GID play ball? » asked John.

« Yes, the attack on the air base really rattled them: they thought that they had the situation under control… And Ahmad is really, really good: if there's something to find, he will deliver it! »

« You guys go back a long way! »

« Yep, we met on a joint job a while back; he's got an impossible job really: Jordan's at the center of the whole fucking mess… Lunch? »

« Sure. »

« Let me take you to a small joint I haven't visited for a while; it's in the historical center of the city. »

They drove with their tail for twenty minutes and stopped in a small street: there behind an old dusty door started a discreet corridor; it opened on a small restaurant with a terrace and a magnificent view on the city. They sat at an outside table, in a warm sun. Lunch was great with the typical local dishes.

« Tell me, » said Terry over a dark strong coffee: *« what service do you actually come from? »*

John looked around.

« We're secure here; we own the place… » He gulped some coffee. *« You see, Patrick had a look and couldn't place you, nor your boss anywhere… but he had a direct call from the DDO to*

accommodate him… »

« I'm with the Red House. »

« Hmm, so it does exist. I've always thought that it was some kind of internal myth. »

John did not what to say and was saved by Terry's phone. He answered it and, after a few words, rose.

« Come; Ahmad's got something. »

« That was quick. »

« Must be big, » nodded Terry.

They drove thirty minutes to the GID headquarter located west of Amman. The security controls were something else: they had to got through several checkpoints until they could enter the complex.

« Aren't you blowing up your cover? » murmured John.

« I'm officially with DHS[120], so makes sense for me to be here, » replied Terry.

They were taken to a nondescript meeting room. *« The same all over the world… »* snickered internally John.

Colonel Saleh entered, followed by two men. He seemed more focused and concerned than earlier in the day. The laidback suaveness had given way to some ruthless intensity.

---

[120] US Department of Homeland Security

* * *

« Ok, here's what we have: we reviewed the guest list and one immediately stood out: Henry Gilbert. You see: we have no trace of his arrival in the country! Border security couldn't place him in any flight or border crossing! »

« How's that possible? » asked John.

« The only explanation is that he entered the country under another identity. I've already sent a team to hotel to interview the maids again and to build a facial composite so that we can have something to work from. »

« How about that woman from the hotel, » said Terry, *« she might know something! »*

Ahmad sent them with an officer back to the hotel while he was monitoring the investigation from his office.

Finding her was easy, the lady in charge of the spa knew her very well and gave them her name and address at the urging of a deferent Head of Security.

« Jennifer Collons, English citizen » said Terry; *« gonna be interesting knowing the context… »*

She lived in one of the plush neighborhoods of Amman, staging large houses and gardens hidden behind high walls.

John rang at the door.

« Who's this? » answered a woman in Arabic.

« Major Hassan, GID, open the door! » said briskly our escort.

* * *

The door buzzed and opened. We walked across a large yard and reached the entrance where a frightened young maid was waiting for us.

« Mrs Collins, is she here? » asked the Major.

The maid nodded and said that she would go and get her.

Moments later, a great-looking woman in her forties entered and said rather arrogantly: *« yes gentlemen, what do you want? »*

« We would rather talk in private » said the Major.

She dismissed her maid with a disdainful hand.

« We want to talk to you about the man you met at the Marriot two weeks ago. »

She flinched and paled: *« I do not see what you're talking about! »*

John had enough: *« fuck it lady, either you spill the beans now and here or the Major will be happy to take you to his HQ and inform you husband of the issue at question! »*

She had tears in her eyes… *« How dare you! Do you know who I… »*

« A whore who likes to get fucked in hotels? » snickered John.

« I suggest that you sit down and that you tell us what happened; we will be gone quickly and confidentiality will remain » said a

rather diplomatic Major.

She fell rather than sat in a chair: looking miserable, she asked John « *what do you want to know?* »

« *Everything: where did you meet him and what happened?* »

« *We met at the pool: he was swimming and I… I talked to him; he invited me to his room; we had sex and that was it.* »

« *What did he look like?* »

« *Err, average height, short dark hair, very fit.* »

John raised an eyebrow.

She sighed: « *not like a bodybuilder, more like a runner or a triathlete…* »

« *Anything else? What language did he speak?* »

« *He had several scars on his belly and he spoke English with a little accent.* »

« *Scars? Slashes, plaques or more like dots?* »

« *I would say slashes and dots; what's the difference anyway?* » she was slowly recovering and the arrogance was creeping back.

« *What kind of accent?* » Asked John.

« *Maybe French.* »

« *Belgian?* »

* * *

« Maybe, whatever... »

« Did you note anything else in his room? »

Her eyes clouded at the memory: *« it's not like I was attentive to the room... »*

« Did he say anything? »

Her face reddened.

« Lady, I don't give a shit about you fucking him, » lashed out John, *« did he say anything that could help identify him? »*

The tears were back now: she sobbed quietly *« no... »*

« Major, do you think your team can come here and work on the composite? »

« Yes, » replied the Major, *« as soon as they are finished at the Marriot. »* He turned towards the woman. *« Stay here until they arrive, help them and I will guaranty that it will go no further! »*

The distraught woman nodded.

On the drive back to the GID HQ, Terry smirked: *« she's fucked, literarily, if she doesn't leave the country; Ahmad has her now in his files; he might even have a little fun with her... »*

« Right, so maybe not such a nice guy after all... » thought John.

Back in the meeting room, Colonel Saleh had some additional information for John:

* * *

« We might have something else: during Mr Gilbert stay in Amman, there was an incident in the old town; according to witnesses, a foreigner was chased and shot at near the Grand Husseini Mosque. We deployed our emergency response teams in the area and they were involved in a gun fight that left two suspects dead, both with known links to Al Qaeda. »

« What happened to the foreigner? » asked John.

« That's where it get interesting: we have no trace of a complaint or anything: the guy just vanished… »

« Were you able to get a description? »

« Very basic: white male, under six feet, twenties to forties… We were able to get a partial image from a camera in a shop. » the colonel handed a black and white photo; there was something familiar to it but John couldn't put his finger on it…

Terry chimed in: *« you've got this look I know well Colonel: you've kept the best for the end… »*

The man smiled: *« you know me too well my friend! »* He turned towards one of his aides who laid carefully a transparent plastic bag on the table, in it a bag pack.

« The foreigner dropped that bag during the chase; there's nothing that stands out of place: a French travel guide, a water bottle, a camera with pictures of Petra and the old town… »

John leaned in: *« but prints, DNA maybe? »*

He nodded: *« My technicians are working on the book and the bottle as we speak; as soon as we have something, you'll get it! »*

They agreed on the follow-up on both sides and as they were about to exit the building, the Jordanian officer stopped them: *« One last thing, the two men killed in the old town were quite experienced operators, not very good but probably the best that AQ have in Amman at the moment: that foreigner clearly had a high value to justify risking such a shoot-out and losing those assets... »*

After a final briefing at the Embassy, Terry drove John back to the hotel to pick up his luggage and dropped him at the airport. Whatever prints, DNA, material that would be recovered by Colonel Saleh would be sent to his secure email address ASAP.

From there on, John would run it through the various governmental databases: the guy had to appear somewhere...

An excited John flew back to DC: the chase was on!

International Bank of Indochina
Account Number: 7011114642
Balance: US$ 189,574.89

CHAPTER 21

Paris, France

February 2017

It was getting tough for me to travel: I didn't feel safe anywhere; the comfort of my different 'perfect' passports couldn't relieve me of a permanent fear. We had decided that my system would stay for good in Paris as it could too easily fall into the wrong hands, especially as the organisation seemed to have a mole.

Updating it, adding accounts, modifying banking rules was still necessary and quite time consuming; we had agreed that I would only travel in places with no AQ[121] presence: Africa and the Middle-East were out of the equation. Those trips were taxing: the call of the Panama beaches or the Andorran ski slopes were lost on me; outside the bank meetings, I would remain in my hotel room, drinking myself in a stupor until the moment came for me to return to Paris. I was barely sticking to my morning routine run, a final lifeline for my

---

[121] Al-Qaeda

sanity…

Yet it was inevitable that one day they asked to see me in person! Kazem informed me that I was to come and meet with a common friend; I knew that the system was working very well. The dwindling resources of the organization, thanks to the concerted efforts of the international coalition was achieving its goal and weakening ISIS everyday. Expanding the reach of the banking AI was crucial and they couldn't let it unchecked in my hands, even after five years of absolute loyalty and ruthless efficiency.

Surprisingly, or maybe not, given the state of the fight, Kazem didn't ask me to go to Syria nor Baghdad: no, Kenya was my cover destination, the real one being obviously somewhere in Somalia! The country had been without a functioning government for years: to be fair, it did function within a few kilometers around the presidency and that was it… The rest of the country was owned by various tribal militias and mainly the Shebabs, a sister organisation that was just as pure as ours. It was only logical for some brothers to hide or at least use it as a temporary base: its proximity to the Indian Ocean and Kenya made travels easier than in Syria and Iraq, especially as the US were less interested in the area or so we hoped.

The message from Kazem was simple and full déjà-vu: I was expected to be at a specific place at a specific date; in that case, a hotel in Garissa, east of Kenya, close to the Somalian border, in May!

I organized the trip to Nairobi, the capital city; getting there from Paris was easy: millions of tourists visit Kenya every year and I would just be an extra one coming to enjoy the safaris in the amazing wildlife reserves. The idea was for me to visit one or two main parks close to Nairobi, then to venture into the more remote ones eastward, incidentally closer to Garissa…

The preparation for the trip took several weeks; Louise and I had several conversations about what I would see, where I should go; she had been more present in my life since the attack in Jordan and it was comforting to have her support, even though we never discussed my job: she simply never asked about it…

I expected to be taken to Kismayo, a coastal city two hundred kilometers from the border; officially liberated from the Shebabs, it remained in their sphere of influence; entering the area was probably easy for whoever I was going to meet.

I had opted for a week long safari in the Maasai Mara National Park: I would land in Nairobi, tour the park with a guide and, once back to the capital city, rent a car and drive east, officially to stop at some reserves on the way.

On paper, easy until I was taken care of, which I wasn't looking forward to. Kazem had been adamant that there would be no uninvited guest; he had found the mole and the guy's final hours were probably stuff made out of nightmares…

I left Brussels one morning: I had a quick stop-over at Frankfurt Airport and then a direct flight to Nairobi. The plane was packed with tourists, heading for safaris and sunny beaches. As expected, I was just one amongst many, though an astute observer would have noticed that my clothes and gear were more rugged and sober than that of my fellow adventurers' whose safari outfits screamed of fashion magazines!

We landed on time and, due to some unexpected but welcomed efficiency, I was quickly in my hotel shuttle; the weather was fair and cool thanks to the city's altitude at nearly two thousand meters above the sea. I met the safari company representative at the hotel: she confirmed that my driver would pick me up the next morning at eight to start the journey. I had opted for an high-end individual ride for the whole week: I didn't feel like talking to strangers and it would limit my exposure; besides, the locals would easily forgive a rich tourist's misanthropy.

The next morning, at eight o'clock sharp, I was packed and ready, waiting for my guide in the lobby. He arrived after a few minutes and introduced himself: « *Absko Maina, nice to meet you Sir.* » He had an open face and carried a smile that hard to resist. My stuff was quickly stored away in the car, a ubiquitous Safari Toyota Land Cruiser, and we drove away. I had opted to sit in front: it allowed for conversation and for keeping an eye on our surroundings. Absko explained that we would have a rather long drive on the first day to reach the lodge where we would be based for a few days and plan our daily tours. That was fine by me: I had one week to prepare myself for the ride east and needed to gather as much information about road conditions and the local driving culture as possible; I had no intention to get stranded somewhere out of gas or worse in an accident.

I had driven 4x4s in Africa before and it quickly downed on me that these roads were not really different but for the left side driving: there would be all kinds of traffic whatever the road and chicken would, as everywhere else on the planet, permanently try to get run over when driving by little villages... What I had not encountered yet was the risk of getting in a collision with a zebra or god-forbid an elephant!

Absko, apart from being a fine driver, had a wonderful way with stories, and I had my first heartfelt laugh in a long time as he described in very colorful details the undignified retreat of a British tourist, pants on her ankles as she had insisted on having a pee in the bush and finding herself facing an equally surprised warthog! That her husband did not stopped filming and laughing had made for an interesting conversation for the couple all the way back to Nairobi!

We drove north around Mount Suswa, hidden in a crown of clouds, and reached the lodge after six hours of eventless driving. I had told Absko on the way that I wanted to keep away from the crowds of tourists that some time flock around an animal and that I was happy to explore the remote areas, rising very early and driving back late. He had frowned then beamed: « *Good, good, I think that I know exactly what we're going to do, Pierre! Since there are only the two of us in the car, would you like that we camp one or two nights out? There's this place near the Sand River that could be perfect!* »

« *The further away, the better* » had I replied. I was going under a new alias: Pierre Jean, for once with a French passport.

« *Perfect, I need to make arrangements and have a special permit but my cousin is a ranger in the Park and he will get it for me.* » This was followed a long call on his cellphone, as we had parked on top of a little hill: a good guide had to know where to get cell connections for his guests...

The week went by fast: we ended up spending most nights

out, including one spent on a foot patrol with his cousin, looking for an elephant injured by a poacher. As we had stopped for a break in the hills, his cousin, looking at me, had said something in Swahili; Absko had turned to me and said: « *My cousin thinks that you are a hunter or maybe a soldier… Didn't you tell me that you were an accountant?* »

I smiled to hide my uneasiness: « *Where does he get that? I just like to do trail runs back in France.* »

« *He says that you walk like him; you don't make noise; you feel the animals almost like him…* »

I was saved by a radio call: a ranger had found the elephant and we hurried to find it, put it out of its misery and destroy its tusks.

On the ride back to Nairobi, Absko was mostly quiet, which was fine by me as the tension of the days to come was creeping back slowly.

« *It was good to meet you Mr Pierre* » said Absko, as we parted: « *I hope we can stay in touch!* »

« *Yes, let's do that !* » as I gave him a email address that I would probably never use. I tipped him generously and he left the hotel.

The following morning, I took a cab to the rental agency where a sturdy white Toyota was waiting for me; I filled in the reservation documents under my fake identity, telling the clerk that I intended to drive around Mount Kenya, which got me an increase in price: « *premium insurance Sir,* » had he said unapologetically « *too many tourists think that they can play safari here… »*

I then drove back to the hotel and checked out, keeping my charade alive there as well.

The highway out of Nairobi was rather hectic until I reached Kenyatta University; in all, an hour went by until I reached Thika and turned east. I had now left the highway and the A3 Road had turned to a dusty asphalt ribbon surrounded by fields, bush and the occasional village.

Petrol stations were the local hives of activity with crowds waiting upon buses of all sizes and colors; restaurants and small guesthouses made for the rest of the surrounding buildings. I had decided to stop for gas every time I would have consumed one-third of the tank: I'd stay on the safe side and it would break the monotony of the drive. The temperature was in the high twenties which made for open windows, except when driving behind a vehicle; I had to slow down briefly at a few police checkpoints but got quickly waved through by the odd bored policeman or woman.

Taller trees, thicker bush and greener grass announced the Tana River, a green ribbon cutting through brown land, and the city of Garissa, my destination. After navigating through some traffic, I easily found the hotel that I had booked, a nice oasis of green and calm. I checked in and quickly enjoyed the coolness of the pool: the heat had gone up dramatically since driving down from Nairobi; the sun was mostly hidden behind thick waves of clouds but it did little to alleviate the high heat…

I had told the lady at the registration desk that I would be staying a few days organizing my trip to the Rahole National

Reserve to the north of the city. She had made the expected offer of a guide well known to the hotel but, thanking her, I had said that I had a guide recommended by some friends living in Nairobi.

The tension that had left me as I slept under the stars in the middle of the Masai Mara had slowly creeped back up as I had driven closer to my destination: now was the time to wait and eventually to let go my near future in unknown hands. For the first time, I had taken with me a satellite phone, an Iridium, to stay in touch with my handlers should a situation arise: for some reason, Somalia felt a lot less safer than war-thorn Syria! I sent a quick message letting them know that I had arrived and powered it off. It was a testament to the slow decrepitude of the organization that I would never be searched in the following days: because of the relentless efforts of the international forces, my bosses had to rely increasingly on sub-par partners.

The wait lasted two boring days until, one morning, the phone rang in my room: the concierge informed me that a visitor had left me a message; I walked down to the reception desk, retrieved the envelope and waited until I was back in my room to open it.

« Chek out hotel tonite at 8, take car and turn right lamu road. Stop at blu water truck » The words were scribbled in broken English on a yellowish paper but the instructions were clear.

That evening, at eight pm, I drove out of the hotel and turned right on Lamu Road. I drove slowly, partly to avoid pedestrians or bikers on the poorly lit road, but also not to miss my target. A mile out, the paved road turned into a dirt track with street lights hundreds of yards apart, slowing me.

A few minutes later, I saw it inside a right bend of the road: a blue water tanker was parked in the shadows; I stopped next to it. A man appeared:

« Pierre? »

« Yes! »

« Come, take your bag! Leave the keys on the car…»

I hopped out of the Toyota and grabbed a light rucksack that I had prepared for the occasion, the rest of my clothes were in a suitcase in the car.

I climbed in the truck and sat next to the driver who, not saying a word, spurred the engine and drove off on a side track that I had not seen. We drove for an hour in absolute darkness and I might just as well had been under a hood: every dirt track that we would turn into was similar to the one that we had left.

We suddenly turned into a bigger road with a little more traffic; on a hunch, I asked : *« A3? »* The driver grumped an acknowledgment.

Ok, it made sense: we had avoided the city center and potential police with the additional tail detection and we were now driving east towards the Somalian border. A few hours later, we turned left at a sign indicating Ifo refugee camp. We were entering one of the biggest refugee camps in the world: the driver stopped at a checkpoint; a policeman appeared on the side of the truck, shook the driver's hand, made sure not to look at me and waved us through.

* * *

After driving a few minutes in a maze of brownish and blue tents, the driver stopped and indicated that I exit the truck. I closed the door and turned away from the dust raised by the departing truck. A man was waiting for me and signaled that was to follow him. After a few turns in dark alleys, he finally entered a tent where I was given some food and water and a poor blanket to use as a makeshift mattress, my bag serving as a pillow. I fell asleep and was woken up by the noise of the camp city waking up. My handler gave me some food and water again then threw a thobe and a scarf at me: I put the thobe on and tied the scarf around my head and face. He nodded and we waited again.

A truck approached; he rose, looked outside and made a sign. The truck stopped right next to the tent; he looked at me and said « *come, come!* »

I walked out and climbed in the back of a… garbage truck!

« *Oh putain*[122]… » I almost threw up because of the horrendous smell and tried to find a place to stand near the truck's cab. In a sense, it was perfect: I was hidden in plain sight; none of the people here would spend more than a second looking at the truck as it drove across the camp and back on the A3 for several kilometers. After throwing the thobe away in a bush, I was switched to the back of another truck carrying construction material. There was a little wind and the shadow made by the canopy made the temperature almost bearable. I quickly understood why they had given me a three liter jerrycan of dirty water…

A couple hours on the A3, we turned off the road into a wadi,

---

[122] French: « oh fuck! »

the dry river bed; our speed dropped dramatically making the heat surge brutally. The ride was rough and, trough the bumps and the holes, I struggled to find a comfortable position to rest in. After yet another hour, we exited the wadi onto a small road and started making way north, eventually joining a bigger and somewhat smoother road and accelerating.

I dozed on and off and, at some point along a boring opens of sandy grounds and meager bush, emptied the jerrycan; we drove across several small villages and stopped only once, in a makeshift petrol station where a sweaty guy had pumped some petrol in our tank under the bored glaze of a fifteen year old holding an AK74[123]. The kid had kept his head low, his eyes protected from the blazing sun by a Yankee cap, in all places!

We arrived to our destination, probably Kismayo, around four in the afternoon; I suddenly felt a welcome coolness in the air, in a contrast with the desertlike surroundings. We stopped on top of a hill; the sea glittered in the distance and I could see a sprawling city a few miles away. The driver asked me to come in the cab and we drove off again; the cab stank of sweat and stale tobacco.

As we descended, the houses were few, small and far apart; then, suddenly, we were surrounded by traffic, pedestrians and one or two stories buildings. We turned into a small neighborhood and stopped in front of a house: a kid opened a rusty gate and we entered, only to stop under the cooling shade of a lone myrrh tree.

* * *

---

[123] Kalashnikov AK74 assault rifle

I opened the door and went out of the truck, happy to stretch my legs after a long day. The courtyard was a rather even square, twenty yards by twenty, with high walls on three sides, the last side being the house, a two stories building with shaded windows, a long patio and opened doors. A man appeared and waved at me from the shadow: I grabbed my rucksack and walked to him. As I approached with the sun in the eyes, something about him seemed familiar.

« Hello my brother! »

« Kazem? Is that you? »

We embraced like long lost brothers; it felt good to find a known face after such a journey. We sat on some couches inside the house and were served some tea by a veiled woman. We took our time savoring our hot drink. Kazem had aged since the last I had seen him: he was disheveled and looked tired. Gone was the arrogant man full of assurance that I had met last in Raqqa. In a way, he was a metaphor of the ISIS fight: from strong and threatening to hidden and maybe, maybe even scared!

To be fair, I certainly didn't look great myself: besides the long and hot trip, the stress of the past years clearly showed to the few people who had known me since my first discussions with Kamaal. When I reflected on the journey, I had been incredibly successful and no one would have expected me to do so well in the organisation… But still, what should have been a source of pride did little to offset the permanent tension and I couldn't help but think that somewhere ahead lay my end, one way of the other!

We prayed together of some worn-out mats then enjoyed a

poor meal. Then, as the lights went out - « *we use no generator,* » had said Kazem, « *no need to attract unwanted attention!* » - I was shown my room, on the far left side of the house and on the first floor, with a window overlooking a quiet adjacent courtyard. Before falling asleep, I powered my sat phone and got a fix of my position: as expected, I was in the center of Kismayo. As agreed, I kept the phone powered.

I slept surprisingly well: in the hands of Kazem's allies, nothing could really happen; it was very unlikely that they had any idea of my role in the fight against the kafirs and, being invited by Kazem made me a honorable man in their eyes.

The next morning, I woke with the sun and joined Kazem again to pray. We had breakfast and sat to discuss the next steps.

« *We are strapped for money my friend,* » had he started; « *we need to find ways to increase the transfers… This system is slowly becoming the only one that still works, thanks to your dedication! We have lost control of the oil and the territories that we control are reducing by the day…* »

« *And I have noticed a worrisome trend; our brothers seem to give less every day…* »

He remained quiet for a while: « *yes, I noticed as well: one finds it difficult to make all these efforts if one feels that the fight is lost!* »

I was shocked: « *surely, that is not the case!* »

« *No, rest assured my friend, the Caliph will make a call to them in the next weeks to renew their faith in our fight…* » He sighed.

« Thank God that you can still work and travel... I still don't know how you can do that: it seems easy. I envy you... »

« As I told you in Raqqa, I have the best forger; he was presented to me by Kamaal; he is very, very expensive but in the end, I've never had a problem; if you want, I can explain again how much I pay him and... »

Kazem raised a hand: *« Please, please, do not apologize: I am not one of those Amni thugs who can trust no one! I for one, know how much you have contributed! »*

He smiled. *« Besides I can tell you that the place where you live in Paris was checked several times and that we never had any doubts about you... »*

« What? Several times? » I knew that he was lying as my camera system had only once caught some unwanted visitors...

He smiled again and handed me a paper. *« There are some more amounts to send: to some accounts; here's the list. »*

« Ok, I'll go scramble them. » I stood and headed for the stairs.

Kazem stood as well and said: *« I'll be out on the patio; I need to see the sky for once... »*

I arrived in my bedroom and started looking for my notebook: I had created my own cypher, some accounting documents that would look innocuous enough to a border guard or an unsuspecting police officer.

*   *   *

* * *

It was a cool dark room full of men and women seated in front of screens.

« Sir! We have a male out of the house, in the courtyard under the tree! »

A forty year old man in camos walked up to the console and looked at the screen: *« the same guy as yesterday? Do we have a positive id? »*

« Negative Sir, different individual, smaller and fatter; workin on it Sir! He's moved out of the shade. »

A pause…

« We have a good image of his face… Running facial recognition. »

Tenses minutes went by.

« Postive ident Sir: Hassan Al-Moktar! »

A rush of excitement stirred the room.

« Any school or mosque around the target house? Any gatherings? » Not that the guy really had to be careful: he had after all a lot of leeway built in his ROEs[124], especially for a HVT[125], especially in such a godforsaken dump… But still, better to know in advance if this was going to need mitigation or not…

« Negative Sir! » A small crowd had assembled around the

---

[124] Rules of Engagement
[125] High value target

console, a mix of civilians and soldiers. A blond guy stood in the back frowning…

« Ok, take him out! »

High above Kismayo, A MQ9 Reaper broke its patrol pattern and came in hot on a 044 vector…

The blond guy moved back and walked briskly out of the container-turned into building. Once out on the brown pavement of Camp Lemonnier[126], facing the Subway restaurant, he glanced around and pulled out a phone.

*   *   *

A ring pulled me out of my concentration; it took me a few seconds to realize that it was coming from my sat phone!

I picked it up and read the text message that had just arrived: *« Bingo »*

I froze for a few seconds, then grabbed my bag, ran to the window and opened it.

A curious swoosh filled the quiet neighborhood.

I jumped!

The house blew apart behind me, throwing me under a tree. I landed hard, loosing my breath, my ears ringing. Lying there, it took me some time to realize that the house was gone: what

---

[126] United States Naval Base alongside of Djibouti international airport

was left of it was a raging inferno full of smoke.

After a few minutes, I managed to sit, then stand; by some miracle apart from the many bruises and cuts, I had only hurt my left ankle… What was left of my rucksack was lying a few yards away. I struggled to it, picked it up and was relieved to find my emergency stash undamaged.

A man appeared and spoke to me in Somali; I shrugged and … fainted!

I woke up to find the water tanker driver standing above me: *« You ok? »*

I was lying in a small room and struggled to sit. *« Err, I thin… What, what happened? »*

« American drone… » He was shaking with rage.

« Kazem? »

« Everyone dead! You leave! Too dangerous for us! »

« How, where? »

« Dhow[127] *this afternoon; take you to Lamu! »*

« Where? »

« Lamu, Kenya… »

I laid back exhausted.

____

[127] Traditional Red Sea and Indian Ocean sailing vessel

* * *

I have few memories of the following hours but for a constant ringing in my ears and a body that seemed to hurt everywhere… They half-dragged, half-carried me into a car and onboard a dhow that was moored in the harbor. There, I was unceremoniously dropped below deck onto a smelly and damp mattress stuck between crates.

We sailed off immediately. I didn't see the crew, apart from the few times they brought me some food and some water. I lost track of time, gently rolled by the sea and buried in the noise and foul smell of the engine.

After what must have been a day, we arrived in the Lamu harbor. They waited for the night to fall and waved me away. I headed painfully along the quay, looking for a hotel that would host me for the night. As I was about to turn away from the water into the city, I saw a boat leaving the harbor: my transports were apparently eager to get away from me!

After a half an hour, I stumbled upon a guesthouse; the lady at the entrance wasn't too happy when she saw me appear, but reluctantly agreed to rent me a room after I had waved a weeklong worth of cash at her.

A painful night later, I bought some clothes, painkillers and a suitcase at a local supermarket, then boarded a bus to Nairobi. The ride was uneventful and the ringing slowly became just another sound of my environment.

I went straight from the bus terminal to the airport where I changed my ticket back to Brussels, arguing easily for a benign illness. My hollowed and pale face was an easy facilitator and I was able to board the evening flight.

However exhausted I might have been at the time, I just couldn't sleep: I seem to discover new bruises each time I moved and, each time I closed my eyes, I seemed to live again and again the blast that had killed my only link to the organization.

Finally arriving home, I called Louise who showed up and took care of me, cleaning some cuts that had reopened and soothing my mind, finally helping me to sleep…

CHAPTER 22

Unspecified location,

February 2017

It was an urgent meeting, in a secure room, called for by the recent events in Somalia.

« It was close; if our man hadn't been in the OPS room in Djibouti, we would have lost him! »

« Was he targeted specifically? »

« No, the Americans were aiming at Hassan Al-Moktar. We don't think that the Americans are aware of…»

« Yes, » the older man interrupted, slowly exhaling some smoke from his cigarette, *« but you were careful and wise… Hassan will be replaced but we cannot stop the operation: the system works well and is giving results! »*

There was a pause.

« Is he still holding on? »

* * *

« From what Louise tells me, yes, but she's never seen him so tense... »

« Protecting him will get more difficult everyday and will require more resources and people... Resources I can get them for you, but people talk... »

The old man picked up another cigarette.

« Keep an eye on him and no international travel anymore for him without my authorization. »

Unspoken but well understood was the fact that Alain was now living on a count-down, one day left less after another...

CHAPTER 23

Washington DC,

June 2017

As he was approaching his house, John was running hard, turning the final five hundred yards into a full sprint. Encouraged by Jenna, he had decided a while back to give it a go at triathlon: he would run or ride a bike to the office, either coming back home in a long loop or, twice a week, doing laps in a swimming pool not too far from his commute.

He relished that feeling of exhaustion that threatened to destroy his still imperfect balance; it was also a good way for him to get rid of a growing frustration: the Devil's guy was somewhere, he was sure of that, but there was nothing to prove he even existed. There was nothing obvious but he was quite sure that his fellow workers were laughing at him in his back…

It's not that he didn't have any successes; thanks to a tip from the DGSE[128] and some fine work with DIGA, he had been able to identify a guy who went by the name of Kazem, Hassan Al-Moktar, a high level ISIS leader. US forces had failed to nail him as he was leaving Iraq, thanks to a maddening inter-agency fuck-up, but John had managed to reposition him in Somalia and the CIA guys in Djibouti had efficiently droned him back to his creator…

What the guy had been doing in Somalia was the million dollar question! It must have been important for Al-Moktar to take such a risk… « *The Banker* » had relentlessly thought John.

That was when the snickering had really started in the office!

Of course there had been that suspicious sat phone ping from an hidden number, right before the strike, but nothing could be made of it: the number was attributed to a company that did not exist in Belgium and paid for two years in advance from an account that did not exist anymore. The phone had been offline since, most certainly destroyed…

Colonel Saleh had been true to his word after the trip to Jordan the previous year: he had delivered a set of print and even a DNA sample. He had run them through the various US databases to no avail, which was rather expected; what wasn't was the absence of a ping in the Five Eyes[129,] knowledge bases as well: it was surprising that such a high level player did not appear in any of them. An amicable

---

[128] « Direction Générale de la Sécurité Extérieure » : French equivalent of the CIA
[129] Alliance of Australia, Canada, New Zealand, the United Kingdom, and the United States' secret services

request to the French and the Belgians had been equally fruitless; the Germans hadn't bothered to answer which was hardly surprising in the light of the rendition debate…

Then, one Sunday morning, DIGA struck gold: it highlighted the interview of a Yazid woman, now freed from ISIS and safe in Turkey in a UNHCR[130] camp; amidst the sordid tell of her ordeal, she had mentioned her luck of being pretty, which got her being married to an important foreigner instead of a low-level thug; the woman had overheard a man she knew as Kazem call him « *the banker* »…

The Monday morning reading of the DIGA treasure trove froze John: he had his smoking gun! He read and read again the interview: there were no details; he had to get more!

His find raised an eyebrow on Mike's usually impassible face: « *You need to follow that lead; I'll organize it asap with our guys in Istanbul.* » An elated and arrogant John walked across the office back to his cubicle: he was right, had been right from the beginning!

The mood wasn't lost on a « *Punk isn't dead* » tee-shirted Bubba: « *Found yourself a bone to chew? Your banker?* »

John nodded, beaming.

« *Go at it slow man, you're gonna burn yourself: if that guy exists, it's probably gonna take a while before you find him… And, advice from a buddy, carefully with that smug look, some guys here might resent it!* »

* * *

---

[130] United Nations Refugee Agency

« *Honestly?* » Thought John walking away, « *I don't give a fuck!* »

A week later, he landed in Gaziantep around noon. A station officer had travelled with him from Istanbul. They were met by a local intelligence official who didn't introduce himself. The ride to Kilis took less than an hour on a fine highway.

The city of Kilis stood a few miles north of the Syrian border. It had involuntarily welcomed thousands of refugees from Syria in the past years and several camps had been built to accommodate them.

The Turkish officer drove them into a camp that was surprisingly well organized, thousands of containers turned into housing, nicely lined up, with some small shops. The set-up did little, though, to hide the despair and absence of hope that oozed from the people living there.

« *The Camp Chief has organized the meeting with the woman in half an hour,* » said the officer.

« *Is she willing to talk?* » asked John.

« *If she doesn't, they'll get kicked out of the camp back to the border!* » Smirked the guy.

« *They?* »

« *She's got a son…* »

They turned into what looked like the parking of an official building, one of the few two story buildings, next to the mosque and its blue minaret.

* * *

They exited the car and walked in the freezing rain to the Camp administration building. A weary looking man in his fifties welcomed them and took them to a meeting room without asking questions.

« Man, she's beautiful! » That was John's first thought when the woman entered he room. She was 5'8", with a dark scarf that played with her black hair, and had a figure most woman would die for. That it was probably due to the dreadful life of a refugee was a dark irony that was lost on John…

« Good morning, » said John. *« Thank you for coming to speak to me. »*

The translator who had walked in with her spoke. She smiled wearily and answered.

« She says you're welcome and happy to meet you… »

She frowned and said in good English: *« That's not what I said! I said that I had no choice and that I was tired of being abused! »*

The translator breathed in through his teeth; John raised a hand: *« I guess we don't need you; out! »* The guy stormed out.

« I'm going to pay for that, » sighed the woman *« but these creeps get on my nerves! »* She paused: *« what do you want from me? »*

There was a force behind those weary black eyes that impressed John.

« I studied in England for a year when I was eighteen… » She said, answering the unspoken question.

* * *

« Miss, err »

« Layla »

« Layla, I wanted to talk to you about a man that you were married to; the man that you referred to as the banker! »

« I was never married to him; he was forced upon me by those bastards! » A murderous burst of rage went though her. *« It was that or get raped everyday in a brothel… »* She had a dignity that shamed John for being a fellow male.

« Err, what can you tell me about him? »

« What do you want to know? I only saw him a few days and many years ago.»

« What does he look like? For a start, what's his size? »

« A little taller than I am, maybe one meter eighty[131]; brown short hair, brown eyes… »

« Anything else? »

« Scars, quite a few scars… »

« Scars? Where? » John had startled.

She reddened and lowered her face.

« Where? »

---

[131] 5'10"

* * *

« His belly, his back... »

« Like dots or slashes? »

« Both, bullets and knives... » John had forgotten that she had been living in a country at war for years... but damnit, it felt like the same guy in Jordan!

He powered his laptop and retrieved a face rendering that he had received from Colonel Saleh: *« is that him? »*

« Yes, it looks like him... »

« Man... » John took some time to get his thoughts in order.

« Do you know where he comes from? »

« No, he spoke very good English; maybe French? »

« French? Why »

« I remember that Kazem » - she shivered at his name - *« Kazem and him mentioned French thugs; Mourad seemed to take it personally... »*

« When did he come? »

« Mid-September 2015 »

« Wow, you've got a great memory! »

Her eyes filled with tears, a first display of weakness: *« You don't forget your first execution... And my son was born in May*

2016… »

John let that sink in… and suddenly jumped: « *your son? »*

« *Yes, my son is… »* She lowered her head in shame and couldn't end her sentence.

« *Damn, »* thought John, « *DN-fucking jackpot-A… »*

The interview went on but she couldn't give much more. She had agreed to have the DNA of her one year old son to be harvested.

« *Thank you for your help Layla, »* said John, « *you're really helped us! You should be happy: we're going to nail this bastard and make him pay. »*

She looked up and surprised him: « *he was gentle to me, he gave me my only reason to live! »*

She spoke again: « *can you take us to America, get us visas? »* Then, looking at John, smiled bitterly, « *no, of course not, no one cares about us. We are just collateral damage… »*

She left the room, full of sorrow and dignity.

John took a while to gather his thoughts: that woman had impressed, no, troubled him more than he expected. Yet, the trip had been a resounding success: corroboration of the guy's existence, DNA, maybe even a French origin…

Wait, did she say public execution? He would have to research that as well…

* * *

*   *   *

As soon as he got back to DC, John turned into a machine: DIGA got him several hits on public executions, one of which matched the details given by Layla; he actually remembered storing that video away…

What he saw of the face slip was consistent with the rendition from Jordan that Layla had also approved; with DNA and prints, he was getting as close as he could to the Banker: he ONLY missed his name…

He also had found an interview of a French ISIS sympathizer who had gotten captured by the Turks as he was trying to enter the country and leave the fight: clueless and scared shitless, the bastard had tried to give away as much information as he could to get on the good side of his capturers; it's in that context that he had told a story of finding a guy hidden in the trunk of a car, trying to snick into Raqqa:

« *I'm sure he was French* » had he said in his poor Arabic.

« *Why?* » had said his interrogator, hidden from the camera.

« *His Arabic was very good, much better than mine, but he made the mistake I always make when he got angry and told us to stop sucking dogs' dicks: too much « in » on* [132]جنس فموي *! My Algerian friends always made fun of me…* »

The DNA from the kid had finally spoken and it was a good match with the Jordan mystery man, one additional mail on

---

[132] Arabic: blowjob

the guy's coffin…

Another request, complete with face rendering, DNA and prints, went out again to the French services, DGSE[133] and DGSI[134], to no avail: this was not a known customer to them but both agencies clearly expressed their interests: why was the CIA interested in that person? What did the US have on him? John's understanding was that the CIA had remained rather elusive, a nice strategy to keep them frustrated and actively looking for the guy… It was a subtle game played both ways between very close players: the French had been at the tip of the fight against radical Islam since the eighties and John had real respect for their troops for their skills and courage back in Afghanistan.

Dead ends all over again, doors after doors closing on him!

A dead stop after such an increase in speed of the hunt was tough to live with; Bubba had been right and John was boiling…

Another one to slap a door in his face in a major way had been Kate: she had found out that John was fooling around in the most caricatural way, a forgotten very risqué red thong, lost under the bed of his Palisades home. That had turned into the expected ugly scene. Kate, furious and distraught, had stormed out of the house and, within a week, had filled for divorce. The fight was ugly: she was going for his money, wouldn't let him see Josh and had picked a white shark of a

---

[133] « Direction Générale de la Sécurité Extérieure » : French equivalent of the CIA
[134] « Direction Générale de la Sécurité Intérieur » : French equivalent of the CIA

lawyer.

Jenna had noticed his fury and asked about it once: he had chickened out and explained that, after all these years, his wife had finally filed for divorce and wouldn't let him see his son. « *Oh,* » had she said, « *I didn't think that you would be so upset about that; you were complete strangers now, weren't you?* » She had eyed him carefully and warned him, ever tough as steel: « *don't even think of popping me the question! I'm not marrying material ok? Fooling around is fine, period!* » That had chilled John and they hadn't spoken for a week when he left to meet his bunch in West Virginia for a few days.

*   *   *

John had settled comfortably within the group and had become the official Wild Westerners' CQB[135] trainer. He would run the guys through drills over and over again and had selected a few who had become the Standard's guard, his own little fighting unit... Those guys were rougher than the rest of the members, some of which were little more than would be campers.

When he arrived near the camp located in the heart of the Monongahela National Forest, he turned right onto a narrow track that most would have missed but for the « Private property, trespassers will be shot on sight » sign. After driving a mile deep into the forest, John parked his Cherokee in a clearing next to a village of small cabins, curled by a big pond under the watchful gaze of the surrounding mountains. A mountain of a man was standing by the water, only turning as John approached.

---

[135] Close Quarter Battle

* * *

« Morning Sergeant! »

« Morning Major! How are you doing! »

The Major was the group's founder, a guy made of the hardest wood. He ran the WW like a military unit and had a seemingly rough, undisclosed military past and strong political acumen. John had seen him kick a member out of the Unit, as the Major called it, literarily kicking him back to his car, cursing and ranting: the ex-member's mistake had been admitting voting Clinton in the 2016 election.

« Sergeant, I've been thinking lately: I need a second in command and you're the right guy for it. Will you take the job? »

From up the trees fell the call of a lone bold eagle.

*   *   *

The following week, John struck gold again: following a call to all ISIS sympathizers to send cash to their cause, Xavi, the quasi-autistic analyst had dropped a bomb on John's desk: two Western banks under INGOT surveillance were sending cash to an account in the Bahamas, an account that was closely monitored since the incident in Amman. For John, it was proof that there was a system in place to transfer cash from different sources back to Iraq and ISIS.

Now came the hard part: convince Mike to take it up at Langley and make it a strategic goal to catch the banker…

It was surprisingly easy: John quickly realized that Mike had been very closely monitoring his work; so closely indeed that

Mike had replied to John's request for a targeting team to be set up by telling him that they had an appointment at Langley four days later with the DCI[136] and DDO[137]!

The meeting had been stressful but a resounding success: first met with skepticism, the Banker's existence had been reluctantly acknowledged thanks to Mike's persistence and pure luck!

The CIA had been increasingly puzzled by ISIS' ability to purchase equipment, weapons and pay its fighters… The constant targeting of petrol logistics had reduced that source of income to close to zero; the art smuggling couldn't account for much and the Mosul bank heist was regularly downplayed… In fact, there had been an in-house analysis that went as far as saying that 70% of the organization's income was unexplained… The Banker was Occam's razor[138] bingo!

John was now the leader of a glorious team of three, based in a Langley office, whose mission, codename PHORMIO[139], was simple: catch or kill the Banker!

*   * *

« *Second in command… What do you think?* » Asked Uncle William, through the thick and rich smoke of a Cuban cigar.

* * *

---

[136] Director, CIA

[137] Deputy Director of Operations

[138] The simplest explanation is usually the right one (attributed to English friar William of Ockham)

[139] 4th century bc Greek slave turned banker

« He's on a very thin line: you know how dangerous that Major is! » replied Mike as they sat in comfortable leather club chairs on a quiet patio of the Army and Navy Country Club.

« Yes, I've read his FBI file, suspected of a few homicides and armed robbery, one might even call that domestic terrorism… »

« And hardly no military past… » frowned Mike…

International Bank of Indochina
Account Number: 7011114642
Balance: US$ 1,526,354.00

INTERLUDE

Forward, forward, forward, forward,
Without ever retreating, never surrender,
Forward, forward, forward, forward,
Undefeated Warrior, sword in hand kill them!

Kill the traitors, attack them by surprise,
Slaughter them, make them pay for their treachery,
Identify the hypocrite with the beating guise,
That beats only for the interests of this earthly.

He thinks that Allah is not going to reveal it,
What a real fool, unconscious with a veiled heart,
Kill him with a bullet in the head,
Such is the fate of the stubborn criminal!

Forward, forward, forward, forward,
Never retreat, never surrender,
Forward, forward, forward, forward,
Undefeated Warrior, sword in hand kill them.

Forward!

CHAPTER 24

Paris, France

September 1st, 2017

The ringing in my ears had finally stopped after a few weeks…

Coming back to Paris, I had fallen into a trance: I was afraid of going out, seeing people. I would wake up in the middle of the night, shivering with fear; once, I even came close to jumping through the window after a particularly vivid nightmare, a dramatic rendition of my near death exit of the house in Kismayo…

Thank God for Louise: her quiet presence was probably what that kept me sane during those weeks. She came everyday, brought me food, dried my tears, provided me with my cocktail of pills… She's the one who forced me out one beautiful Saturday morning for the first time in weeks…

I still had a job to do and, reluctantly, I slowly came out of the black hole I had fallen into. To be fair, I was probably safe in Paris: no one, apart from my bosses, knew my identity, nor my responsibility in the system, the Beast as I had started calling it; I had had no contact with Chuppa in ages, no one to link me to my brothers and my old mentor, Kamaal, had died of a sudden heart attack in jail…

So, one Monday morning, I walked to my small office and sat in front of my computer. If the server was always on and actively allocating the cash as expected, I still needed to update the system with changing banking regulations or answer requests from the various banks. I was cautiously hidden behind VPNs, bouncing from one to the other in a way that my IT guy had described as « *impenetrable* » the last time I had spoken to him a year ago. The tone of his voice had alerted me and I had pressed him: he had reluctantly told me that he had needed to twinkle with the system following an incident with one VPN a while back but that « *I needn't worry as it was now foolproof!* » The fact that I was alive today was probably a testament to his talent…

I also checked my company emails as I needed to declare some taxes and prepare the coming closing of my fiscal year. Because of my retreat from the world, I was late on a lot of things and had a dozens of emails waiting for me in my inbox.

I froze: there, stuck between two spams, an innocuous request for contact and a commercial proposition for remote accounting services from a company based in Turkey! Kazem's words came back to me from the dead: « *My friend, if one day, Inch'Allah, you receive a message offering accounting services, it will mean that I am dead… You will call the company and ask for Abdallah. He will not be there; just leave a message regarding his accounting offer. This will trigger the emergency contact procedure…* »

* * *

I debated it for a few days, finally talking about it to Louise: I was done in; I didn't want to experience the absolute panic and could probably still do the job from far away…   After many late hours, she persuaded me to make the call: « *one last time!* » I said « *and you'll tell them that you want out.* »

My heart was beating and with a sweaty hand, I picked the office phone and dialed the company number.

A woman answered: « *Salman accounting services, Tünaydın*[140]*!* »

« *Err, could I speak to Abdallah please?* »

There was a silence. Then the lady replied in poor English.

« *He is not here now; can I take a message?* »

« *Yes, tell him that Mourad has called regarding his accounting proposition.* »

« *Yes, yes, I will do that.* » She hung up!

One week later precisely, I logged onto a Pakistani website; in the comments of the Quran quote of the day, an anonymous account had left a long message; hidden in it were an email address and a password.

I switched to the domain webmail, identified myself and found a message in the draft section: « *impossible to travel to Syria or Iraq; all communication now by physical courier; this will*

---

[140] Turkish: good afternoon

be the last email contact. »

It was getting sketchier by the day, a sure sign that the organisation was struggling: I was to be at Abu Sultan harbor some six weeks later at noon, on the beach facing a fish restaurant...

« Where the fuck is Abu Sultan? »

Muttering, I had to Google it: *« Egypt... You've got to be kidding! Come on, do they think I'm a travel agency? »*

It turned out that the meeting point was in the middle of the Suez Canal, on the shores of the Great Bitter Lake[141]. There was indeed a fish restaurant there... and a beach. The only positive thing was that there were thousands of tourists entering the country everyday and the former colonial city of Ismailia, just a few kilometers north of the meeting point, had some museums and was the place of birth of a famous French singer; I guessed that I would be able to disappear quietly, without raising too much suspicion. Cairo being less than two hours driving away, the easiest was going to be renting a car and dumping it somewhere. I'd need to take a ninety day visa to be on the safe side: I could always pretend that I was sick to cut my visit short.

Ok, the beach, then what? A ship? That called for some extra preparation...

So, three weeks later, I landed in Cairo and played the French tourist for a few days under yet another different name... Playing a role was getting so taxing now that I had opted to

---

[141] Saltwater lake, located in the middle of the Suez Canal, Egypt

stay as close as possible from my real personae: French, with a financial occupation. I toured the various world-famous sites for a few days with a group whose members, after a few failed attempts for conversation, quickly left me on my own. One evening, I came back to my small hotel and found that the equipment that I had asked for, back in Paris, had been delivered during the day: it felt like overkill and was, in its essence, dangerous should I encounter a nosy police officer but I wouldn't have moved with less!

Then came the day I had dreaded for close to a month: I rented a car, checked out and drove north-east towards Ismailia: it was a short ride, less than two hours. On the left, I could see the green halo of the Nile delta, on the right, endless desert. Thirty-two kilometers from Ismailia, I turned right and headed to Abu Sultan. Finding the fish restaurant was easy: I drove past it on the road that followed the Great Bitter Lake shores and found a discreet parking spot nearby in the unexpected shade of a tree. I was two hours in advance and, after sitting restlessly in the car for a while, went to look for a coffee nearby; after locking the car and looking around, I discreetly left the key hidden within the right wheel bumper. Someone would handle the drive back to the rental agency. No need to attract too much attention with a missing tourist…

A quarter to noon, I stood up, paid for the light food I had hardly been able to eat and walked along the road, a heavy rucksack on one shoulder. Trafic was light because of lunch and there were few pedestrians. I turned right and followed a narrow canal leading to the lake; the air was damp and from the dirty water rose a smell of rotting fish and mud… I arrived on a beach littered with debris and rubbish. Small fishing boats had been randomly dragged ashore, most of them in a poor state; a couple were moored and quiet on the water. I could make out a few ships anchored a couple kilometers in the distance.

I walked slowly along the beach and finally rested against an old wreck, keeping an eye on the water and on the quiet traffic on the road a hundred yards away. I was the only one on the beach.

After twenty minutes, a small boat appeared from nowhere and made way for the beach; it came to a gentle stop on the sand a few yards away from me: « *Mourad?* » asked the guy onboard.

« *Yes!* »

« *Come!* »

I boarded the fishing boat and we left the beach in a puff of black smoke. Our destination soon became clear as we headed towards a lone freighter. She stood low over the water and had obviously seen better days: her sides had been painted in a worn-out black paint and rust oozed from every rivet in a forest of small red springs falling to the sea. The bridge was a dirty white and the two loading cranes a yellowish brown. Some smoke pouring away from the funnel was the only indication of life aboard.

We stopped by a pilot ladder: I adjusted the rucksack on my shoulders, grabbed the rough side ropes and started the ten meter climb. As soon as my feet left the boat, I heard its engine power up and drift away. I finally reached the top of the ladder and jumped on the desk. A tall muscular guy was waiting in the shadow and waved me in. I followed him to a small room on the starboard side where he signaled me to wait, closed the door… and locked it!

There was a bunk against the opposite partition of the porthole, a closet with a few drawers and, behind an orange curtain, a foul-smelling toilet; the white walls were bare with remnants of tape where pictures or posters had been displayed. The floor was a grey linoleum that had known better times, displaying a few suspicious stains.

I dropped my bag on the floor and leaned on the bunk.

*   *   *

On the shore, a man lowered his binoculars and murmured to himself: « [142]قمر أبيض it is, » then walked away to drive Alain's car back to the rental agency.

*   *   *

I must have dozed off: I was awaken by a rattling noise, chains being dragged, a rumble coming from down below; we were under way. The temperature in the room was cool thanks to a gentle breeze coming from the porthole. I stood and looked outside: we were slowly leaving the Great Bitter Lake and heading into the Suez Canal.

Around three, the same man appeared with some food and some water. He closed the porthole and dragged the curtain across: « *Too many people on board* » he reluctantly said in bad English, « *pilot and docking crew. Stay way from window.* » I was locked up again…

---

[142] Arabic: white moon

* * *

A few hours later, I gently pushed the curtain on the side: we were fully engaged in the canal now with the side of the canal not more than eighty yards from me. The sun was setting down and the ship was bathed in a beautiful orange light.

I sat back on the bunk and waited.

It must have been ten when the door opened again: the same man asked me to follow him. We went up some steep stairs and arrived in front of a larger room: I entered and saw a man seated at a dining table. He was fiftyish, bald and had a Pakistani look about him.

« *Come in Mr Mourad. Please sit.* »

I grabbed a chair and sat in front of him.

« *I am the captain of this ship. I am sorry that you couldn't not come out earlier but your presence aboard my ship must remain confidential. Egyptians are very nosy and, even if we keep the docking crew in front of porn videos in the crew common room, I wanted to be sure that no-one saw you.* »

He drank some tea.

« *Here is what will happen: we will sail for several days until we reach a point at which you will disembark my ship and I will never see you again. In the mean time, you will take your meals in your room and will only leave it at night to refresh yourself for an hour. If you don't like it, your problem. If it becomes my problem? Well, no one knows you're onboard… * »

I nodded.

* * *

« Can I have books? Would you have a Quran? »

The Captain looked at me, nodded and made a sign. The muscular man was back at my side.

« Now my boatswain will escort back to your room. »

I was quickly back in my cabin. The bosun[143] opened the door and a young man, still a teenager, appeared with some food that he lay on the bunk, then returned with a Quran and several books in English. I was locked up again.

We sailed for six boring eventless days; three times a day, the young Filipino would appear with a meal, only to return forty minutes after to retrieve the leftovers. Every night, the boson would accompany me on the deck where I exercised under his watchful eyes: it was a relief to be out, in the breeze. The weather was fair, the ship gently hitting the long and small swell head on.

It all changed one night. Around midnight Egypt time, the bosun woke me up and told me to prepare to leave the ship. I put on my clothes quickly, grabbed my kit and followed him to port.

The swell had gotten stronger and longer: we had left the Red Sea and were probably somewhere along Yemen. I moved closer to the rail; ten meters below, I could make out the shadow of a boat.

* * *

---

[143] A petty officer on a merchant ship who controls the work of the seamen

« *Now?* » I asked the bosun. He nodded. I climbed above the rail and started the descent. The waves made the journey perilous and I made sure that I always had three points of contact, hands and feet, on the ladder. As I got down, I saw that I was about to board a small dhow. The three meter swell pushed it up then dragged it down: I had to time my jump perfectly for fear of crashing on the small deck or worse getting crushed between the two hulls. I had done it the past and my training took over: I waited for a large wave to arrive and, right before I felt it upon us, I jumped!

I landed on all fours on the smelly deck but, all things considered, was rather happy with myself. I immediately felt the dhow move away from the freighter, its large mass disappearing in an eternity of waves and stars.

I looked around and saw three men; the smell and the wet nets that I had landed on were self-explanatory: fishermen! One of them waved me inside the small cabin. It was a few hours before I felt the swell settle. The same man came in and put his finger on his lips: I nodded, no noise, got it! The engine stopped. I could hear some men speak outside and what could be crates being dragged. After forty minutes, the cabin door opened and I was asked to come out.

The night was still dark but a faint light could be perceived, the premise of a hot day. The dhow, one of many, was berthed alongside a small jetty. I walked off the boat and followed the man to a small military truck; I climbed in the back onto the platform and we drove away. The drive was short, maybe twenty minutes, before we stopped; the tarp was raised off the back of the truck and I jumped out into a quiet dead end. I was whisked through inside a compound. A man was waiting for me and spoke in heavily accented English:

* * *

« Welcome brother, my name is Saleh Nasser! » The guy stank of arrogance and scorn. *« You will stay here for a few days until your visitor arrives; don't leave your room without authorization! »*

I followed him to a small bedroom where I dropped my bag, then, after checking a small compass, prayed on the floor. I stood up and checked my environment in the morning light: I raised the bottom shelf of a small cabinet and was able to hide a small sat pager, after making sure that it was powered and connected; it was my one and only lifeline!

Some time later, I heard the house wake up. A young man brought me some food.

I settled into a routine: a boring day came after another, interrupted by prayers and meals with a rowdy bunch of guys, Nasser's guards, who called him Prince; I had kept the Quran from the freighter and spent my time reading and exercising, often with Ahmed, a young guy who had taken an improbable liking to me and with whom I would go into impromptu pushup contests in the courtyard, under the shade of a tree…

One morning, when most of the guys had left with Prince and the rest was lethargic, chewing khat[144] for hours, he came to me, looked around and said: *« Come, I show you secret! »*

We walked across the main room where the guys spent most of their time watching television or playing video games,

---

[144] Khat users chew leaves for hours, inducing mild euphoria and excitement. It is classified as a drug of abuse by the World Health Organization.

and, at the end of a narrow corridor, entered a small storage room. There were shelves filled with indiscriminate stuff on two sides, the last one, facing the entrance, was covered by a dirty mattress.

« *Here!* » He pointed at the mattress. « *Secret hole to next house!* »

I extended a hand.

« *No, no touch!* »

I stopped a few inches from the mattress but could feel a flow of air coming from it.

« *And next house, there is cave!* »

« *Cave? Tunnel? Going where?* »

« *Yes, yes, going to mosque.* »

South then, that was invaluable! The complex was a small group of two story houses stuck together with a large east-facing courtyard, last in a dead end. There was a small mosque nearby, blazing its prayers through dreadful loud speakers. I had been able to sneak up once on the roof: after tying up a beige cheiche around my head to hide my face, I had climbed a shaking ladder, and set foot on a burning roof. I looked around: to the North, a few kilometers away, some mountains, to the East, a small fort perched on top of a small hill and a city, to the South a maze of brown ancient and old houses, roads and further away, the sea, and to the West endless flat land, sand and dust.

* * *

Ahmed was about to lose his life, but, that day, unknowingly, he saved mine!

CHAPTER 25

PHORMIO briefing room
  Langley Virginia,
  CIA HQ

October 28th, 2017

Six months, six fucking months stuck in a windowless room and nothing to show for…

The PHORMIO group had been at work for six months and was yet to find any evidence of the Banker's identity, yet alone its existence. John could hear the little music in the corridors at Langley: « *another wild goose chase from those jerks at the Red House…* » Even Mike was pressing now for more, any information that the team could lay its hands on.

Going nowhere and having his two supports about to be reassigned, John had gone for the basic of any investigation: start again from the beginning and review all the evidences and see if any could shed new light on the target.

It was a boring, tedious job that turned the tide one morning:

* * *

« John? » Said Lea, a data analyst who had been assigned to him to the PHORMIO op. Only in her late twenties, she had plain looks and weird blurry eyes; her awkward social skills hid a natural talent for data management and an incredible memory.

« Yes? »

« Remember that Belgian company that had a sat phone operating in Kismayo when the target was there? » For some reason, she had never wanted to use the Banker nickname.

« Yes, the one that doesn't exist anymore? What? »

« Well, I was reviewing the contract that had been signed at the time and I noticed that they also had a sat pager under the same conditions… »

« You mean prepaid? »

« Yes, and guess what? » John raised an eyebrow.

« I checked and it's active! »

John rose and walked to her desk: *« What do you mean active? »*

« It's been live for a few days and we've got a location! »

« Are you kidding me? » John looked at the data and she was right: the data indicated 4°33'31.8"N 49°08'00.7"E.

« Ok, where the fuck is that? »

* * *

« Yemen, I already checked, a place called Al Mukalla. »

John's brain went in overdrive: *« We need some visuals on the location to place the target there. I'll check it with the bosses. »*

The good thing about having an official mission tag was that the brass could support what you were doing, the bad thing was that you had to tell them first what you were doing… *« God, I hate politics! »* thought John as he was waiting for a lift to the 7th floor where Mike, incidentally, also had an office.

Convincing Mike was fast and, to John's surprise, he quickly got him some visuals from the NRO and the promise of an aerial asset within ten hours. It was, for the Agency, an area of interest due to the strong Al-Qaeda and ISIS presence, favored by the ongoing civil war…

Twenty-four hours later, an elated John was looking at a video of a guy partially hidden under a tree: his face had been visible for a few seconds but that had been enough for the MQ9 to give them a perfect match with the Jordanian face rendering. The guy was 5'10 according to the analysts, was probably from Southern Europe and had a hollowed face.

« I've got you bastard! » thought John.

The following days few days were a blur: the bosses had decided that the banker should be interrogated as he probably had invaluable information on ISIS financing; luckily the location made it possible to arrest him, whereas a land raid in Somalia had been deemed too DC-sensitive for Hassan Al-Moktar: no one still wanted a remake of « Black

Hawk down[145] »... Here though, there were no Russians nor any Iraqi to get in the way as in Syria, and the house was isolated enough to allow for a forceful grab and avoid steep fighting!

And the flailing Yemen government would only be too happy to get any public help from the US!

US SOCOM[146] was brought into the loop: they tasked a Navy SEAL team, opportunistically based on Arta beach, Djibouti for some training with the local French Navy Commandos.

A Wasp-class amphibious Marine assault ship was repositioned from its northern patrol position in order to shorten the flight time of the raid helicopters; a couple of Ospreys[147] flew in with the SEAL team from Djibouti to the warship.

Forty eight hours later, one late afternoon, on an underground floor at Langley, John and Mike entered a situation room to follow the raid in real time...

---

[145] A 1993 failed raid in Somalia that saw 19 rangers killed
[146] US Special Operation Command
[147] US multi-mission, tilt rotor military aircraft

CHAPTER 26

Al Mukalla, Yemen

November 1st, 2017

I was seated on a bench, outside my parents' house, basking in the spring sun, facing a gentle slope that reached out to the woods below. My father was seated next to me and asked me: « *What are you doing these days? Your mom and I haven't seen you in a long time… * »

I told him: he paled and was soon white with fury or fear; which? I would never know: as he was about to speak, an annoying beeping interrupted him!

I woke up, my heart beating in a tense rhythm; the beep was coming from under the closet: the sat pager! Suddenly awake, I jumped out of the bed and grabbed the device; the message was short: « *R* ».

« *Putain de merde*[148]*!* »

---

[148] French: « fucking hell » (not literal)

* * *

I urgently put my clothes on and grabbed my rucksack. I removed a light tactical vest and swiftly put it on; it was already fitted with two flash bangs, a Glock 19 on a side holster, along with several magazines and a Gerber combat knife. I then put on some night vision goggles and, breathing slowly, stopped to listen.

The window was slightly opened to let some air in.

A discreet engine noise slowly approaching!

I ran out of my room, yelling and raising the alarm.

The noise turned into a roar!

At least two helicopters landed around us, probably just north of the compound, and, had I been in charge, probably on top of us! The guys were waking up around me and were running around half naked, each with an AK in the hand. Several detonations were heard then a major explosion: the courtyard gate had been breached!

The whole place instantly turned into a full blown firefight; I had a few escape routes: the main gate was out; I could hear some movement above so the oppo would keep an eye on the street for jumpers or runners and they certainly had legs on the ground there… I only had one solution left: Ahmed's secret way!

I ran across the community room amongst gun shots and flying wood and cement splinters; two of Prince's guys were already down: this was not going to last long… My goal was simple: avoid capture as long as possible; the US, it had to be them, couldn't afford to stay long on the ground: the longer, the higher the danger of local militants to arrive, and literally everyone had guns in Yemen…

As I was approaching the storage room, I heard some breaching noise coming from the room opposite of my escape door; I stopped and crouched.

A figure was moving slowly over the broken window frame; a body was slouched on the floor: Ahmed had vainly attempted to resist… I threw a flash bang in the room and closed my eyes, my hands pressing my ears, my mouth slightly opened. There was a thunder of noise and light. It took me a while to reorient myself but I moved forward: one soldier was stuck on the window frame: I shot him center mass and he fell backwards.

The other soldier who had entered first jumped at me from the left; still under the shock of the grenade, his attempt was clumsy and I was able to elbow him in the throat. He made a gurgling sound and his hands went to his throat. I grabbed him and, using him as a shield, withdrew backwards out of the room as quickly as possible. I threw my second flash bang, kick the door closed and moved into the storage room.

I dropped the guy who was visibly choking and pushed the mattress aside: there was a three foot hole at the base of the wall. I crouched then stopped and sighed.

I quickly crawled back to the guy, grabbed my knife, positioned two fingers above his supra-sternal notch and slit his throat opened. There was a small hiss; I looked around and found a hollow piece of plastic: I inserted it in his throat and moved back to the hole. I tried to move the mattress back into position and ran…

I could hear the battle waning down behind me; Prince's men were no match for the US soldiers!

The hole gave way to another cellar and, on the side, an underground corridor. I followed it quickly. The noise were quickly muffled and I was soon in complete silence. I kept walking until I reached another cellar. I climbed the steps into an empty room and listened. People were yelling in the street and the gun fire that had receded seemed to ignite again. I grabbed my pager and keyed *RV*; a minute later, a message came back with some coordinates. I entered them it my GPS handheld and powered the pager off.

A few minutes later, I heard several explosions and the infamous rattling of a chain gun: A gunship had opened fire… The helicopters took off and flew away, out of a wildfire.

I carefully opened a door leading to the street: men were walking around, cursing and shooting randomly in the air. I removed my goggles and stored them back into my bag. I quickly wrapped my cheiche around my head and walked quietly away in the dark. At a corner, I saw a guy seating alone on a motorbike; its engine was running. I moved in before he could see me and held him into a choke hold. As he struggled, the bike fell on its side. He fainted rapidly and I lay him on the ground. Seconds later, I was off!

I had a quick look at the GPS handheld to get a rough idea of my destination: south-east it was. There was a little traffic, mostly men in arms in cars and I was easily lost in the mayhem. Five minutes later, I was near my destination, a deserted beach, away from the road, the nearest building a few hundred yards south. I laid the bike gently on the dusty ground in a small ditch and walked the final distance in the darkness.

The air was cool and damp; a gentle breeze blew from the sea; I sat on the sand and shook for some time before finally calming down.

I waited there for an hour until two men appeared out of nowhere: my ride had arrived!

CHAPTER 27

Washington DC,

November 10th, 2017

A fucking clusterfuck!

John didn't know what to say: the raid had been a complete failure; there was no trace of the target; the Banker had disappeared without leaving a trace! Four SEALs had been injured, including one who had miraculously been saved; an estimated thirty locals had been killed: militants or civilians, the margin was thin... The guys had landed into a hornet's nest and the raid had clearly been compromised from the start.

The SEALs had recovered some documents, a few phones and a computer; the CIA analysts were busy working on it but it all seemed to pertain to a local warlord called Prince... The SEALs had also been able to quickly interrogate a militant, who had led them to a room where a foreigner had lived: the Banker had been there and a Quran was recovered with his finger prints on it!

* * *

John had lived the raid as if he was there with them: the smell of his days in Iraq or Afghanistan had filled the situation room: the sweat of his fellow soldiers, the cordite, the blood… He had stopped breathing when all hell had broken loose in the cul-de-sac; he had frozen upon the « *man down* » calls over the radio and started to breath again when the helos had gotten feet wet…

He drove down to Norfolk to interview the SEAL team leader. After presenting his credentials at the base entrance, he was escorted to the Naval Special Warfare Command building. A sailor was waiting for him at the door of the building and walked him to the CO[149]'s office. A stern looking Commander looked up from a stack of paper and waved him in. A tall, sturdy officer was seated on the side.

« *Mister Quirston? Come in and have a seat!* »

« *Morning Sir!* »

« *Now, what are you doing here exactly?* »

« *Well, I read the report from the officer in command of the raid, Lieutenant-Commander Morrison if I remember well, and I wanted to… * »

The CO interrupted him: « *This, here, is Lieutenant-Commander Morrison and let's get something straight right away; if your intention is for him, or us, to take the flack for whatever game you're playing, you might as well drive back to your comfy DC desk!* »

* * *

---

[149] Commanding Officer

« With or without your permission Sir, I don't give a fuck! » The two officers' eyes widened! *« I've been there, done that, left a leg there… I don't give a fuck about politics and bullshit. I want to nail the bastard and I will! I just want to get as much info as I can get… and not from a fucking action report… »*

The CO smiled but his eyes didn't: *« Tell me you were not in the Army! »*

« MARSOC, 1rst Battalion » John beamed.

« Right, Morrison here is going to forget that you don't-give-a-fucked me and will walk you through the raid. Dismissed! »

The two men rose, saluted and left the office. Morrison was grinning: *« Come to the briefing room, my 2iC[150] is waiting for us; coffee? »*

« Yep, black, no sugar… »

« Of course »

They reviewed the operation for an hour, going through the intelligence that they had gathered. The conclusion was already known but needed saying: the target had been there; his room had been searched and a bag found with some clothes and toiletry items. DNA was recovered on a toothbrush and matched with the Banker's file.

« PHORMIO probably exited through an underground passage; he never went through the gate, nor the street. One of my guy found a hole in a room, leading to a house next door and some extra exits…

---

[150] Second in command

We simply did not have time to follow them through... »

John nodded: searching cellars, tunnels and caves was a long and hard job; not one that you could do from a feeble fire base in the middle of a hostile suburb.

Morrison stretched and said: *« What is strange though is that we clearly had the element of surprise: every single militant that we killed was in a state of partial undress; yet, PHORMIO's shoes were missing; there were clothes folded in the closet but none left behind on the floor... »*

« He had time... » muttered John. *« How's that possible? »*

« Your call! » Morrison shrugged.

They walked back to John's car.

« I forgot to ask: how are your guys doing? »

« They'll be ok; I mean, two had minor stuff and will be back within a week; we got real lucky with two: a crushed larynx doesn't normally give you much chance; without the tracheotomy, he wouldn't have made it... »

« Yep, good call from your guys! »

« Except that, you know what is interesting? None of my guys did it... »

« You mean... »

« Yes, one of the militants did it... »
* * *

« Err… You said two were lucky? »

« Yes, my larynx operator? His buddy was shot, 9 mill, double tap center of the chest, less than half an inch across impacts, by the same guy who did the tracheo… »

He stopped and faced John: *« Want to know what I think? »* Morrison stopped: *« in the middle of a hellish gunfight, two great shots like that? With that level of skill, the guy should have aimed at the head: better chance to take down an operator… And yet, they were right in the center of the body armor, the most protected spot… And on top of that, a life saving medical procedure on the fly… »*

He paused: *« Call me crazy but your PHORMIO has serious special forces written all over him! »*

« And why didn't he kill your men? »

Morrison grinned: *« That's the question, isn't it? »*

« None of it makes sense, » thought John on the four hour drive back to Palisades. It took a lot to impress a SEAL officer in the field and PHORMIO clearly had. But a guy with that set of skills had to appear on databases somewhere…

Then it down on him: a special forces operator in any top level unit will get injured at some point of his service; being injured on a mission means medical assistance, maybe rehab, definitely hospital databases…

Hospitals are easy to hack, unfortunately for them: everyone will tell you. Military hospitals are a little less so but nothing that would stop a dedicated TAO[151] team from the NSA…

Three weeks later, they found a trace: a DNA pinged positive in a civilian hospital database in Biarritz, a costal city south of France. The country had been their first target as some of the evidence pointed there.

John was reviewing the information; they had little: a lone DNA correspondence with no patient identity…

In Mike's office on the seventh floor at Langley, John was presenting the evidence: the Banker had to be French, yet, all calls to French intelligence had been fruitless.

« *It's time to up the game!* » said Mike.

« *What do you mean Sir?* »

« *If the Banker is French, then there must be something in their files on him; forget the Bataclan[152], those guys are really good…* » He nodded to himself: « *The guys at NSA are not going to like it!* »

They didn't: it took an explicit request from the DCI[153]! Hacking a friendly Intelligence service isn't something to do casually: get caught in the act and experience serious political consequences… The DGSI[154] network had a backdoor: it had

---

[151] Tailored Access Operations: NSA cyber-warfare intelligence-gathering unit

[152] On 13 November 2015, 130 people were killed in a coordinated terrorist attack in the Bataclan theatre and various places in Paris

[153] Director, CIA

[154] Direction Générale de la Sécurité Intérieure: French equivalent of the FBI

been discreetly inserted by an IT consultant very keen on building a swimming pool in his house down in the south of France! It was yet to be used…

The hack came up with a surprising result: the face recognition software had a match!

Alain Paul, white male, 1,80 m, brown eyes dark hair, born in 1983 in Toulouse. « S » rated[155], suspected but never convicted of a killing at the age of fifteen, multiple convictions for minor drug offenses and violence. Current whereabouts unknown.

« *Alain Paul* » murmured John finally able to put a name on the guy as he looked at a familiar face on the screen.

« *If only you had the right DNA… * »

---

[155] Indicator used by French law enforcement agencies to flag an individual considered to be a serious threat to National Security.

CHAPTER 28

Paris, France

November 18th, 2017

It was a late Saturday evening; a drizzle fell on the capital city; city lights were glistening on the Grands Boulevards[156] and the few people still out were hurrying back home in the cold.

An ensemble of grayish buildings stood on both sides of Boulevard Mortier. Its high walls were carefully monitored via dozens of street cameras. The few entrances were barricaded and fortified against ramming vehicles. Parking along those walls was illegal and insured an immediate visit from cops who had zero sense of humor. It was the Piscine[157], the nickname of the headquarters of the Direction Générale

---

[156] First ring around Paris, each boulevard is named after a Napoleon General

[157] French: swimming pool; the nickname comes from an adjacent swimming complex

de la Sécurité Extérieure, the French CIA.

At the heart of the complex, a few men were assembled in a secure meeting room: amongst them, the most powerful of the French Intelligence community: *le DGSE*[158], *le DGSI*[159] and the Secrétaire Général[160] of the President of the French Republic. They all knew each other well and had attended the famous ENA, the Ecole Nationale d'Administration, the required school for ambitious civil servants.

The DGSE cleared his throat:

« *Nicolas, Alexis, thank you for coming at such a short notice! We've had some major developments on Wanda and I think that we need to move quickly to a new stage, but, Alexis, in order to bring you up to date, I suggest that we hear first what the DGSI IT guys have to say!* »

A nervous man in his forties entered the room. He sat at one end of the table:

« *Erm… Messieurs, my name is Henri Marche; I am the Director of Systems at the DGSI. We have noticed a breach of our systems yesterday. The perpetuators were interested in our criminal database and especially the « S » section. They came back a second time and focused on one file.* » He looked at a paper: « *One Alain Paul.* »

« *What, how could they enter our system so easily? I thought that they were completely safe?* » erupted the Secrétaire Général.

---

[158] Equivalent of DCI
[159] Equivalent of the Director of the FBI
[160] Chief of staff

* * *

« It's all right Alexis, » said the DGSI, *« We have been aware of that backdoor since its conception… »*

That startled him!

« What do you mean, Nicolas? »

He nodded to the IT guy who went on:

« A couple years ago, a computer consultant working on our systems was approached by an unknown party asking him to insert that specific backdoor. He informed us immediately of the contact and we were able to identify a US consular agent during the cash transfer! We have been monitoring the breach ever since and we have been slowly reducing its access to the less sensitive data… »

« I get it: better leave open a door that you guard than not knowing where another one might be… »

« Oui, and we are not high priority for the US so they won't spent resources to create a second one if they think that the original is still active… » smirked the DGSE…

« Ok, this is changing the game isn't it? » asked Alexis.

« Merely accelerating it I would think! It was inevitable and frankly, no one thought that it would last so long. » answered the DGSE.

The system specialist was dismissed and four men remained in the room.

« What's your opinion on the next steps, Jean? »

* * *

The fourth man who hadn't spoken yet was bald and in his fifties; he leaned back:

« I think that we have to tell the Americans: they are getting too close and we will lose Wanda if we don't move quickly! We tell them and we ask them to help us maintain the charade... »

The men remained silent and nodded their ascent.

Alexis leaned forward: *« What about your agent, Bernard? How will he react? »*

« Alexis, I would suggest that you do not get too involved in the operational matters. » Said the DGSE.

« Plausible deniability? »

« Yes, even Nicolas here doesn't know everything... »

Nicolas nodded: *« I especially don't want to know everything... »*

The DGSE went on: *« I think that you need to bring the PR[161] up to speed on the operation, especially on the political and financial implications: we need his green light. »*

They agreed on the course of action and left in the first hours of a cold Sunday.

The following afternoon, after receiving a formal approval from the President, the DGSE picked up his phone: *« Gabrielle, could you please call the CIA? I need to speak to Gina*

---

[161] Président de la République

Haspel urgently. »

Forty minutes later, his phone rang.

« Yes? Put her through! Hello Gina, how are you? »

« … »

« Good, listen, I need to talk to you in person ; I have an interesting story for you… »

« … »

« Rather quickly I'm afraid! Would Wednesday suit you? »

*   *   *

Forty-eight hours later, the DGSE was driven to Villacoublay, a military airport south-west of Paris and boarded a French Republic Falcon 7X. *« You know Jean, back in the days, »* said the DGSE as he sat comfortably in his seat, *« there used to be a reserved seat for the French Republic on every Air France Concorde flight to New York, seat A1, until fifteen minutes before departure. I flew it once for an urgent meeting at the UN… Classy aircraft but awfully noisy… Is your presentation ready? »*

« Yes Monsieur le Directeur; it will be a relief for Wanda when he hears about it… »

« Hmmm, yes, I can understand that; we need to stay on course a little more though, whatever the endgame… »

Their eyes met, cold and calculating. The DGSE lit a cigar, his only vice…

* * *

The flight took less than eight hours and was quiet, both men managed whatever sleep they could.

They landed at Andrews Air Force base and were walked by a CIA agent to two black suburbans. The convoy, lights blazing, siren blaring, cut through the morning rush hour and arrived at the CIA headquarters in a record thirty minutes.

The two men were ushered quickly to the seventh floor and the office of the DCI; as they walked in, the Director of the CIA rose and shook their hands.

« *Bertrand, it is nice to see you!* »

« *The pleasure is mine Gina; please let me introduce Colonel Kermeur!* »

« *Nice to meet you Colonel,* » they sat at a meeting table, « *Now Bernard, you have me very intrigued: it's not everyday that I throw my schedule up in the air like that…* »

The DGSE smiled: « *I gather you will find it worth it! But first, I would like your word that this will not be discussed with your President! He has spread gossip around the Oval Office[162] or God knows where in the past and I think that he will love talking about this specific topic!* »

The DCI cringed and spoke carefully: « *I have a duty to the*

---

[162] President Donald Trump discussed classified information provided by a U.S. ally regarding a planned Islamic State operation during an Oval Office meeting on May 10, 2017 with several Russian officials, endangering the operation.

Constitution, but you will have to trust me to make that call… »

The DGSE nodded knowingly: *« How familiar are you with ISIS finances? »*

« Rather well, we've been wondering a lot about it lately… » She paused and her eyes narrowed. *« Would you be thinking about their unidentified sources of income and the so-called Banker? »*

« If that's what you call him, I think so… »

« Let me call someone then. » She picked a phone: *« Ask Mike Willow to come here right now, please! »*

They waited a few minutes until he arrived; after quick introductions, the DCI said: *« So this Banker, can you help us get rid of him? »*

« Actually, You must protect him… »

A sigh betrayed her intensity…

« Now that's a very interesting story… Do tell! »

Mike leaned in…

Jean spoke for fifteen minutes… When he stopped, there was a silence: both Americans needed some time to digest the bomb that the French had thrown at them. They discussed it for about an hour in order to coordinate the next steps and, especially, who to bring in the loop.

« One last thing, » said then DGSE, *« again, I insist, please keep it from President Trump… »*

* * *

« How much money is involved? » asked the DCI.

« Currently, over a billion euros… »

She paused and nodded: *« Yes, I understand your request… »*

*   *   *

On the flight back to Paris, the DGSE told Jean: *« You need to activate Angel! »*

« Yes, Monsieur le Directeur, I'll get her in the loop… One billion you said? » He chuckled.

The DGSE smiled knowingly and closed his eyes.

*   *   *

« What do you mean, we can't have any support from our Paris Station! What bullshit is this? Can't they get their fingers away from the petits fours [163]*at the Embassy and actually do some work? »*

John slammed the phone down and swore: *« They won't send a team in Toulouse to investigate the Alain Paul lead; can you believe that? They don't have the fucking resources! What a fucking bunch of incompetent bureaucrats! »*

Lea looked at her colleague, sighed and walked out of the PHORMIO room…

---

[163] small bite-sized confectionery or savory appetizers

International Bank of Indochina
Account Number: 7011114642
Balance: US$ 17,598,251.00

CHAPTER 29

Paris, France

January 7th, 2018

I think I fainted, then I cried for what felt like an hour!

When I came back to my senses, I was lying on a bed and my head was resting on Louise's lap. She had called me one morning and said that she wanted to see me. I had used a Velib, the Parisian shared ubiquitous bike, to go to her place; the effort and the fresh air were a welcome relief after coming back from Yemen.

*   *   *

Thinking back about it, the exfiltration had been remarkably smooth: the two Hubert[164] combat swimmers, who had risen out of the black sea, had geared me with a wetsuit, a FROGS breathing apparatus, and all the equipment required for the

---

[164] Commando Hubert: French unit equivalent to the US Navy SEALs

346

rest of the journey. While I had undressed and geared up, the two operators had kept a vigilant eye on the perimeter.

Once ready, I cast away all my stuff in a waterproof pouch. I clicked my tongue twice; the two operators walked back to me almost casually, one after the other; we entered the sea: I checked my balance, added some weight to reach zero buoyancy and was checked again by one of the guys. The drill was simple: I was to let myself be manipulated and do nothing, especially nothing.

They dragged me under the surface a few yards away from the shore, where a swimmer tractor was resting on the ocean floor. I knew that the lead swimmer would drive it and that I would be dead weight, cast to it. The other swimmer probably clamped himself to a second vehicle. I felt the tractor rise slowly and move forward, the pressure of the water on my mask and cheeks the only indicator of movement. I concentrated on breathing slowly: it had been quite a few years since I had done that and, though I knew what to expect, it showed in my heart rate…

Both swimmers had pingers emitting on different frequencies and a meeting point; once at the right location, they were to ditch the tractors, release a ten meter long line and wait; the submarine was going to sail right between the pingers at minimum speed, catch the line and drag us along until the swimmers turned the pingers off and we could get in…

We rode for some time in pitch darkness: it could have been from fifteen to fifty minutes such I was lost; we finally stopped and waited with a hand on the mask and the other on the rebreather. I felt rather than hear something close to me. The shock came unexpectedly and we were dragged along for a few minutes until the oppressing flow of water eased. The lead swimmer came to me and, by touch indicated that I was supposed to hold the mask and rebreather on my face. He dragged me for a short while, positioned me horizontally, pushed me forward and followed. There was some new noises, a strong hiss as the water was flushed away and I suddenly felt some air on my face; a door opened at my feet: I was resting in a long metal tube!

« *Welcome on board the Emeraude*[165] » said a guy in French; he wore a French Navy uniform. I was home and, at least for a while, safe…

*   *   *

Louise had told me that the Americans had been made aware of my special status and that they wouldn't be targeting me anymore… The relief was extraordinary and my reaction to that news displayed more than anything else the tensions I had been under for months, years actually!

For the first time in years, I saw a light ahead of me, a faint hope that I might get out of it alive…

---

[165] French nuclear attack submarine

CHAPTER 30

Washington DC,

February 8th, 2018

John's life was a mess: as expected, Kate had easily destroyed him in court; she had full custody of their son, a nice alimony and, the cherry on the cake, had obtained that John would be under the careful watch of a psychologist until what seemed like a heavy dose of PTSD[166] was under control… Not until then would he be able to see Josh!

« A fucking shrink, Jenna, she forces me to see a fucking drink! Can you believe that? » had he ranted one evening at his place, pushing his fury on another glass of whisky.

As a matter of fact, Jenna understood that really well and, in retrospect, probably should have kept it for herself; he erupted when she told him so and a nasty exchange followed, concluded by his yelling Jenna out of the house! She had quite logically refused to pick up the phone ever since…

---

[166] Post-traumatic stress disorder

* * *

Uncle William had summoned him the next evening at his place: he had been brutal; there was one shrink who was on CIA payroll and John would go and visit him every week! John had ranted, pacing back and forth, under the cold glare of his uncle. He had only calmed, actually broken, down when he had heard that even his colleagues had asked to stop working with him: he was persona non grata at the Red House…

« *What, you can't take that from me: it's the only thing I have left; I've been working so much to get there…* »

« *We are not taking it away: you'll be working from the PHORMIO room at Langley, only you'll be on your own, with a weekly briefing with Mike!* »

John had let himself fall on a deep chair…

« *And you will stop going to Virginia! Your Major has been arrested by the FBI for various crimes, including two homicides and, on a side note, impersonating an officer, under UCMJ Article 106…* » He paused: « *You see, your Major was an administrative Army clerk, never left the USA and never saw any action more dangerous than clipping paper…* »

John didn't know what to think: everything was crumbling down around him…

« *But, but, what am I going to do? I…* » He was at loss for words!

« *So what you are going to do is simple: you're going act like a fucking soldier and do your job and earn back peoples' respect, one fucking hour at a time! »*

That was the first time John had ever heard his uncle swear; there was only one answer: *« Yes Sir! »* And he had left picking up whatever was left of his dignity!

After his departure, uncle William had picked up his ringing mobile phone: *« Mike? He just left. »*

« … »

« Yes, he's hurt, worse than I thought but I think you should keep him on the job: he's still the best you have, isn't he? »

« … »

« Yes, on a very short leash! »

John had seen the shrink the following day: he was obviously a high priority case of the Agency! John had entered the plush office with mixed feelings, fear, resentment and anger steaming in a strange maelstrom of emotions. They had talked for a few minutes and agreed on a schedule.

Then on the morning of the 10th, Mike had called him to his office. He had entered warily.

« You will take a plane tonight with me. Be ready at your place at eight pm, bag for two or three days; a car will pick you up! »

« Where are we going Sir? »

« Paris »

* * *

Mikes's tone didn't call for more conversation; John nodded and left.

The flight was quiet and they didn't exchange more than ten words.

They landed at Villacoublay Air Force base, just outside Paris and were greeted in perfect English by a French officer: Colonel Kermeur.

« Good morning Gentlemen, welcome in Paris; I hope that you had a good flight. »

« No problem Colonel, thank you, this is John Quirston, our lead analyst on the matter. John, this is Colonel Kermeur, from the DGSE. »

« Nice to meet you Sir! »

« Pleasure is mine Mr Quirston. Please follow me! »

They walked in the sunny but cold weather to a building a hundred yards away. The French officer led them to a large room where a typical French breakfast had been served, croissants, pains au chocolate and jugs of black coffee.

« Please make yourself comfortable, I guess that we'll have about an hour before Wanda arrives. We have to run a precise operation to make sure that no-one is tailing him. »

The room was a training center of some kind, with old posters and educational material plastered on the walls ; the curtains were drawn. John went to raise one but the Colonel asked him not to: *« Please, don't; we'd rather no one sees our asset here; an accident happens so fast these days with all those smartphones around... »*

A phone rang; Colonel Kermeur brought out it from his pocket: « *Oui ? Quelle est votre HPA ? Parfait.*[167] »

« *Pickup is complete, they'll be there in thirty minutes.* »

True to his word, they heard a vehicle stop next to the building half an hour later; the door of the room opened and a lone masked man entered; he looked around, saw Colonel Kermeur and nodded.

« *Good morning!* » said the guy in excellent English.

« *Good morning Wanda, you may remove your hood; we are amongst people of confidence... »*

The guy removed his hood and raised his head.

John froze: the guy was the spitting image of the...

« *Gentlemen, let me introduce you to Alain Paul, also known but very much less so as the Banker!* »

Mike extended his hand: « *Mike Willow, it's an honor to meet you!* »

« *Thank you Sir* »

The guy turned towards John: « *Alain Paul, good morning!* »

* * *

---

[167] French: What's your ETA (estimated time of arrival)? Perfect!

John shook his hand tentatively and remained mum.

« *You'll have to excuse John here,* » said Mike, « *he's been after you for quite a few years, at a time no one even believed that you existed…* »

« *Yeah, we've been very, very careful all this time!* » he chuckled « *Though I guess I owe him some tense moments!* »

« *The banker is a French mole?* » finally said John. « *But… How long ago did you turn him?* »

« *Oh,* » said the Colonel, « *we never turned him: he's always been an operator from the Division Action[168]!* »

John's head was spinning…

« *I think that we need to bring John here up to date, Colonel!* » smiled Mike.

« *Yes, you're right Mike! You see Mr Quirston, err … May I call you John? You see John, a while back, we were able to position Alain in the recruitment process of the French ISIS environment. The operation started in a very low profile and served only to identify local ISIS contacts and map their branches.* »

« *Then the unexpected happened…* » the Banker cut him bitterly.

« *Yes, we realized that we had a better way to fight: monitor the money trails, actually create and control them! That's when the Banker was born… We knew that in the long run, ISIS would need*

____

[168] DGSE service in charge of planning and running clandestine operations

money and that the military might of allied forces would destroy them on the ground. So we helped Alain, provided perfect covers, removed a few obstacles, and created a perfect finance system... »

« But, err... Why help them? » John was lost!

The Colonel beamed: « *We are not, actually, we are fighting them daily... »* He smiled knowingly.

« *Everyday, ISIS' income from our system is reducing: you might call it death by a thousand cuts... We managed to become essential to them and we are now, slowly, randomly, perversely, reducing the flow! »*

« *But why not cut it off? I mean, you're sending them money and they can still fight! »*

« *So they start up somewhere else we don't know? You see, ISIS supporters have never sent as much money as today; there are weekly calls for more money to be sent... And yet, less and less arrives, not even fifty per cent these days... But they haven't noticed it! »*

« *And then, sympathizers send more and more and have less for domestic operations... »* smiled Mike, « *this is wickedly clever Colonel! »*

« *And we identify them easily having ids of all accounts sending in money... »*

Alain, who was eating a croissant on the side, grinned: « *And even when we stop, the local collectors won't know that the bank accounts are compromised and this will go on, and on... »*

* * *

John couldn't believe what he was hearing: « *But how does it work? I mean, there must be … »*

« *Hundreds of accounts, yes; we run an AI that decides how to allocate the funds in a random way: sometimes one flow will bring money, some times it will dry up, only to pick up again a little later… With a global decrease overtime. »*

They worked the next hour on the strategy, how Wanda would react when his ISIS masters ask to see him again, what communication protocols would be used between the CIA and the DGSE, what would be used in case of an emergency, etc.

Once back in the air, John finally burst out: « *Mike, we're going to work with that man? He's a murderer, a rapist; I mean, you saw the video of that execution back in Mosul… »*

« *John, remember the missile strike in Kismayo? What was the damage count? Eight civilians killed, a dozen injured… Tell me that we are so much better! »*

« *But it was different, it was… »* John stopped.

« *Raison d'état*[169]*… »* finished Mike. « *Those guys are protecting their country exactly the way we do… And at a much greater risk to their operator, I would add… »*

He smiled: « *The French would say that you won't do an omelette*

---

[169] French: national interest, a concept defended by 17th century philosopher Jean de Silhon as « *a mean between what conscience permits and affairs require. »*

without breaking eggs… Don't you just love the way they put food at the center of all things serious! »

« *No, that doesn't work!* » thought John. « *That guy's a monster… There's no way he can get away with that!* »

*   *   *

« *Do you trust the Americans?* » asked Alain after they had left.

« *Not at all,* » replied Colonel Kermeur, « *You are safer now but that doesn't mean that they will play ball…* »

« *So that's the reason why you didn't give them my real name…* »

« *Yes, and didn't mention Angel!* »

Alain nodded lost in his thoughts.

CHAPTER 31

Baghdad, Iraq,

September 5th, 2012

We had arrived in Baghdad a few days before after a long drive and had settled in an apartment in the Karrada district; our identity was fairly straightforward: we were just another bunch of Algerian NGO workers who had arrived to gorge on the spending frenzy of the US reconstruction effort.

Our place was small, in one of the low-key buildings of the district, away from the restaurants and bars, and far from the US forces. The four story building had a flat per floor and a ground floor garage where one could park a few cars. We were located on the second floor, with two bedrooms and a small south-oriented living room. My two colleagues shared a room with bunk beds while I, the op chief, had the luxurious master bedroom at a glorious eighty square feet!

I knew Joss and Axel well: we had run a couple of jobs the previous year in Afghanistan and all originated from the same unit before being transferred to the Action Division of the DGSE; calling ourselves the three musketeers, full of bravado and hunting every girl in the region, we had trained restlessly together in Bayonne, a coastal city south-west of France and home of the 1er RPIMA[170], the French SAS regiment...

I had joined the regiment a few months after my eighteenth birthday. As a kid, I was living in Biarritz, the city next door. I had always loved the outdoors: I would surf in the summer, ski in the winter, play rugby at school and climb whatever block of rock anytime I could get away from school... I had permanently stained hands, thanks to an endless fight with a reluctant dirt bike that sputtered me to school. At the age of sixteen, I was the Junior French national rock climbing champion and, one day, as I was watching the television on a cold day in Biarritz, I saw the final hundred meters of the Hawaï Ironman... Eighteen months later, I finished my first long distance triathlon in Marseilles.

One afternoon, I was having fun at home, away from the prying and worried eyes of my mother: As I was about to reach the top of the facade of our family house, a guy walked by and stopped.

« Nice climb! »

« Thanks » I couldn't help grinning then frowned: *« don't tell my mum ok? »*

Our neighbor nodded and grinned: *« As long as you don't fall... »*

---

[170] French: Premier Régiment Parachutiste d'Infanterie de Marine (1st Marine Infantry Parachute Regiment), one of the three special forces regiments in the French Army

* * *

He had just moved in with his wife the previous month and seemed to be a decent guy: there hadn't been any of the juicy gossip that small provincial dwellers loved; they were polite and blended in quietly.

The next morning, I met him in the street; he was wearing a camouflage uniform.

« *How old are you?* » he asked.

« *Seventeen.* »

He smiled: « *oh, the bacc*[171] *is coming…* »

He saw me cringe: « *Tough isn't it? Any ideas as to what you're going to do next year?* »

« *Not really, maybe university? My dad is an accountant and he thinks that I should study business…* »

« *What do you think yourself?* »

I somehow felt I could trust him: « *Argh, am gonna die if I'm stuck behind a desk…* »

I was wearing my triathlon finisher teeshirt. He pointed at it: « *Are you showing off or are you the real deal?* »

I couldn't help it: I bragged; My whole climbing and triathlon track record was thrown at him…

* * *

---

[171] French: short for Baccalauréat: important end of high school exam

He smiled knowingly: « *I know something that you cou*
do… But I don't know whether you'd be tough enough… »

Man, was I hooked, badly so!

Our neighbor told me that he was an operator at a regime
had never heard of in Bayonne, the city on the Adour Ri
just a few kilometers away and the ultimate rugby enemy
school… I knew no one in the Army and had never given an
thought to it apart from thinking on a scheme to avoid th
then compulsory National Service. Alban invited me over a
few weeks later for an open house day: I was left speechless
by the parachute team, the gun show, the display of an
exfiltration of a diplomat… My seventeen year blood was
boiling…

That evening, I announced to my parents that, not only I
would be joining the Army, but that I would join the toughest
unit in the country! My dad found that funny, another
passing fad; my mum remained silent, looking at me
worryingly.

Two weeks after my eighteen birthday, I was standing on the
Citadelle[172] ground along with a group of aspiring operators
I had spent many weekends in the eight months before wit'
my new friend Alban; we usually left on the Friday night an
return exhausted, dirty on the Sunday evening. He h
taught me how to shoot, hunt, dress an animal, orient mys
in the foggy hills at the Spanish border. I taught him how
rock climb; I was cold, hot, wet, dry, thirsty and I loved e
minute of it. My parents were quite skeptical at first
facing a stark improvement at school, just couldn't oppc

---

[172] A 17th century fort, home of the 1rst RPIMA

Alban had been very clear: I'd better study and pass my bacc with honors; « *no room for illiterate idiots in the team…* »

I ran to his place one afternoon of July and yelled that I had passed with a mention « Bien »[173]! He congratulated me and asked how my parents had taken the news; I paused - « Oh merde[174] » - and ran home to tell them…

September was grueling: the selection process was damning. I thought that I was going to find it easy but had to dig deep to cope. I never saw Alban as he was off to some job somewhere. There were fifty of us at the beginning and only four at the end, one of them a lanky redhead, Joss!

The day I learned that I had been selected is engraved in my memory: I was called in the Selection Course Officer's office; standing at attention, scared shitless and trying to hide it, I stood in front of a group of officers and NCOs. « *Congratulation Porte, you've made it, first of your group; we are taking you in!* »

My heart was beating so fast: I couldn't say anything.

One of the older NCOs leaned towards the officer and spoke to him briefly; the officer's smile froze and his face darkened. « *You know Alban?* »

I nodded and beamed: « *He's the reason why I am facing you today, Sir!* »

Alban had been killed a couple days ago in a futile skirmish

---

[173] French: A- minus honors
[174] French: oh shit

in a remote village of Afghanistan... I wore my full dress uniform for the first time to his funeral.

I dove restlessly into my training and, after a year and a half of intense learning, I became a full-pledge operator; my first deployment overseas was Afghanistan in a bodyguard capacity to the French Ambassador; it was an interesting job with a few tense moments, including my first ambush with shooters up in some hills. The job had a lot of quiet time and I started to learn Pashto, only to discover that I had a knack for it...

I had a very proud dad and a very worried mother; I had to tell my dad to stop advertising my belonging to the regiment and kept telling my mum that I was extra-careful.

It's a somber irony that I, living through numerous tours in combat zones, got a few scratches and just enough scar to impress the girls back home and that, on a quiet day in a peaceful country, my parents fell to the very demon I was fighting... On the 16th of May 2003, Casablanca, the largest city of Morocco, a group of terrorist killed dozens of locals and tourists. My parents had gone there to visit some friends and celebrate their twentieth wedding anniversary, leaving France for the first time; reluctant at first, they had agreed to go when I had presented them with the non-refundable plane tickets that I had purchased... It was pure bad luck that they chose a Spanish restaurant that evening.

Facing their graves alone on a windy and wet morning, my heart in a storm of rage and sorrow, I swore to keep fighting. Deep inside, I felt the need to get outright dirty and inflict pain! I applied and joined the Division Action that same year.

* * *

My selection buddy, Joss, had been the first one to answer the call of the « Moustaches[175] » and transfer to Cercottes, the French training ground for clandestine operations a couple years before; Axel, a loud Marseillais[176], had followed him the following year. I applied to and was selected to the French Navy combat swimmer course and, after a year without alcohol and no bed-time past ten pm unless when training, I graduated. After extensive training in Cercottes and other places, It was time for me to enter the grey world of wet work. I was twenty-five, single and still in a rage.

Flash forward several years, I had become a kill team leader; France was very active in the infamous War against terror, having been the target of the radical islamic terrorists for decades. Several hundred French nationals had left France to fight alongside the Talibans and other extremists. Those who were captured by allied forces were flown back and judged in France; some were killed in aerial bombings; my job was to go after the high-level and unreachable ones in Afghanistan, Syria or Iraq… I was now fluent in Pashto and Arabic and lived south of Paris. I had no one in my life; the occasional girlfriend lasted a few months at most: I was probably not the most lovable man, prone to burst of rage, hateful at the sight of a burka, consumed with a fire no kiss nor smile could put out.

My team had been sent to kill a guy named Alain Paul, a late convert and terrorist. From the small infractions as a young teenager in Toulouse, he had moved to smalltime drug trafficking; usually partially dosed-out, he hadn't been very successful and had spent most of his time between jail and his

---

[175] French: mustache; nickname of French spies
[176] Inhabitant of Marseilles, a coastal city South of France

parents' apartment where he and his friends would pass the day, drinking and watching porn.

Born in 1983, he had been suspected, but never convicted of a revenge murder; the turn of his life was the ten year conviction for assault and unintentional homicide after a drug deal turned sour; sent to a prison in the north of France, he had discovered Islam and bought himself a righteous future; he had also gotten two BTS[177] in accounting and IT. Bahadur, as he insisted on being called now, was released for good conduct after a few years and settled back in Toulouse at the fringe of his previous world, hardly ever seeing his sinful sad parents. Around 2006, he disappeared and was rumored to be studying in a madrassa in Afghanistan; he had returned to France in 2008, only to be interrogated by the DGSI and sent back to jail for an assault on a bar tender who had opened during Ramadan...

Six months later, upon his release, he had disappeared again, only to be seen briefly in Peshawar. We could only imagine that he had then travelled across the border back to his buddies in a Taliban stronghold, somewhere in the Helmand province. From there, he had turned himself into a preacher, calling the French speaking to arms. He was known as the Black Preacher as his face never appeared on the videos that were smuggled discreetly out of Afghanistan and released on Youtube...

The day his videos recorded over one hundred thousand views, a decision was made in Paris. I was called to the

---

[177] French: Brevet de Technicien Supérieur; professional post-highschool diploma

« Piscine[178] » in the spring of 2012 and delivered my marching orders: kill Alain Paul! Operation Vipère[179] was born. Once our analysts could place him in a specific location, I would enter the local theater with a small team and wait for the right opportunity.

We flew to Afghanistan and settled within the French forces, lost in the myriad of soldiers, contractors and civilians living in Camp Eggers, Kabul; the French Embassy was literarily next door and the proximity allowed for quick trips to the DGSE center in the underground floors. We were also in close contact with the team in charge of hunting the tribal leaders responsible for the Uzbin[180] attack.

We had an opportunity once: we had been inserted in a night halo jump six kilometers in the north of Waja, a small village close to the Helmand River. After a quiet and slow walk to our basecamp, we chose an observation point on the top of a small hill, eight hundred yards from a small group of houses where Alain was rumored to spend his time. There were four of us, Joss and a sniper duo from the 1er, our former regiment.

After two days, the sniper had the guy in his scope; I made a quick sat call to confirm the green light for the kill and, to my frustration, never got it! The French government was apparently engaged in secret negotiations with the Talibans to allow for a swift and safe exit of French forces out of Afghanistan... Then was apparently not the time to stoke their anger! We were increasingly at risk of being

---

[178] French: swimming pool; the DGSE HQ's nickname
[179] French: viper
[180] A 2008 ambush that killed ten French soldiers

compromised and walked away the following night to be picked up by a chopper. We lost Alain Paul the following week: he just disappeared in the aftermath of the 15th of April attacks[181].

It was back to Paris and wait until the analysts could locate him again…

A few months went by until we got a lead from a surprising location: Baghdad! Alain Paul only had one relative left, an ailing mother, and her phone line was obviously under close surveillance. On her seventieth birthday, she received a short call from her son: during the brief conversation, a muezzin could be heard in the background; the time of the prayer call and the accent of the Imam positioned Alain in Iraq; the local DGSE station was alerted and was able to cable back to Paris some local gossip about a French fighter looking for work: that was enough to get us moving in country.

Our days since we had arrived in Baghdad were quiet: we remained hidden in the apartment apart from a quick shopping trip to the local supermarket. It all changed on the 3rd of September with a call from the station on our sat phone: an informant had given them an address in Sadr City! Joss, Alex and I drove off in an old dusty Toyota for a quick morning recon; our tanned skin and dark beards gave us a local flavor as long as we avoided close scrutiny. We went north, carefully stopping to let an American convoy drive away, and, close to the Martyr Monument park, turned right into a quiet neighborhood. The address we had been given was in a narrow one way street, in the heart of Shiite

----

[181] Major coordinated Taliban attacks throughout Afghanistan in 2012

country…

« Let's drive in front of the place; Axel, we'll let you off at the next intersection and we'll circle back via a parallel road to pick you up at the end of the street. »

We drove slowly thanks to a small truck that was delivering some goods to a small workshop and had to stop twenty yards before the target; our windows were half opened and we had some local preacher on the radio in the background. The location was a two story brown building on the south side that had, like most of the city, seen better days: its door was left ajar and shades were opened on all floors.

We crossed a street and drove a few dozen yards before stopping and letting Axel exit the car in a relaxed way, just a friend parting. He walked back and we lost him. We drove to the next intersection and turned right; the blocks were perfect square and getting lost was impossible.There was some traffic and it took us five minutes to circle back. We found Axel leaning against a wall, in the cool shade. We barely stopped and drove away casually.

« Did you get the rock in place? » I asked. We had seen a pile of rubbles almost facing the house and jumped on the occasion. We had a couple cool devices with us, one of which an innocent looking rock, hosting a small digital camera.

Axel grinned: *« Yes, easy… »*

We ran a counter-surveillance drive before heading home before the morning prayer. Back in our apartment, we powered a computer and were able to access the rock GSM feed in real time; the street filled and emptied to the rhythm of the prayer call and… Bingo! We got Alain entering the house and, seconds later, shades closing on the second floor to block the burning sun. No one entered the building for the following hours.

I had a quick sat call with Paris and got the green light: we were going in that evening, quick and dirty; we should have run a surveillance for a few days before moving in but, in this neighborhood, that was impossible; placing the rock was already pushing our luck and I wanted some left for the raid!

The plan was simple: Axel and I would walk down the street reverse of traffic, enter the building and do our deed; Joss would drop us off first, drive past the target as a final safety check and circle back to a waiting position close to a petrol station, ready to move in fast and pick us up. If the shit hit the fan, there was little backup and we would be on our own! It wasn't my first roadshow and I had gone through a few hairy close calls but, all in all, had done pretty well, if you forgot a couple scars…

That evening, we monitored the rock feed up to the mast moment: no need to crash an empty apartment. We drove in again, this time all geared up and hoping to avoid the occasional checkpoint thanks to an Embassy recon vehicle ahead of us, who didn't know anything about us, only that they were supposed to run a specific route and radio in checkpoints: we would have found it difficult to explain the Glocks, the SilencerCo suppressors, our night goggles, our comms gear and our lack of ids… Playing the French Embassy staff card was allowed, only as an absolute final last resort, and only before the hit!

We exited the car and walked up the street. I had my gear in a black backpack, Alex in a dark brown side satchel.

« *Juliet, target clear!* » announced Joss a few minutes later in our earphones.

« *Roger Juliet, Kilo moving in.* »

We arrived at the door of the house that was still unlocked, visibly broken. We entered a small corridor in pitch darkness and removed quickly our night goggles from our bags. Guns were next and, to a wave of my hand, we climbed the stairs in absolute silence. There was only one door per floor and we were quickly in front of the second floor door. There was a thin ray of light coming from the threshold: Alain was awake!

Improvisation is my forte: I removed my goggle and knocked at the door three times; Axel was crouched on the other side of the door, facing the stairs.

The door opened and Alain Paul appeared; he was dressed as if about to leave home, a bag was on the floor behind him.

I barely noticed that and simply shot him twice in the chest. He fell backwards in a loud thud.

I moved in quickly, shot him a third time in the head and checked the room: he was alone. Alex entered behind me and remained close to the threshold ready to pounce on anyone climbing up the stairs. The suppressors, even with subsonic bullets, were still quite loud: this was not a Hollywood movie.

« *Kilo, Juliet, incoming!* » Joss's urgent voice broke the silence. I went to the window and saw a car stop in front of the house:

a man walked out.

« Kilo, Roger, stand by »

I turned to Axel: *« Close the door! »*

I dragged Paul's body away into the bathroom and removed my earphone.

We heard steps in the stairs and someone knocked and spoke in Arabic: *« Bahadur? »*

« Yes. »

Why I replied, I would never know!

« My name is Amir. Are you ready? I've come to pick you up and introduce you to the sheikh. »

« Wait, Coming! » I put a finger to my mouth and looked at Axel: his eyes were wide but he kept his cool and moved to the side behind the door.

I opened the door: a thirty year old man was standing there. He looked at me, at the gun in my hand and smiled.

« We were told that you are a fighter: do you always welcome your guests like that? Come, take your bag, we need to hurry! »

I grabbed Alain's bag, followed him and closed the door behind me…

CHAPTER 32

Cercottes, France

April 15th, 2018

My ISIS bosses were pressing me to come and meet them in Iraq; Colonel Kermeur informed the Americans and we agreed on another meeting, this time in a forest debriefing house[182] on the Cercottes DGSE base, south of Paris.

John Quirston landed in a CIA Learjet at the local Air Force base and was swiftly transferred to the plain house. I had arrived a couple hours earlier after a complex counter-surveillance operation, with several teams in charge of making sure that no one followed me.

The grounds were familiar: I had trained and been debriefed here multiple times.

« *Welcome to Cercottes, did you have a good trip?* »

---

[182] Known to be used for the debriefing of long-held French hostages

* * *

« *Yes,* » grumbled John.

« *Your room is on the left there, if you want to freshen up. I'll be in the living room; err, one thing: if you want to go out, stay within the clearing; we are in a secured enclave within the base and guards have zero sense of tolerance, nor humor,* » I chuckled, « *their dogs even less so...!* »

He joined me in the living room a few minutes later; I was seated in a deep comfortable chair, enjoying a glass of thirty years old Lagavulin pure malt whisky, Colonel Kermeur's traditional way of welcoming me back into my world. A fire was burning in a corner and its glow and warmth was basking me comfortably, the smoke smell blending nicely with the tar flavors.

He sat next to me. « *Whisky?* » he said.

I nodded and poured him a generous glass. He took a sip and his eyes were suddenly alight.

« *Amazing, hu?* »

« *Incredible; what is it?* »

I showed him the bottle.

« *We opened that bottle on the day the Banker mission was decided; each time we meet, Colonel Kermeur brings it and we have a sip, even if we see each other only over breakfast... And funnily, the bottle never empties...* »

We spent the next minutes in silence enjoying the fire within and without.

After some time, he looked at me, playing with his glass:

« Why? »

« Why am I doing that? »

He nodded.

I told him about my parents without going into too many details; the words came easily: it had been a long time and my life in the recent years had maimed those emotions. He was looking at me deeply, vengeance seemed like a very fine explanation to him.

« But what I don't understand is: you're not Alain Paul, are you? How did you create that persona? The charade is perfect... »

« We didn't: he was real; we just grabbed an opportunity! »

« Pour me another whisky! »

I told him about the real Alan Paul, how he had radicalized, how he had turned into a recruiter for the Talibans.

« We tracked him down to Baghdad and... »

« You killed him ! » There was understanding in his tone!

« Yes, » and I told him how a guy had arrived and how I had left with him. How he had driven me to a location south of Baghdad where I had met his Sheikh, Yozi Al-Khoury.

* * *

John opened his eyes: « *the Butcher?* »

« *Yes, he wanted to meet the French fighter from Helmand… I guess I was somewhat of a curiosity…* »

« *But this was crazy, I mean, some people could recognize you, err, discover you weren't Alain Paul…* »

I nodded and smiled: « *Yeah, I still don't know what made me do this… You should have seen the face of my partner at Alain's place!* »

I smelled my glass and enjoyed the flavors.

« *I knew Alain was a loner; he had turned away from all his friends back from his early days in Toulouse. He only had a mother who hadn't seen him in years and his only two buddies who had left with him for Afghanistan were killed in an aerial bombing near Kandahar.* »

I paused: « *no, my main problem was his body.* »

« *His body?* »

« *Yes, after I left the apartment in Kabul, my team dumped it somewhere and there was a risk that he would be identified…* »

John had suddenly tensed! « *So?* »

« *So, the Sheikh believed my story but wanted some proof of allegiance…* »

Deep down, John knew what I was going to say.

* * *

« So, I offered to blow the local morgue! »

John couldn't breathe... I went on, unknowingly, lost in my thoughts.

« We stole an old ambulance and parked it next to the building with two hundred pounds of Semtex and a detonator triggered by a paging signal; my goal was to blow the IED[183] at night to reduce collateral damage but they wouldn't have it. The Butcher wanted maximum chaos! »

I paused, my eyes lost in the past.

« We were positioned in a flat north-west of the morgue, looking at it through broken down shades; I had a basic cellular phone and was about to blow the bomb when the militant with me said: wait, there's an American convoy coming; we can take them out! »

The fire was slowly dwindling away... The sun had set down and we were now in near total obscurity.

« It was a nightmare: refusing to blow the IED would kill me and I couldn't let them kill your soldiers... I mean, I had met some rangers back in Afghanistan and had really appreciated working with them... So, err, so in the end, I cheated: I made the call early enough that it could attributed to nerves and hopefully early enough for your guys. I didn't look at the aftermath as we were sprinting away... I spent the following weeks fighting against Iraqi forces before getting wounded and driven away from Baghdad. I managed to get back to Paris and settled in my new role, as a bait for the local radicals... The rest is history as they say... »

* * *

---

[183] Improvised explosive device

There was a long silence, then John rose and left out of the house without a word.

*   *   *

No, there's no way; no, no, that bastard…

I couldn't stay in the same room with the mother fucker who had ruined my life!

I walked out of the house and headed away in the pitch darkness; I walked for a few hundred yards before I reached a fence: I stopped, sat against it and started crying…

The irony was crushing; the Devil must have been laughing at me so much… Here I was, having searched indiscriminate vengeance for years only to find that I had to protect the very person responsible for my curse…

I yelled in the night.

Minutes later, I heard some people approaching and a growl; a powerful light beamed in my eyes.

« Monsieur, ca va[184] *? »*

« Leave me alone, get the fuck away! »

The lead patrolman was apparently used to strange behaviors and didn't take offense: « *please Monsieur, no crossing the barrier.* » His accent was comically horrendous. He looked at me for a few more second until I nodded. He then left talking

---

[184] French: Sir, are you alright?

in his radio, his attack dog turning to look at me a few times.

After an hour or so, I was freezing and found my way back to the house. I went to my room and fell on my bed without undressing; I probably fell asleep when the sun rose and awoke with a bitter taste in my mouth when someone knocked at the door.

Colonel Kermeur looked at me when I appeared and offered a cup of coffee. His prying eyes never left me; Mike had told me that he was something of a legend in the intelligence community, rising from the ranks in the DGSE to heading the most sensitive operations; he had personally killed the men who had organized the assassination of the French Ambassador in Lebanon in 1981 and had been in Khartoum when Carlos, the world renowned terrorist, had been drugged and airlifted back to Paris from Sudan…

« *Tough night,* » It wasn't a question. He nodded to himself: « *I know those!* »

Alain appeared later: he had been on a run and had removed his shirt to enjoy the fresh air. I was struck at how damaged his body was, the number of scars, at how, in a sick perverse way, we were similar. We had no life anymore and our bodies carried the stigmas of our work.

And our minds, what about our minds…

I moved that day like a robot, working on Alain's next trip to Iraq, how to work on deconfliction while he was in the area, how we would be able to follow him around and possibly exfiltrate him if needed…

* * *

I flew that evening back to DC: I was utterly confused and furious at myself, Alain, the world in general!

And I drank, oh boy, did I drink!

*   *   *

« *What's wrong with him?* » I asked Colonel Kermeur when John finally left.

« *Did you tell him how you became Alain?* »

« *Err, Yeah, a little; to build some connection I guess. Why?* »

« *The morgue job?* »

« *Yes, so?* »

« *I asked our US team to research him; he was a Marine in Iraq.* »

I had a growing knot in my stomach: « *The morgue?* »

« *That's where he lost his leg.* »

« *Putain, c'est pas possible[185]…* »

My life was in the hands of a man who had to hate me, rightfully so…

The following nights were full of nightmares and bitter remorse.

---

[185] French: fuck, that can't be true

International Bank of Indochina
Account Number: 7011114642
Balance: US$ 27,235,879.21

CHAPTER 33

June 3rd, 2018

Paris, France

Chuppa is dead!

It took me a while to take it all in; it was on all news channels : there had been a terrorist threat related raid that morning in Bobigny, a Paris suburb. A prosecutor from the anti-terrorist specialized group at the Paris Criminal court had apparently signed an arrest warrant for several individuals, including one Diego Martinez, the supposed leader of a terrorist finance ring.

The RAID, the French Police Nationale elite SWAT, had been sent to arrest him and a dramatic gunfight had followed, ending up in one suspect dead, three police officers injured and one other suspect apprehended!

The television was full of the details medias crave for: how the raid had been compromised early on and that Diego had had time to barricade himself in his apartment, how he had refused to negotiate, how he had displayed unexpected skills during the assault. The screen yelled of blasts, gun shots, masked ninjas and police sirens.

I smiled bitterly as I remembered the uncut Chuppa playing gangsta on the day I met him, an amateur drug dealer looking for a conscience at the local mosque, how I had kicked his ass when he had tried to jump me one Monday morning as I was returning from a recovery run.

He had walked up to me with Mohammed, his school buddy, a big, burly black man; their swagger and their pseudo rapper baddies looks would have been comical but for their obvious malicious intent and the knuckle breakers they held; fortunately for me, they weren't discreet and I had time to alter slightly my course to the right: I was aiming at the bigger guy's outside shoulder. The money I had collected was in a small bag hanging from my left shoulder; I slowly let go the bag to carry it directly in my left hand, a casual gesture that should have warned them.

When they got near me, the smaller one spat on the side and opened his mouth; I didn't let him say anything and threw the bag at him, then, in the same move, kicked the big guy in the balls.

He let go a high squeal and just dropped on the ground; his buddy was eyeing me with shock: they had gone in to inflict violence on an average size man and he had not prepared for the potential inversion of situation.

« C'est bon ? Arrête tes conneries et occupe-toi de ton pote. »[186]

---

[186] French: *« are you done? Stop your bullshit and take care of your buddy! »*

* * *

He was shocked but courageous, I had to give him that, stupid but courageous…

So he came at me: I easily blocked his punch and hit him hard in the solar plexus…

This memory brought a smile to my face: his face then and later, his eagerness to learn, the time he actually saved the day shooting at a guy I hadn't seen; he had missed obviously but had brought me time to cover and ditch the run…

I frowned remembering our last conversation… It had hurt to part from him!

He was my friend: we had worked together, laughed together, even chatted up girls, not very effectively so, together; he was raucous, fun, light hearted, in essence, every thing I was not anymore…

He was my friend, my only friend!

He had been…

*   *   *

A phone rang in a bland impersonal office, devoid of any decoration apart from world maps, each oddly centered: an astute observer would notice that each country map was centered on the capital city of the country

« *Yes Yves, I've seen the news; how are your men?* »

« *Good morning Jean, Thanks for asking: they are all right, nothing that will prevent them from coming back to active duty in the next month, but they had a tough time: the operation was brutal! »*

« Oh good, as I had told you, the intelligence that we got pointed to a certain level of skills… »

« Yes, And thank god you did, my guys prepared for that: you wouldn't believe the number of hits their ballistic shield took! It wasn't the twenty seven from the Bataclan but still, it saved their beacon! »

« The media say that you got people in custody? »

« Yes, one guy, Mohammed Bernard, slightly injured; Does the name ring any bell to you? »

« Not immediately, I'll have to check with the intelligence teams; I'll get back to you if they have anything. »

« Great, he seems to be willing to talk: we'll see what he comes up with! And thanks for the tipoff: the judge was happily surprised; you know she generally has a moderate opinion of the DGSE! »

« Moderate! You've always been the diplomat, Yves; Anyway, happy to hear that; we're in the same boat in the end! »

« Take care Jean! »

« Yes, you too, Bonne journée. »

Colonel Kermeur hung up and leaned back in his chair.

« Merde… »

One loose end removed, one on the run…

CHAPTER 34

September 15th, 2018

Paris, France

For the first time in years, I had a partner who knew pretty much everything about me; I still saw Louise once in a while for a quickie but she rightfully felt she was being kept out of the loop and resented it: running an agent for years and using sex as a soothing tool was a thing, being reduced to a convenient sex worker was not what she had signed for.

John and I had now our own safe house in Paris, where we would meet once in a while and our own communication canal.

He had followed me every step of the way on my previous Iraq trip, making sure that there would be no aerial bombing in my area, and it had been comforting for me to know that a rather dark angel was reluctantly caring for me.

We never discussed the morgue job: we both knew that there were subjects that should be best forgotten, buried deep under a veil of feigned ignorance. Surprisingly, we discussed our families quite a lot: he showed me some pictures of his kid, a cute little guy he saw every four weeks for a week-end, flown in from Providence by his father-in-law. I told him about my parents, how we would drive to the beach, how I took my first surfing lessons, how utterly boring they lives were…

One morning, I asked him about his prosthesis, surprised at how well he could hide it and walk:

« You should have seen me run with my blade, man, that was something! » he said, playing with his glass of malt whisky.

« Not running anymore? »

« Nope, no envy, no… » He chuckled somberly: *« I've gotten fat and ugly again! »*

« I know what it feels like: got shot in, err, Western Africa, a while back. »

« Those scars on your torso? »

« Yep, I was on a job and the local guide betrayed us; I ended up separated from the team and it took them several hours to recover me… » I froze for a second and shook. *« Anyway, it took me six months back in Paris to get back in shape; when I got out of the hospital, I had a cab waiting for me, I nearly collapsed on the fifty yard walk to the car… I felt, err… »*

« Useless! »

We drank to that depressing conclusion.

* * *

The next day we started working on a Syria trip: my ISIS bosses wanted to see me again which was worrying: were they becoming suspicious?

Colonel Kermeur suggested that there might be a way to secure my position in the organization and explained his plan.

I hated it; John loved it…

CHAPTER 35

November 11th, 2018

Creech Air Force Base, Nevada

Forty-seven miles north-west on the US95 from the Strip in Las Vegas lies an Air Force base which, contrary to its famous northern neighbors, does not harbor any alien activity. Creech Air Force Base is one of the main drone flying base; its pilots, while never leaving Nevada, fly, observe and deliver ordinance in every corner of the world!

One of the pilot was a first Lieutenant; she had arrived at eleven pm the previous evening and, to her surprise, had been taken away from the mass briefing to an individual room where a civilian had been waiting for her. There, suddenly not needing her coffee anymore to clear her head, she had learned that she would be flying a special mission under CIA operational control. Though she had heard that it happened once in a while, it was a first for her and the specific non-disclosure document that she had sign had made it very real!

After getting acquainted with the region of operation,

weather, flight plannings, she then went to a separate Ground Control Room where she found her squadron leader - flying swings[187], wow, that was seriously unusual stuff - piloting the Reaper over the sky of Syria. Two civilians were standing in the room talking to a Major General she had never seen.

She stood to attention until her boss called her over.

« Lieutenant, come over here! »

« Morning Sir! »

He spoke in a low voice.

« Cynthia, the spooks in the back have control; the guy with the red tie is the boss; the brass is babysitting them! »

« A Major General, Sir? »

He chuckled:

« Yeah, has to be new to him. »

He frowned: *« Keep a clear head on this one; I don't know what this is all about but this is big! Middelson will replace you at 8am. »*

Jesus, the 2IC[188] flying on the same job as the CO[189]! Cynthia's head was spinning…

She knew Jack, the sensor operator well: he was the most

---

[187] The 4pm - 12pm shift
[188] Second officer in command
[189] Commanding Officer

experienced NCO in the squadron and, besides the difference in rank and in experience, they worked well together: it made sense to pair him with her, the bright young kid.

She went through the transfer protocol with her boss, rank forgotten, two pilots exchanging information, and finally sat in the pilot chair. Seating into a warm chair had been a strangely intimate feeling the first time she had done it, but that was two years ago, and she quickly entered into her routine: the reaper was on autopilot and hovering high above Syria, on a lazy oval trajectory above the south suburb of Raqqa.

They were surveilling a small compound, monitoring it for movement. It was going to be, as usual, a boring job but Cynthia was used to that: long hours of patrol with an occasional bursts of violence had been her life for the past two years.

In an other room, thousands of miles away, John was chatting with Colonel Kermeur; the Frenchman had arrived in DC the day before on a regular Air France flight. He had been taken to a situation room at Langley to monitor the operation that had been agreed upon and prepared for several weeks.

The plan was surprisingly simple: consolidate Alain's position by playing a Kismayo déjà vu all again; only this time, the Reaper would be careful to shoot once Alain would have exited the house or the vehicle…

Alain had been equipped with an SCT, a subcutaneous transmitter, that was, according to both CIA and impressed DGSE techies, undetectable, but that would allow a hovering drone to follow him, especially in the open, and deconflict his area of operation; no-one wanted their asset to be accidentally killed in a side run by a stray fighter jet.

He had been smuggled into Syria by a lone guide, a complex operation as ISIS was falling through hard times: the territory that it controlled had been reduced to tatters by the joint Russian and Allied bombings and the relentless ground fights by the National Syrian Army and from the Kurds. He expected to meet a close deputy of ISIS leader, Abu Bakr al-Baghdadi, or maybe, though very unlikely, even the man himself.

Alain had been understandably reluctant to crawl back in the hell that Syria now was, doubly so as the organisation was unpredictably paranoid and could decide on a whim that he was a danger to its survival and end his amazing run in a dusty and dark room with a quick headshot or, more probably, after an extensive and dreadful interrogation…

Colonel Kermeur hadn't appealed to his sense of duty: that would have been beyond stupid in the light of those past seven years spent under deep cover, not mentioning his previous life as an army operator. He had just depicted ISIS' situation, how close Allies were from really driving a final nail into its coffin and how, once that done, Alain could turn a heavy page in his life… Kermeur had been running agents for a quarter of century and he, once again, was successful into driving Alain into danger!

The first five hours of patrol were eventless: Cynthia was now two hours away from flying the drone back to its base in Baghdad. Nothing had moved in the house: Target Alpha was inside the compound, on the east side of a rectangular house; there had been no traffic, pedestrians or vehicle, near the house.

At four thirty pm local time, Jack twitched, leaned in and called: « *We have movement! Incoming vehicle.* »

« *Roger that, do you need me to move to have better angle?* »

« *No, we're fine so far.* »

A car drove from the north on the small road and turned right into the courtyard.

« *Confirmed, vehicle in target house yard. Provisional call sign Beta.* »

The CIA agent who had remained with them so far briskly left the room and came back with his boss who had probably been dozing somewhere near.

« *Any movement from Target Alpha?* » asked Red Tie.

« *Negative Sir* » answered Jack. « *Wait... Err... Yes, Target's moving in the house.* »

The digitally enhanced picture displayed a grey house at the center of a dusty courtyard, surrounded by green fields, a mile south of the Euphrates. A red spot, labelled « A » was indeed moving west into the house; the car stopped between two buildings, made a text-book perfect three point turn and waited there facing the exit.

The « A » blip turned into a dark figure that quickly disappeared in the white car.

* * *

« Colonel, something's happening! » said John. Kermeur woke up instantly, the result of many sleepless nights and followed John into the situation room.

« Target Alpha driving south! » said an invisible male voice.

« Roger, heading change to 290; that should give us a good coverage for now, » answered a woman. Her voice was suave and exulted confidence.

« Do we have visual confirmation? » asked John in a microphone.

« Affirm, observed individual' size and tracking device in line with op details; no visual id, the angle was wrong. »

John looked at the French officer who nodded.

« Roger that, activate plan. »

« Roger, waiting for Target Alpha to exit Beta. »

They followed the car in near silence; the only voices heard were those of the reaper team coordinating the tail. The car turned west on the main road following the river and drove a few miles. It travelled across several small villages, then seemed to slow down.

« Beta turning left into a small village; initiating firing sequence! » said the invisible woman.

« What? » Said John; he picked the mike and asked: *« what are you doing? Wait until Alpha exits. »*

* * *

« *Target Beta locked; incoming; range in thirty seconds.* »

« *Creech, do you hear me?* » Yelled John in the mike. He turned towards the technician who had been there since the beginning of the operation. « *What the fuck is wrong with the comm?* »

« *I don't know Sir; everything seems fine; they've maybe locked us out!* »

« *Do something for Chrissake! Creech, do you copy; hold fire, I repeat, hold fire!* »

They were looking at the screen: a targeting lock was focused on the car; the « A » bleep seemed to waiver.

The lovely voice spoke again: « *Target Beta locked, incoming in five, four, three, two and impact!* »

The car disappeared in a massive explosion!

« *No!* » Yelled John; he fell on a seat, breathless and in disbelief.

Kermeur's face was expressionless and didn't say a word.

A few minutes passed.

Kermeur spoke in a cold, cold voice: « *I have nothing to do here anymore; I have to inform my boss of the situation. Please escort me out!* »

John escorted him back to the entrance where a drive was quickly arranged. When Kermeur climbed into the Suburban,

John said: « *I, I don't know what to say… I…* »

« *What is done is done! Forget about this; the Banker never existed!* »

His ruthlessness shocked him to the core: « *but… He was your agent; don't you…* »

Kermeur interrupted him: « *I lost an asset: it's not the first time, nor the last. Get back to your job!* »

The car drove away.

Thousands of miles away, a confused pilot was about to land her Reaper.

« *What the fuck was that?* » she asked her colleague.

« *No idea,* » replied Jack, « *but that was weird LT; never seen such a change in plans!* »

They hadn't screwed up, that was for sure: Mr. Red Tie had walked to her and said: « *Good job there Lieutenant! You make your CO proud.* »

« *Err… Thank you, err, Sir?* »

« *Mike* »

« *Err, Mike, Sir, what went wrong?* »

« *Nothing, absolutely nothing! Everything is as it should be!* » and he left.

* * *

Cynthia looked at Jack who raised his shoulders: « *Spooks…* »

*   *   *

« *Sir, Wanda is gone!* » said Kermeur on an encrypted phone.

« *That was to be expected… I guess we should retrieve the system quickly; come back to Paris and sanitize everything!* »

« *Yes, Sir* ».

A few days later, a DGSE team visited the office that Alain had rented; under the false identity of electricity workers, they entered the two room location and found it empty of electronic devices! A similar visit to his apartment failed to find anything of interest, apart from a gun and a few ids in a cache. A letter was sent to the owner terminating the rent and the apartment was left bare.

The following week, a small massage parlor closed in the 14th arrondissement and was put on the rental market.

Within three weeks, all proof of Alain's existence was gone…

CHAPTER 36

December 1st, 2018

Paris, France

At 11:59 am, a small server was humming nicely in the fifteenth arrondissement of Paris.

At 12 am, a query was launched and, having found no proof of contact within the past two weeks, executed a small program: all bank accounts received a transfer order reallocating the funds permanently.

At 12:10, having received confirmation from the banks, the server shut down and the Beast burst into flames!

At 12:25, alerted by worried neighbors, a team of firefighters broke the door and entered a small apartment filled with acrid smoke; they quickly founds the source of the fire: a burning piece of electronics set directly on the concrete floor as if to minimize its extension.

Forty minutes later, a team of operators wearing police armbands appeared to retrieve the debris.

CHAPTER 37

Paris, France

December 15th, 2018

A smiling Bruno Le Maire, French Finance Minister, was standing in the media conference room of his ministry in front of a small crowd of journalists.

« I am happy to announced you that, thanks to improved tax procedures and unexpected better economic activity, the final deficit numbers for 2018 will be four billions euros lower than expected. It is the proof of the efficiency of the government policies » he said *« and a proof of the sincerity of our budget! »*

That same week, major raids were conducted across Europe; discreet arrests were made in Saudi Arabia and in other Gulf countries...

On the 19th, the Director of the CIA drove to the White House for a specific ultra-secret briefing. A tweet followed shortly:

« We have defeated ISIS in Syria, my only reason for being there

during the Trump Presidency. »
Donald J. Trump (@realDonaldTrump) December 19, 2018

International Bank of Indochina
Account Number: 7011114642
Balance: US$ -

Account terminated per customer request
January 4th, 2019

CONCLUSION

Forward, forward, forward, forward,
Never retreat, never surrender,
Forward, forward, forward, forward,
Undefeated Warrior, sword in hand kill them.

Forward!

Extract from a French nasheed[190],
ISIS claim of responsibility,
2015 Paris terror attacks

---

[190] Acappela rap favored by Jihadis

First and above all, I thank you, oh dear adventurous reader, to have wandered in my universe; I hope that you enjoyed reading this book as much as I enjoyed writing (well, most days…)! If you did, it would mean the world to me that you tell at least two people around you!

Oh, and also please leave a comment on the book page!

Love you guys!

*   *   *

Now, this book owes much to a few people who chose to remain anonymous: they know who they are and what they mean to me!

Special thanks to B, a former Navy Seal CO, for his validation of my crazy ideas; thanks to my beta-readers whose initial enthusiasms melted my very worried heart! Thanks to PO who, stubbornly, corrected each typo, mistake and word omission: whatever is left is mine only…

And finally, this book wouldn't have been for the infinite patience of my wonderful wife, who never sighed when I told her that I was writing a novel and doing nothing else…